SKYLARK
A MYSTERY

SKYLARK
A MYSTERY

◆ ◆ ◆ ◆ ◆

SHEILA SIMONSON

ST. MARTIN'S PRESS
NEW YORK

Design by Dawn Niles

Library of Congress Cataloging-in-Publication Data

Simonson, Sheila.
    Skylark / Sheila Simonson.
        p.   cm.
    "A Thomas Dunne book."
    ISBN 0-312-08294-0
    I. Title.
PS3569.I48766S58   1992
813'.54—dc20   92-24912
                                                CIP

First Edition: October 1992

10 9 8 7 6 5 4 3 2 1

For Louise Smith, without whom this book would never have got off the ground.

SKYLARK
A MYSTERY

LONDON, 1989

I simply take the side of truth against any lie. . . .
—Vaclav Havel

♦   ♦   ♦   ♦   ♦   ♦

History is an ocean. Events—the kind that make headlines—are whitecaps. Other forces deep below the surface of awareness, tides and currents, move the mass of water at their will, warming, shaping, destroying. We notice the waves, though.

If the events of 1989 had been presented as fiction, nobody would have believed them. I'm a private person. As a rule, public events pass me by. I tut-tut or give a mild cheer and get on with my own life, but in the spring of 1989, a wave of events slopped over into my private life. I got my feet wet.

1

Spring 1989

◆ ◆ ◆ ◆ ◆ ◆

Ann Veryan put her tray down by mine and let the strap of her vast purse slide from her shoulder. She hung the bag over the back of her chair, sat down, and inspected my plate. "Prawn salad?"

"Salmon," I said glumly. "Canned." I should have known better than to choose salmon salad in a London cafeteria, or, in fact, any salad. *Salad* is one of those words like *knickers* and *napkin* and *bum* that Americans trip over in England.

"Where's Milos?" Ann wore large pink-tinted glasses. She peered around.

"Still talking to his friend, I guess. Yes, there he is." I pointed out the window.

Ann craned. "Well, he'd better hurry if he wants to eat before six. Wasn't that a great production?"

I took a sip from my glass. The wine was French and good, the food English. "I liked Lady Macbeth's dress."

"Lord, yes. Bloodred, wasn't it?" Ann's pasta casserole looked marginally more interesting than my canned salmon. She babbled on about the costumes.

We had just attended a matinee of the RSC's *Macbeth* at the

Barbican Centre. The set was interesting and the acting competent, but I thought this *MacBeth* was a little like Hamlet—having a hard time making up its mind what it wanted to do.

I live in northern California, within a hundred miles of the oldest Shakespeare festival in the country, and I grew up in upstate New York within driving distance of the Stratford, Ontario, festival, not to mention Broadway. Ann, poor thing, had taught *Macbeth* to high school seniors in Purvey, Georgia, for fifteen years without once seeing the play onstage. I didn't intend to spoil her pleasure with critical carping, so I listened to her and looked out the tall window at the rain-swept plaza.

Red and yellow tulips made a brave show against the gray stonework, but it was nasty out, blowing up a storm. A coachload of determined Japanese tourists were taking pictures of each other. Milos and his friend huddled in the lee of a kiosk. Everyone else had ᵎdently sought shelter.

ᵎ was marveling over the raked stage and the set—very vertical and claustrophobic. I watched Milos's friend hand him something; it looked like a green plastic bag of the sort Harrods supplied with purchases. Milos gave the man's shoulder a pat as he went off, bent into the storm.

The glass door to the cafeteria opened and shut on a gust of wind and Milos strode over to us, beaming. " 'They have tied me to a stake. I cannot fly, but bearlike I must fight the course.' " He shook himself, spraying water, tossed his raincoat over the extra chair, placed his furled umbrella and the parcel on the seat, and sat down.

Ann gave him a warm smile. "Wasn't the play wonderful?"

" 'Aroint thee, witch! the rump-fed runyon cries.' "

" 'The devil damn thee black, thou cream-faced loon!' " Ann shot back without missing a beat.

" 'Cream-faced loon,' " Milos repeated. "Even in tragedy, such a playful sense of language."

"How do you remember useful quotes like that, Milos?" I asked, sipping my wine.

"Simple genius." The wind had whipped a healthy color across Milos's high cheekbones and tousled his hair. For a moment, he looked almost romantic. Then he smoothed his mustache with one finger, took a slurp of wine, dived into the quiche I had selected for him, and became once more himself—a middle-aged Middle European waiter who served dinner nightly at the Hanover Hotel and studied accounting in the daytime.

2

Ann and I, who were sharing a flat to cut costs, had attended a booksellers' convention at the Hanover the week before. It was an expensive hotel and Milos was a good waiter—but romantic? No.

The English do not strike up casual acquaintances, especially not with Americans, whose social class they can't gauge. I had since called on two of my mother's old friends and been welcomed kindly, but Ann knew no one in London except Milos and me, and she didn't know me well. The booking agency for the flat had put us in touch with each other. Ann was lonely and newly divorced—looking for diversion. She had bumped into Milos at a pub on his night off and, on impulse, invited him to join us at the play. She liked him. So did I, but I wondered at his motives. Was he perhaps angling for an American wife and passport?

He said, between bites, "In prison, I am translating *Macbeth* into Czech to keep myself from dying of boredom. Prison is very boring." He popped a bit of quiche into his mouth, keeping the fork in his left hand.

European table manners were beginning to look normal to me after ten days away from home. I raised a forkful of salmon with my left hand. The pale pink flesh fell onto my lap. I dabbed. "Were you in prison long?" He'd told us he had been a political prisoner, a dissident.

He shrugged. "Is a year long? I am twenty the first time—that is in '68—and it seems forever. This time—two years ago, you understand—my mind is better fortified. I have memorized *Macbeth* and so I amuse myself well enough."

" 'The mind is its own place,' " Ann murmured.

"What is that?"

She flushed. "Milton. 'The mind is its own place and in itself / Can make a heaven of hell, a hell of heaven.' "

"Ah, of course. *Paradise Lost*. You are comparing me to Lucifer."

Ann's eyes widened.

"Devil that I am." Milos laughed. "You ask how I like this production of *Macbeth*, Ann. The scene at the end with the spears . . . is that the right word?"

"Lances," I murmured.

"Yes, with the lances coming through the stone wall of the castle. That is very good. Also I like Lady Macbeth's gown."

It was my turn to laugh.

He cocked an eyebrow.

"That was my reaction, too."

3

He turned back to Ann. "Ah, my poor friend, it is your first time to see the play, and Lark and I are making light of it."

A spot of color showed on Ann's cheek. "I could see that it wasn't perfect. Malcolm fluffed one of his lines and I didn't like the banquet scene. All the same, I thought it was wonderful."

"And so it was," Milos said. "A wonderful way to spend a rainy afternoon. Eat, ladies. I must be at work in an hour."

We ate, gathered our belongings together, and left. Outside the complex, Milos swung the green Harrods bag to his left hand and tried to open his large black umbrella one-handed with his right.

"Why don't you let me tuck your sack into my handbag?" Ann asked. "There's plenty of room."

There was. Ann's purse was the size of an airline tote and covered in needlepoint. It shouted, American Tourist, Snatch Me. Milos eyed it without enthusiasm, but a gust of wind tore at his umbrella, so he shrugged and handed Ann the plastic bag. It *was* a Harrods bag, and rather battered, as if it had been used several times.

"Not very heavy." Ann stowed it and settled her purse on her shoulder. She was wearing one of those pleated plastic rain hats, useful but ugly.

"Just some papers," Milos muttered, wrestling his umbrella into submission.

I tied a scarf over my head. "Shall I hail a taxi?"

"Nonsense." Milos led the way. "The tube station is not far and the underground is quicker than a taxi this time of day." He set a rapid pace. Londoners, even dissident Czech Londoners, walk fast. We dashed along in his wake.

Ann and I had passes, so we jostled through the crowd at the ticket taker's booth while Milos zipped through the automatic turnstile. He waited for us with leashed impatience. The station was crowded with commuters in raincoats and suits. We went with the flow and found the right Circle Line platform. The day before, I had hopped on a train going west when I wanted to go to Victoria from South Kensington. I was in Bayswater before I figured out what I'd done.

There was no question of finding a seat. We squished through the double-width doors and stood together in the middle of the car, held upright by the press of people. The doors shut and the car lurched into motion.

I kept my eyes on the map of the underground above the windows. When we flashed through the Mansion House station, I

4

relaxed and let my gaze wander. We were going the right way for South Kensington. Milos would get off at Gloucester Road, one stop after South Kensington.

He was standing beside me, balancing easily as the train swayed. His damp coat gave off a faint smoky smell. I was holding one of those skyhooks—the equivalent of straps—that are intended to help standees keep their balance. It worked fine for me, but Ann was too short to reach the plastic knobs without dislocating her shoulder joint.

She sidled over to the panel that separated the entry area from the seats and clung to the metal edge. Her purse sagged and the little plastic bonnet dripped. She looked tired. I gave her a smile but was just too far from her to say anything without shouting. At Charing Cross, with access to the main-line station, there was a general turmoil as passengers swarmed on and off the car. Milos and I were shoved farther along, away from Ann. She clung to her panel and smiled.

The train rushed and rattled through the dark. The lights of our car lit up patches of sooty stonework. The window gave back a reflection of the packed-in passengers.

A woman facing me was reading the *Evening Standard* with avid concentration. Something about Princess Di's knees merited a screamer headline and a half-page photo. The woman's briefcase jabbed at my hip. I inched sideways. "Sorry," she said without looking at me.

Londoners say *sorry* with no inflection at all when they cross in front of you in the theater or jostle you on the street, and sometimes when you jostle them. It isn't even a politeness, because there's no feeling in the expression at all, not even fake feeling. They aren't sorry. They're just letting you know Mum brought them up right.

They also avoid eye contact. Nobody in that crammed car was looking at any one else unless they worked in the same office and had gone to the right schools together. Then they murmured. Mostly, they didn't say anything. They just stood there, swaying against each other, avoiding each other's eyes by reading their tabloids or the adverts above the windows, or looking down at their feet. Each was enclosed in a sheath of privacy. It was strange and entertaining. When I first arrived in London, I invented a game. I stared until someone met my eyes by accident, then I smiled. My victims always looked away at once—as if I had farted.

Neat snippets of poetry were printed on placards among the commercial messages—some ingenious civil servant bringing culture to the masses. A much anthologized poem of my mother's had stared me right in the face on the way in from Heathrow Airport. This car displayed Thomas Hardy's "In Time of 'The Breaking of Nations.' " I read with critical attention.

> Yonder a maid and her wight
> Come whispering by;
> War's annals will fade into night
> Ere their story die.

"Maid" and "wight": self-consciously archaic diction by the time Hardy was writing. The car swayed. The lights flickered.

Abruptly, the train came to a dead halt in the dark tunnel. The air conditioner whirred, the electric engine hummed, and a few commuters murmured. Someone near me cleared his throat.

Only that morning, the *Independent,* my newspaper of choice, had given extensive space to the inquiry into the King's Cross fire of the year before. Gruesome details floated to the surface of my mind: charred corpses, corpses dead of smoke inhalation, corpses trampled by other corpses. I am not as a rule claustrophobic, but I began to sweat. I glanced at Ann. She was pale. I grimaced at her, comically, I hoped. She smiled. Beside me, Milos clucked his tongue.

"Did you say something?"

"Perhaps a taxi would have been faster, after all. This is the third time I am delayed this week on the tube. They are having troubles in the electrical system."

"Wonderful."

We lapsed into silence. Apart from one or two hushed murmurs, no one said anything. We just stood there sweating in our rain gear waiting. No one looked at anyone else.

I stared at the reflection of our faces in the window and thought what fools human beings were. I was paying our Miss Beale an outrageous sum for half a tiny flat with no shower and a refrigerator the size of a TV set—all in order to stand below tons of English dirt, sweating beside a hundred or so English citizens, none of whom would give me the time of day. Dumb idea. The lady with the briefcase lowered her paper, turned the page, and began reading something about a horse race. I wished I was at a horse race. I was willing to bet Dick Francis didn't ride the tube.

The car shuddered and jolted about three feet forward. Right direction. It groaned to a halt again. Tabloid Tessy read on.

Just as I was bracing myself for the next train to crash into ours, the car gave a series of jolts and squawks and started to move. There was a soft simultaneous sigh of relief from the commuters. They were going to live, after all. The tabloid fancier had turned to the football scores.

At Victoria—white tile on the walls, blue edging—half the passengers got off and twice as many pushed aboard. They were less homogenous than the City commuters—fewer pinstripes, more jeans and sweatshirts, more women with shopping bags, fewer with briefcases, a sprinkling of tourists in bright colors.

We were jammed in cheek by jowl by briefcase. I wriggled around so I was facing the open door and yanked my scarf down. The door stood open, but no one else got on. The people on the platform seemed resigned to waiting for the next train.

"Hot?" Milos and I were now facing each other, eyeball-to-eyeball. "It's stuffy, no?"

" 'The mind is its own place,' " I muttered.

His mustache quirked in a grin. "Breathe lightly and think of your so-tall redwoods. How is Ann? Can you see her?"

I peered. She had removed the plastic bonnet and shifted the bag to her left shoulder. She gave me a wan smile.

On the platform, the public-address system garbled out a warning to stand clear of the doors. They slid shut and the train began to move. I caught my reflection as we entered the tunnel—short black hair standing up in tufts, raincoat collar askew beneath the loud scarf. Strange, the scarf hadn't looked loud when I'd bought it in San Francisco.

I clung to the skyhook and swayed with the movement of the train. The lights flickered. The train slowed, sped up again. Just a curve in the roadbed. I breathed.

I decided to distract myself by sorting out the other passengers. They were individuals, after all, not a huge mindless organism.

The lady directly in front of me, beside Milos, had to be an upscale housewife—hair like Maggie Thatcher's, shopping bags from Harrods and Peter Jones. The small, intense man in the seedy blue suit and black raincoat was an Iranian terrorist who would leave the train at High Street Kensington to throw bombs at the headquarters of Penguin Books. Salman Rushdie, watch out.

That was a bad thought. A shop in Charing Cross Road had been firebombed the week before. I tried not to look like the proprietor of a bookstore.

I forced my mind back to the scene before me. The kid in the Oxford gray blazer was a clerk at Lincoln's Inn. The tall woman in gray ultrasuede was a television executive; ferret-face by the door, a racetrack tout. I turned the idea over in my mind. If a bookie was a turf accountant in English parlance, what did they call touts?

We bucketed into Sloane Square. Pea green tiles and little white arches like lattices were set in mosaic for the ages. Symbolizing what? The Chelsea Flower Show, probably. Half a dozen passengers got off, including the TV executive and the quondam terrorist. One man squeezed aboard.

Ferret-face was standing in the doorway. The public-address announcement crackled out. He didn't move. Nobody said anything to him. He was looking in my direction but not at me. I noticed that because he was staring so intently—rudely, in English terms. The train waited. The automatic doors would not close, the train would not leave until ferret-face cleared the door.

Beside me, Milos gave a grunt. I saw an arm and shoulder move. A man in a brown pinstripe eeled out of the car. With a final stare—at Milos, I thought—the ferrety tout stepped out onto the platform and the doors slid together. As the train began to move, I saw him vanish into the mass of waiting commuters.

"Lark—"

The train lurched and Milos fell against me. I let go of my skyhook and clutched at him, staggering back.

"Bloody foreigners," said the woman with the *Evening Standard.*

2

♦ ♦ ♦ ♦ ♦ ♦

Stop, thief!" the Maggie Thatcher clone was shrieking. "The bugger stole my bag! Pull the emergency lever!"

No one responded, but the murmurings grew louder. Newspapers rustled. The train sped on.

I had regained my balance, but Milos was heavy. "Are you all right? What's the matter?"

He said nothing at all and he was slipping slowly to the floor.

"Somebody help me! He's fainted." I went down on one knee, then fell to my side, cracking my elbow, as the train rounded a curve. I fell, with Milos on top of me.

"Christ, missus, he's bleeding!" A male hand assisted me to a sitting position.

Various murmurs. Pull the lever. Better not, love. It'll just stop between stations. Wait for South Ken. Give 'em air, please. Back off. I heard the chatter, but I was staring at Milos's gray face. A thin trickle of blood seeped from one corner of his mouth. His eyes were half-closed, the whites showing.

"Oh God, let me through! What's wrong, Lark?" Ann fought her way to my side and knelt beside me. Her bag thudded to the floor. "Lordy, he's passed out."

"He's in shock," I said tightly. "Skin's clammy."

She drew in a sharp breath. Above me, the Thatcher clone was telling everyone the thief had stolen a silver trivet she had just bought for her niece's wedding and wasn't it disgraceful. She'd had a good look at the villain and she meant to report him to the police.

"Is he dead, lady?" the kid in the gray blazer asked me. He spoke with an American accent. So much for Lincoln's Inn.

Ann began chafing Milos's hands. "Oh, God, tell me he's not dead."

I shifted so I could hold his head and torso in my lap, pietà-fashion. "I can't find a pulse. Is he breathing?" It was too noisy to tell.

The man who had helped me sit up was kneeling opposite me, by Milos's head. "He looks bad, love. Trouble with his heart?"

I started to tell him I didn't have the faintest idea. Then we pulled into the South Kensington yard, edging toward the crowded platform.

"Will somebody hold the door and call for the station master?" I looked up.

Pandemonium. The doors opened and impatient commuters were pushing on as our lot—the uninvolved, at any rate—tried to slip away.

"Let me off! Make way!" The Thatcher woman battled out the door, followed by the devotee of the *Evening Standard*.

"Somebody do something," I ordered in my best basketball coach voice. I coach a women's team for the junior college at home. We had had a successful season. The helpful man—he was fiftyish and wore the cap and tweed jacket of an older working man—began urging the crowd to move back. The kid in the blazer stood wringing his hands.

Ann got up and used her enormous bag as a battering ram. "Get back. A man has fainted. We need room here."

Other voices joined the chorus. The doors stayed open. At last, the waiting horde parted and a small white-haired man in the black London Transport uniform bustled up.

"Here, now, what's the fuss?"

The man in the tweed jacket began to explain. I concentrated on Milos. It couldn't be a simple faint. He should have come around. And why blood? Had he bitten his tongue? He didn't look like a heart-attack victim, but I was not a paramedic, so what did I know?

"We'll have to move him, missus. The train . . ."

"Do you have a stretcher?"

He looked blank and I wondered what the right word was. Hurdle? Surely not. Gurney? "Uh, a litter to carry him on."

"Right." The official stepped back to the platform and spoke into a walkie-talkie. I heard him say something about a heart-attack victim.

I hugged Milos to me and Ann chafed his hands. Eventually, two uniformed men brought a stretcher and lifted him onto it. The waiting crowd, now swollen by two trainloads from the opposite platform, and God knows how many from the Piccadilly Line below, milled about and murmured. No one shouted or made a fuss. They stood clear of the doors, but they had the same ghoulish curiosity in their eyes that crowds at a disaster showed at home. A group of uniformed schoolchildren swirled around the edge of the crowd, voices piping, until a stern woman rounded them up and removed them from the scene. They had probably been on a field trip to the Natural History Museum. There was a dinosaur exhibit.

The men bore Milos to the center of the platform and the train we had ridden moved out. Commuters eddied around us. Two trains succeeded each other on the eastbound track. At last, the St. John Ambulance crew appeared and began to examine Milos in a thoroughly efficient, professional way.

I had been answering questions more or less at random. No, he was not my husband. I didn't know his medical history. I told the London Transport officer what I knew about Milos, which wasn't much. Ann spelled his last name, Vlacek, and a different transport officer took it down.

Ann was very quiet, big-eyed, sad. She clutched her huge purse to her bosom and mourned.

I was sitting on a bench by the stationmaster's little booth by then, with Ann and the Good Samaritan in tweeds sitting beside me. His name was Bert something and he looked worried. The kid in the blazer was a Mormon missionary. I was too caught up in the wonder of that to register his name.

For no reason at all, I started to think about Milos's umbrella. It must have fallen to the floor of the carriage. And where was my purse? Small flurry of anxiety. Ah, still in my raincoat pocket. Unlike Ann, who toted passport, traveler's checks, identification, and sundry household supplies around with her, I wasn't carrying much of value. I stood up and brushed my coat off—and found the bloodstain. I had opened my mouth to announce that interesting fact when one of the St. John crew came over to the policeman who had materialized at some point in the proceedings.

"This man has been stabbed," the paramedic said with real distaste.

All of a sudden, everyone was looking at me, Ann with her hand at her throat, as if she might choke.

"Well, I wondered," I muttered. "He bled on my coat."

The bobby whipped out his notebook. "You're a foreigner, miss?"

"American."

All of them but Ann nodded, as if my nationality explained everything. With a last accusatory glower, the paramedic strode back to his mates. Someone had wheeled in a gurney from the direction of the station.

The policeman gave us a comprehensive scowl. "Stay where you are." He went over to confer with the ambulance crew, which was busy doing something to Milos's still form.

"My bloody luck," Bert said. The kid in the blazer looked as if he was going to cry. Ann did.

I sat back down beside her and put my arm around her shoulders.

"I just wanted to go to a play," she wailed. "It's not fair!"

Poor Milos had just wanted to go to the play, too. I didn't say that. I was trying to sort things out.

It was all so puzzling. Where was the woman whose bag had been stolen? Had the thief also stabbed Milos? Why stab Milos at all? Especially on a crowded underground train during the rush hour. It didn't make sense. Nothing made sense.

I glanced around at the crowd, which was finally beginning to thin. Trains pulled in on one side of the platform or the other every two or three minutes, blotting up more people than they let off. Where was that lady whose trivet had been snatched?

I patted Ann's shoulders and scanned the crowd. No sign of the woman. She had said her bag had been stolen, not bags. Which one? She'd been carrying a large one from Peter Jones and a smaller Harrods bag.

Memory stirred. It was the Harrods bag. "Ann, do you still have that packet you were carrying for Milos?"

"Y-yes. I'll have to return it to him." She sobbed harder. "I don't even know where he lives."

"Let me see it."

"What?"

I took the handbag and pulled the plastic sack out. It contained papers, all right—a rather messy typescript of fifty or sixty pages in a cardboard folder, the kind with fabric ties. The manuscript looked like a single document, but I couldn't tell because it was in Czech.

At least I assumed the language was Czech—I would have recognized German, French, or Italian, and Russian uses a different alphabet. Parts of it looked like a play, with names in boldface on the left margin. Maybe it was Milos's translation of *Macbeth*. At that thought, I teared up, blinked hard, and stuffed the bag back in Ann's purse.

The policeman returned. He was wearing one of those tall black hats and looked to be about my age, which was thirty-three.

He came right to me. "They'll transport him to St. Botolph's."

"How is he?"

"Breathing with difficulty, madam. Pulse slow and erratic."

"But he's still alive?" I let out a long breath. I hadn't been sure. "Where's St. Botolph's?"

"Near the Fulham Road." He told me the cross street. "You say you don't know the man well." He sounded skeptical. "Whom should we notify?" He had a characterless accent—not BBC and not cockney—and he persisted in addressing me rather than Ann. We had both explained that Milos was Ann's friend and that I barely knew him.

The medics were wheeling Milos's gurney toward an elevator in the terminal building. Ann was still crying, though not as hard as she had been. I said, "I don't know who Milos's next of kin would be. You should call the Hanover. He works there and they probably have records."

"Oh. Right." The constable made a squiggle in his notebook.

"Here, mate, can I leave now?" Bert interjected. "My old lady's waiting for me at the pub. I don't know nothing and I didn't see nothing till the bloke hit the floor."

"You can't leave, Mr. Hoskins. Not until the detectives come. Nor you, Mr. Whipple." He said that to the wretched missionary, who was probably composing a letter to Salt Lake City explaining why he had been wandering around London without his partner— Mormon missionaries are supposed to go in pairs. And how he had gotten himself embroiled in an assault case.

Or would it be classified as attempted murder? I knew English law and U.S. law were similar, but there would be some differences. According to my husband, who had been a cop for twelve years,

U.S. criminal law differs from one state to the next. Even the terminology of British law was bound to be different from the California penal code.

I thought about Jay, not for the first time, with a surge of longing that almost brought me to tears again. He would straighten everything out when he got to London, but he wasn't coming for another week. I fumbled in my pocket for a tissue and blew my nose. The bobby was taking the missionary through the blameless account of what he had seen—nothing—and scribbling in the notebook. Far off, the characteristic *yip, yip, yip* of a British ambulance siren faded on the air and a District Line train pulled in on our side, bound for Ealing Broadway.

A good fifteen minutes later, two plainclothes detectives showed up. Ann had regained her composure, the missionary had lost his, and Bert Hoskins was fit to be tied. I began to feel sorry for Constable Ryan.

I was sorry for myself. The Circle and District Line platform of the South Kensington tube station lies above ground in semi-daylight, not underground. Rain sheeted down on the gleaming tracks. I was cold, my elbow ached, and I was beginning to tremble.

Ryan introduced us to Detective Inspector Cyril Thorne and Detective Sergeant Richard Wilberforce and gave a summary of the incident couched in what sounded like official police jargon. They seemed to be able to follow him.

Thorne was a nondescript man, fortyish—about Ann's age—with what I thought was a faint North Country accent, though I could not have said how far north—not Scotland. Wilberforce was a young black man, well tailored in a conservative way, and crisply London in his speech. Both men wore damp raincoats, and Wilberforce carried an umbrella. Was Milos's umbrella circling London on the floor of the carriage? I wondered whether Circle Line trains ever changed directions. The case of the revolutionary umbrella, I thought, on the edge of hysteria.

Thorne took the two men briskly through their stories, had Sergeant Wilberforce repeat their addresses, and dismissed them. The missionary fled down the Piccadilly Line escalator. I stood up and shook hands with Bert Hoskins. When I tried to thank him for helping, he looked embarrassed but gratified. Ann shook his hand, too, and launched into southern graciousness. A westbound train pulled in and Bert boarded it with red ears. He was a nice man. I hoped his wife was not the worse for waiting in the pub.

"Now, Mrs. Dodge," Thorne began.

I interrupted. "Inspector, our flat is only a few blocks away. I'm feeling shaky and I need a cup of coffee." I eyed him. "And a visit to the loo. Can't we go to the flat? I know you still have questions for us."

"It's irregular. . . ."

"If you cart us off to Scotland Yard, it will take forever. Traffic is bound to be heavy this time of day, and I really don't feel up to par."

Thorne sighed. "Very well, but we were just going to take you to the Chelsea station, not the Yard. We'll drive you to your flat."

I thought of mentioning the parking situation in our neighborhood. Of course, they could park an official car anywhere. "I want to walk."

Beside me, Ann squeaked.

I ignored her. "I need fresh air." I gave him the address. "It's the basement flat. Blue door at the bottom of the stairwell. We'll meet you there in half an hour with hot coffee."

The two men exchanged glances. "If you're ill, Mrs. Dodge, happen we should drive you to hospital." That was Thorne. Wilberforce watched me without expression.

"I just need aspirin. In fact, I'll pop into the chemist's on the Old Brompton Road and buy a bottle on the way home. Come on, Ann."

Ann started to protest, took a look at my face, and shouldered her wretched bag. Thorne and Wilberforce escorted us past the ticket booth, which was fortunate, because Ann couldn't find her pass.

The arcade that forms the main entry to the station is a wide, covered walkway, open at both ends and crammed with vendors of flowers and newspapers. A young violinist from the Royal Conservatory of Music posed by a florist's stand, playing something Baroque. Coins littered her open instrument case. We parted from the two detectives there. They said they had parked their car in the Exhibition Road by the French consulate. I led Ann across the wonky traffic island to the south side of the Old Brompton Road.

"Whatever were you thinking of, Lark? It's raining pitchforks and hammer handles." Ann was getting her second wind and indignation sharpened her soft Georgia drawl.

I trotted past the chemist's and into the stationer's next door, pulling her inside with me. The small shop stayed open until seven for the convenience of the thousands of tourists in the area. There were no other customers by then and the shopkeeper was closing up.

"Give me Milos's papers," I hissed.

"What?" She fumbled to open her purse.

"Yes, madam?" The proprietor was a Pakistani man, middle-aged and dapper.

"Will you please photocopy this document?" I removed the papers from the folder and thrust them at him.

"It will take much paper."

"Fine. Do it. Fast, please. We're in a hurry." To my surprise, because London retailers seem bent on thwarting customers whenever possible, the man didn't argue with me. Of course, I had been rolling around on the floor of a subway carriage and my tan raincoat was smeared with blood. I must have looked like a madwoman.

The man was back with the stack of papers within ten minutes and he charged me only six pounds ten. Ann and I made it to our flat, used the loo in sequence, and heated up the kettle with five minutes to spare.

I hid the extra copy of Milos's papers in my suitcase and put the originals in the hall closet, dashed into the bathroom, and scrubbed my face free of grime. I was running a comb through my hair when the doorbell rang. Though I hadn't had time to change clothes, the raincoat had absorbed the worst of the damage. There was a run in my panty hose, but my wool suit looked presentable.

I met Ann in the hallway. The whites of her eyes showed. The kettle was shrieking.

"I'll make the coffee," I said, "if you'll let them in. Cheer up. We're going to be open as day, except about the photocopies."

"I'll follow your lead, Lark, but you're crazier than a coot."

I patted her arm. "Don't I know it."

3

♦ ♦ ♦ ♦ ♦ ♦

I set out a tray with four cups and the *cafetière* pot, ignoring an ancient percolator that had come with the furnishings. The coffee itself was the standard grind Americans buy in cans, a short step up from the beastly powdered instant the English use. If the water was very hot, the *cafetière* pot made passable coffee. The percolator did not.

I could hear Ann being hospitable in the foyer. I set the cream pitcher and a bowl of Demerara sugar beside the pot and added a stack of paper napkins. Ann's voice grew louder. I carried the tray three steps into the "parlor" (it was also Ann's bedroom) and stopped dead as she entered—with Miss Beale trailing her and directing a vague smile my way.

The police were practically on the doorstep and here was the landlady, a woman of exquisite, even oppressive, gentility, from whom we were renting the flat by the week. Lord love a duck.

"Mrs. Dodge," she murmured when I had greeted her. I had asked her to call me Lark several times, to no avail. Apparently, the rule book in her head forbade such an intimacy between renter and rentee. What her rule book had to say about cops in the living room, I didn't dare think.

Miss Beale (no Ms. about her) went on murmuring. She was a tall, indefinite woman with vague gray eyes and a taste for misty tweeds. She explained that she had brought me the iron I asked for when I discovered my linen suit had creased itself into permanent wrinkles in my suitcase. She hoped it would be satisfactory and asked whether we would take a glass of sherry with her that evening. Nine-ish? Her niece and nephew would like to meet the Americans.

I abhor sherry. I thanked her for the invitation.

Ann's eyebrows were signaling Distress. She was tired. She was sad. She wanted to go to bed with a hot-water bottle. Tough.

Without saying anything so grossly direct, Miss Beale had intimated that we were in her house on sufferance. Ordinarily, she did not let the flat to foreigners. I suspected we were paying twice what she would have charged two Englishwomen. Even that outrageous sum was less than the tariff at hotels with a minimal degree of comfort, however.

"Would you like a cup of coffee?" I couldn't very well avoid offering. The aroma permeated the room.

She eyed the French device, which I had bought at Marks & Spencer, as if it were an artifact from outer space. "Oh, dear, no. I must take Rollo walkies." Rollo was her miniature poodle. She had lately had Rollo wormed, but her account of his sufferings was blessedly brief. Five minutes later, the coffee was brewed and the landlady gone. Ann and I looked at each other.

"I beg your pardon," I said. "It was high-handed of me to accept the invitation, but with Jay coming, I do not want to offend Miss Beale."

Ann sighed and took the iron into the kitchen. "Do you think we should tell her about Milos?"

"When we have to. If we pay next week's rent tonight, she'll be less apt to kick us out when she hears of Milos's, uh, accident."

Ann's eyes narrowed and she nodded. "*Two* weeks' rent, if we can con her into taking it."

The bell rang again. Ann made for the door and I pressed the plunger on the coffee pot.

There was a damp flurry as the detectives shed their rain gear in the hallway. Ann took their coats.

Inspector Thorne entered, rubbing his hands. "Cold. You did say coffee?"

I indicated the sofa, alias Ann's bed. "I can brew a pot of tea, if you prefer."

Thorne said coffee was just the ticket and both men sat on the sofa. Properly speaking, it was a love seat. A full-width Hide-a-Bed would not have fit in the niche it occupied. I let Ann take the scaled-down armchair and pulled a straight chair from the table, only one leaf of which we extended. Using both leaves would have shoved the table into the armchair. It was a small flat.

I poured coffee and creamed and sugared according to instructions. Ann took hers black.

Inspector Thorne sipped and made an appreciative noise. Wilberforce looked less enthusiastic. Perhaps he preferred tea.

"Now, ladies, I must take you through your statements again. This is a bad business."

"Have you heard anything further about Milos's condition?" Ann set her cup on the wide arm of the chair. I hoped she wouldn't knock it off.

"His heart stopped in the ambulance"—Ann gave a gasp—"but they were able to start it again. He's alive, madam, in a critical state."

We were all silent for a moment, sipping our coffee.

Finally, Thorne took a decisive swallow and set his cup on the low coffee table. He turned to Ann. "I don't understand your association with Mr. Vlacek, Mrs. Veryan. Will you explain?"

Ann bristled. "I went to a play with him in Lark's company. I don't see what's so mysterious about that. We saw *Macbeth* at the Barbican—a special matinee. We had a bite to eat at the cafeteria there. Then we got on the subway—I mean the underground—and rode home. That's all there is to the relationship. I like Milos. He's a nice man. But I don't know much about him."

"I see. How did you meet him?"

Sergeant Wilberforce had drawn out his notebook and was taking shorthand. I wondered why he didn't just use a tape recorder.

Ann sat very straight, hands clasped in her lap. "Lark and I attended the booksellers' convention at the Hanover Hotel last week. Milos waited on our table one night. We were having dinner with half a dozen other booksellers. He was a good waiter—animated, bantering with us, not all stiff like the other waiters. They never said anything but 'Yes, moddom.' I thought Milos was witty."

Thorne kept his face blank and his eyes on Ann. No doubt he was wondering why anyone would want an animated waiter.

Ann looked at her hands. "Yesterday evening, I ate supper at the Green Lion in Bredon Street. I was alone, because Lark was dining with a friend of her mother's. I saw Milos, who was also eating alone, and I spoke to him. He joined me. We had a nice conversation, mostly about the theater. He knows a lot about London theater. He hadn't seen this *Macbeth,* though, so I asked him if he wanted to meet us at the Barbican today."

"Do you make a habit of dining with waiters?" The question was offensive and probably meant to be. I stiffened.

Ann stared at Thorne a moment, mouth pursed, then she leaned back in the chair and laughed. The coffee cup wobbled but didn't fall off.

When she had composed herself, she said, still chuckling, "Inspector, honey, I was married for nineteen years to a man who always ordered for me. I don't believe I spoke two words to a waiter in all that time. I've been divorced for six months, mind you, but this is the first time I've gone anywhere with an unattached male, waiter or no waiter, since I was a twenty-year-old bride. After Buford Veryan, I just wasn't interested." She gave another snort of laughter. "I don't reckon once qualifies as a habit."

Thorne was smiling a little, too. "Then you don't know of any enemies Mr. Vlacek may have?"

"Heavens, no, unless the other waiters are jealous. We left him a very large tip."

I cleared my throat.

Thorne glanced at me. "What is it?"

"I gathered that Milos was a political exile, at odds with the present government of Czechoslovakia. It seems a little unlikely, but I suppose, if he has political enemies . . ."

Thorne made a face. "Spies?"

"Just an idea." Putting the thought into words made it sound even more unlikely. Central Europe was thawing, Czechoslovakia more slowly than Poland and Hungary, but the real action was elsewhere—in Iran and China. As far as I knew, Britain had good relations with the Czech Communist regime.

"There was that man he met outside the theater." Ann's eyes gleamed behind the spectacles, as if she liked my scenario. She was sitting up again, though not in the stiff, defensive way she had been earlier. "Do you remember his name, Lark?"

Thorne looked skeptical; Wilberforce, bored.

I shook my head. "Milos said, 'Your pardon, ladies, there's my friend'—something. I didn't catch the name, but it sounded Czech. At least it didn't sound English. Milos stepped outside for only a few minutes."

Thorne raised an eyebrow. "Did you see this 'friend' clearly?"

"No."

"He was much younger than Milos." Ann shoved her glasses up on the bridge of her nose. "That was my impression of him. Slim, like a young man, and darkish. Shorter than Milos. I think he had a little mustache. They talked for a while, then he gave Milos the package and hurried off. It was raining. I remember thinking he needed a decent raincoat—"

"What package?" Thorne interrupted.

Ann explained the Harrods bag with great aplomb and brought it out from the hall closet when Thorne asked to see it.

I opened my mouth to say I thought the writing was Czech, but Thorne would figure that out—Scotland Yard probably had Czech translators. There was no point airing speculations. There was also no point in mentioning that Milos had translated *Macbeth* in prison. It was possible he wouldn't want the English police to know of his imprisonments. If he lived, he could decide what to tell them. If not, I would add to my statement.

I cleared my throat again. "I took the folder out of the sack while we were waiting for you to arrive at the station. I looked at the papers, but I couldn't make head or tail of them. I was curious because of the lady whose bag was stolen."

Both men sat up straight and frowned at me, Wilberforce with his pen poised.

"On the underground. The woman who was standing beside Milos when he was stabbed. Someone stole her silver trivet." I described the way the tout had prevented the doors from closing while the villain did his work. "The whole thing seemed strange to me. Milos was stabbed and the same man stole the trivet. I didn't see the stabbing, but it had to be the same man, because no one else except the accomplice got off the car. The trivet was in a Harrods bag like this one and the woman was about Ann's height and coloring. Afterward, I wondered if the thief might not have mistaken the woman with the bag for Ann, because otherwise, his actions don't make sense."

Thorne pursed his lips in a silent whistle and exchanged glances with Wilberforce. "An odd story. Let's go through the events on the carriage again. You entered the car where?"

Thorne took me through my narrative three times. The third time, I remembered the irrelevant umbrella and the Thatcher clone's indignation. "She said that she'd got a good look at the man and meant to report the theft, but she pushed right off the car when it came to a halt at the South Kensington station, and I didn't see her talking to the constable there."

Thorne looked at his sergeant. "Happen we should check with London Transport."

Wilberforce nodded and made a note.

Then Thorne took Ann's version of events. She hadn't seen much because of the press of passengers, and his questions for her were vague, as if he was thinking things through while she talked. She had noticed the tout in the doorway and described him as short, skinny, and mean-looking.

"Did he look English?"

Ann stared. "My goodness, Inspector, here y'all are sitting in a city full of people from China and Pakistan and Jamaica, not to mention Spain and Greece. Most all of them speak English. Far as I can tell, they *are* English. He didn't wear a turban, if that's what you mean."

"Did he look Anglo-Saxon?" Wilberforce interjected. He kept his face blank and his voice neutral, but Thorne gave him a little side-glance. Thorne's ears were red.

I said, with equal neutrality, "He was Caucasian and probably northern European. I didn't notice anything odd about his nonverbal signals except that he stared. British people don't do that. His clothes were awful, but not foreign awful."

I remembered that the tout's hair was parted just left of center and looked greasy. We went through total recall on his loud brown suit and pale tie, and I recalled that the thief's suit had been brown, too, but darker, with pinstripes.

Thorne let me fill his cup again. Wilberforce passed. So did Ann. Outside, the rain blew hard on the windows and a siren yipped in the Old Brompton Road. I was tired to my bones. Thorne took both of us through our descriptions again and rose to go. He had the sergeant copy our passport numbers and vital statistics but didn't take the passports. I had been half afraid he would. We were supposed to report to the Chelsea station the next morning to be fingerprinted and sign our statements.

I saw the men to the door. Ann looked as if rising from the armchair might do her in.

I was done in, knackered in the local idiom. I collapsed on the couch. It was nearly half past eight by then and we would soon have to trot upstairs to meet strangers over icky sweet wine. I could think of no way out. In fact, I couldn't think at all. My brain was on hold.

"Get rid of the photocopies," Ann said out of nowhere.

I stared at her.

She ran a distracted hand over her blond hair. "I don't want them here, Lark. I think they're dangerous."

"But they're just copies. The police have the originals."

"I don't care. I want them gone, out of here. Now."

I groaned and shoved myself to my feet. "It's pouring and you know there's no garbage can anywhere near. What am I supposed to do with them?"

"Mail them to your husband."

I paused at the arch that led out to the hall. "That's not a bad idea. Do we have a mailer? Wait, weren't you going to send a bunch of brochures home to Georgia?"

She nodded. "I have brown paper and strapping tape. Let me dig it out." She leaned sideways and opened the small chest that served as her dresser. An ugly plastic radio that was tuned permanently to BBC2 lay on top of the chest with a soapstone carving—Inuit work and very nice—beside it. Ann pulled out a drawer and began rummaging in her underwear.

"The post office is closed." I stepped back into the room. "I'll mail the packet off in the morning."

"No. Now. We can guess at the postage. You shipped some stuff home last week. How much did that cost?" She pulled out several sheets of brown paper and a tape dispenser.

"An arm and a leg." I eyed her, but she showed no sign of relenting. "Oh, all right, but I'll send it to Dad, not Jay. Dad will be able to find a translator." My father is a professor of history at a small liberal arts college in upstate New York and there are several universities nearby, some with extensive language programs. I needed to know what the papers contained. Milos would not be up to explanations for a while, and I didn't think the police would satisfy my curiosity.

I scrawled a brief explanatory note to Dad. Ann made up the parcel in short order and dug out all of her stamps. I wrote my parents' address in and slapped on a couple of PAR AVION stickers I found in my wallet. For good measure, I added three one-pound stamps and two 50p ones. Overseas postage was expensive, as I recalled only too well from the previous week. The parcel looked absurd with all those portraits of the queen in different colors plastered over the right-hand corner—a philatelist's nightmare.

What if the papers *were* dangerous? That thought stung my paranoia to life again. Perhaps the KGB would be watching Dad's mail for a parcel from his darling daughter. If so, I couldn't very well use the address of the flat as sender. I didn't want to set my father up.

I brooded over the package.

"Hurry. You'll have to post it before we go upstairs."

"*I'll* have to? I thought this was your idea." I scribbled B. D. Lee, Dept. of History, University of London, WC1 in the upper-left corner. That probably wasn't the proper postal code and the name was an old joke, but Dad was always receiving mail from colleagues abroad. If we had insufficient postage, some University of London history office was in for a surprise.

My maiden name is Dailey. When I was twelve, I started writing a space opera with myself as the thinly disguised heroine. I never got beyond chapter one, but my family thought it was a great joke and kept making up pen names for me. Flash Bunsen (Ma's offering) and Arthur C. Clockwork (from my brother Tod, who was reading Anthony Burgess at the time). Dad's contribution was Birdie Day Lee, the Birdie because of my first name. He still calls me Bird sometimes. He would know at once if the package arrived.

I threw on my raincoat, filthy as it was, and dashed around the corner and down the long block to the post office. I shoved the parcel through the appropriate slot and dashed back. It was five after nine.

Ann met me at the door. I pushed past her. "We're late," she protested.

"I need to comb my hair. It's wet." I dropped the raincoat on the bedroom floor and went into the bathroom to make adjustments. "I didn't see any villains lurking in the street."

4

♦ ♦ ♦ ♦ ♦ ♦

It was twenty past nine before I pushed the button marked BEALE. A buzzer sounded, and I tugged the heavy door open. When we entered the foyer, a forty-watt light came on, disclosing a brown door with a 1 on it and a stairway covered with what looked like poorhouse linoleum. It, too, was brown. The walls may once have been white—or cream or ecru. Now they looked foxed, like the pages of old, old books, and gave off something of the same musty odor. A brown rubber strip about three inches wide edged each step. Half the strips had begun to work loose and several were missing. At the first half-landing sat a metal pail. The handle of a mop rose from it and sagged against the wall.

Ann pointed at the stairs. "Do we have to scale that?"

"That's it. Four flights."

She groaned. Perhaps she had expected a lift.

"Take a deep breath and hold on to the banister," I exhorted in my kindest basketball coach mode. I'd forgotten Ann hadn't seen the Dickensian hallway yet.

I had arrived in London two days before she had. I had scrambled up the stairs, passed Miss Beale's muster, been shown the flat, and paid the first week's rent. Out of pure charity, I met Ann's plane and gave her her key. Though Miss Beale had visited us twice before in our basement snuggery, we had not yet had occasion to pay her a call.

The light went out.

Ann squeaked.

I began to feel real guilt. "It's okay. The light's on a timer. Stand right there." I groped for the rail and slithered past the mop and up another half flight to the first landing. I stumbled once on a loose strip of rubber but regained my balance. When I reached the landing, I brushed my arm along the wall until I found the light button and pressed it.

Another forty-watt bulb lit and I peered at Ann's shadowy face. She gaped up at me, eyeglasses glinting in the dim light.

"Come on. This bulb will go off, too, if you don't step up the pace."

She grasped the banister and charged up the stairs. By the third landing, she was panting. She leaned on the newel, which creaked but held.

I waited.

When she had caught her breath, she murmured in a drawl as thick as samp, "Leave me here, Lark, honey. I'll just sit on this nice stair step and watch that little old light bulb flickering off and on and think about things? If you're feeling kindly, you can bring me down a bottle of sherry. I'm sure the rats and I will get along fine."

I bit back a grin. "*Courage, mon ami.* Let me haul the purse for you." Her handbag must have weighed twenty pounds.

She shoved herself upright just as the light went off again. I punched it on and led the way, more slowly this time, but not as slowly as Ann. I had knocked and the door had opened well before she reached the landing, so I was standing there all by myself, lit by yet another forty-watt bulb, when I first saw Trevor Worth.

He said his own name, adding, "Hullo, hullo, what have we here? When Auntie said American ladies, I envisaged a pair of old tabbies. I am pleasantly surprised."

He was a tall, blue-eyed man, greyhound-lean, with a voice like Michael Caine and a suit that murmured Savile Row, my dears. I think he was wearing an Old School Tie—which old school, I couldn't tell. The poodle, Rollo, gave a halfhearted yelp and snuffled at Worth's heels. Both of us ignored the dog.

Despite the forty-watt bulb, Worth was backlighted so that his smooth hair glowed like a halo. It was that shade of reddish gold no

26

hair dye has ever duplicated. His complexion was as pale as Devonshire cream. He beamed at me and held out his hand.

I almost dropped Ann's tote in my haste to make contact with this strictly British god. "I'm Lark Dodge. You must be Miss Beale's nephew." I was conscious of the run in my panty hose and the fatuity of my comment.

Behind me, Ann wheezed her way onto the landing.

"This is my temporary roommate, Ann Veryan." Now why did I say *temporary*? I felt my cheeks flush. Ann was temporary because Jay, my sole and singular husband, was going to show up a week from Friday, and Ann was staying on three days after Jay arrived.

Before I could utter something even more misleading, such as "Drop in anytime," Ann caught her breath. "Hello."

"Delightful. Two American nymphs." Worth cuffed Rollo out of the way. The poodle retreated, whining.

Ann shook hands, retrieved her bag, and filled the air with southern comfort. I could see her eyes gleaming. It was a wonder the glasses didn't steam up.

Trevor led us down a handsome hallway and into Miss Beale's tasteful parlor. I could hear Rollo giving tongue in another room. The noise ceased. Ann looked around her, blinking at the splendor.

As I had discovered on my earlier visit, there was nothing Dickensian about Miss Beale's flat. The furniture would have stocked a San Francisco antique shop, and there were rather too many porcelain doodads for my taste, but the contrast with the dank stairwell was startling.

A dark woman of about my age rose from among the knickknacks and fixed us with steely gray eyes.

"My sister, Daphne," Trevor murmured.

Daphne Worth shook hands as if she was used to doing her duty. She didn't smile. Perhaps she realized her smile would be invisible in her brother's golden presence.

She was short, round, and dressed in a black gabardine suit that had to have come off the rack at Marks & Spencer. She wore steel earrings and a matching pin that looked as if it might have been designed by an East German boilermaker. The pin was so heavy it dragged her collar askew. Her blouse was a mustard acetate that swore at her delicate coloring. She wore no makeup.

As Trevor seated us with great charm on the horsehair settee, Miss Beale drifted in. She bore a silver tray upon which reposed a decanter, wineglasses, and a plate of digestive biscuits.

"Oh, there you are," she murmured. "So glad you could join us. Daphne, dear, do pour for me."

Daphne took the tray from her and set it on what had to be a tea, as opposed to coffee, table. Miss Beale sat in a wing-backed chair. Her niece poured. Trevor and Ann exchanged politenesses about the dreary weather, the beauty of the tulips in Kensington Gardens, and the variety of plays to be seen that season. He was gently scathing about the RSC production of *Macbeth*. Ann made delighted protests.

Daphne handed out the Waterford wineglasses. Each held a thimbleful of what I took to be Bristol Cream. When she had reseated herself, she passed me the biscuits.

"Americans are daft about Shakespeare." Her voice was low and rather flat, more in expression than timbre.

"Some are." I risked a biscuit.

"Take this Rose Theatre flap." The Rose Theatre, where Shakespeare's first plays may have been produced, and Marlowe's definitely were, had been found in Southwark on the site of a proposed office building. Preservationists, including Sam Wanamaker, invincibly American even after twenty years' residence in London, were doing battle with Thatcher's Department of the Environment to save the remains. Local feeling was at best tepid.

"I've heard of it." I nibbled. The biscuit tasted like sweet, spiced straw.

"Bunch of nonsense. Hundreds of men idled because the Americans want a few bits of rotted timber preserved in amber."

"I noticed an English voice or two among the protesters."

"Actors," she snorted, dismissing Lord Olivier, then nearly on his deathbed, a clutch of other distinguished British thespians, and half the Dames of the British Empire.

"I was rather surprised how few Londoners objected to covering the site with a boring high rise." I took a sip of sherry. It tasted like cough medicine.

"What Londoners need has nothing to do with Shakespeare. Jobs and housing."

I could think of a few other things Londoners needed, like very large litter bins in Trafalgar Square. The populace would benefit from a good stiff jolt of *Macbeth*, too. I made a neutral noise.

"Rents," said Daphne, "are iniquitous."

I had no trouble agreeing with that. "But I don't see how preserving the theater will affect housing. The builders are putting in an office complex. A museum on the site would draw thousands of tourists every summer and that would create jobs."

"Jobs for Spanish cleaning maids and Lebanese waiters. Not real jobs at real wages."

"A true dilemma," I murmured, wishing that someone would rescue me and tuck me into my nice bed. Didn't Lebanese—or Czech—waiters need real wages, too?

"There's no dilemma. We won't be compelled to live in a bloody museum."

Miss Beale clucked. "Really, Daphne dear. Such language. Daphne teaches at the infant school on Greer Street, Mrs. Dodge. Delightful children, and such good families."

"The little girls who wear the boater hats? I saw them walking to the Natural History Museum yesterday." The longer I talked to these people, the more American my accent and vocabulary sounded to me. "Cute kids."

Daphne's mouth twitched in a morose smile. "Little devils."

"Lark . . . what a lovely name." Trevor, blue eyes earnest, turned to me, pleading. "I may call you Lark, mayn't I?"

"Why not?" Call me anything, O prince, but call me.

"This woman has never seen *Cats*. Help me persuade her."

"You should see *Cats*," I echoed, obedient.

Ann gave a faint shriek. "But it's so expensive!"

"Nevertheless." He smiled like a sunny seraph.

"I'd rather see Daniel Day Lewis do Hamlet." Ann batted her eyelashes at him, I would have sworn to it. "But if you insist, Trevor." And they were off on a discussion of the Lloyd Webber musical, then four years into its run and rather stale. Miss Beale beamed at her nephew and he preened and grew even more eloquent.

The word *expensive* had reminded me of the rent. I was groping for a genteel way to raise the subject when Ann segued smoothly from theater to finance. She hauled her giant handbag to her lap and turned her warmest smile on Miss Beale.

"I know this isn't the proper occasion, ma'am, and it's sadly pushing of me, but I'd be just so relieved if you'd let us give you next week's rent?" Her voice rose, turning the statement into a question. "You've been so kind and it's such a lovely apartment, just what we wanted. . . ." And so on.

At the first mention of the word *rent*, Miss Beale stiffened, but she was unprepared for the full battery of Ann's deference. By the time we left, Miss Beale was projecting regal graciousness and had accepted the rent for both weeks. She wrote out the receipt in a clear copperplate hand.

Trevor watched Ann's performance with every appearance of

amused interest, Daphne with sullen distaste. Bloody Americans flashing their wealth. I could almost hear her contempt. I writhed a bit myself, but Ann was so convincing, I bade our hostess good-bye feeling obscurely grateful to her for taking our filthy Yankee lucre.

Trevor offered to accompany us down what he called the Stygian Staircase.

"I'll come, too." Daphne rose. "I must go, Auntie." That delayed us another five or ten minutes while Miss Beale protested and fetched coats. Trevor took his and gave his aunt a kiss on the cheek that made her bridle and blush. I would have blushed, too. Daphne shook hands. Rollo yipped in the distance.

Trevor joggled the light switches with a practiced hand and we descended, Ann much more rapidly than she had come upstairs. While Trevor held the heavy front door against the wind, we slipped out into the rain. Daphne followed close on his heels. We had left the little gate that led to our flat unlocked.

I was so tired by then, I was seeing double, which made fitting the key in the door lock difficult. I turned it and tried the door. Locked. I turned it the other way. Success. I felt a tiny stir of alarm, but switched the hall light on.

Ann was making her adieus in the areaway. I was about to turn and go back out for a farewell or two of my own when I saw that my bedroom door was wide open. A faint draft of fresh air touched my cheek.

I backed out the door and into Ann.

"What is it?" She sounded peeved.

"Something's wrong."

Trevor and Daphne stared at me.

I stared back. "Someone's broken in. They may still be there."

"Are you sure?"

I explained about the bedroom door. I had closed it because the bed was unmade. I didn't mention Milos's papers, but they were on my mind.

I heard Ann give a small moan as the same thought struck her. Rain gusted in our faces.

"There's must be another explanation," Daphne was saying in brisk, no-nonsense tones.

Trevor's hair ruffled in the wind. "The crime rate is rather lower here than in the States, you know. I daresay you left the door ajar and a draft stirred it open."

"There shouldn't be a draft. All the windows were closed. Locked."

"But . . ."

"There's a pay phone on the corner. I'm going to call the police." The flat did not have a phone. I had liked that. No intrusive wrong numbers or telephone solicitors. Now I yearned for a telephone.

"I'll run back up to Auntie's," Daphne offered, reluctance and doubt palpable in her voice.

"Up five flights of stairs? It'll be quicker to call from the corner. Please stay with Ann, though. I don't think she should be here alone." Before they could object, I started down the sidewalk, head bent against the wind.

I was not wearing a raincoat and the cold cut right through my wool suit. By the time I reached the space-age phone booth, I was half-running.

I got there and remembered I hadn't brought my purse with the handy-dandy card for use in pay phones. Sheer frustration made me want to bawl. I huddled for a moment in the dim shelter, panic rising in my throat, teeth chattering. To calm myself, I read the instructions printed on the telephone. No toll necessary for emergency calls.

I lifted the receiver and tapped the number—not 911 but 999. The dispatcher said something.

"I'm sorry. I didn't understand what you said. I'm trying to report a burglary. It may still be in progress."

She had trouble understanding me, too. Eventually, she took the message and told me she would notify the appropriate people. I had to be content with that.

I scurried back to our building and down the steps. Ann and the Worths had gone in. I could hear them talking in the foyer in low voices. I banged on the door and Trevor let me in.

"Did you reach the police?"

"Yes. They're coming. You shouldn't have entered the flat."

"It was bloody cold in that wind." Daphne's voice had an edge and her eyes were cool with disbelief. "Besides, there's nobody here."

"Have you checked?"

"We're about to," Ann said. "We didn't hear anything. I turned on the light in the living room." She could do that from the hallway.

"Then let's go in and sit down and wait for the police. I don't want to mess up the evidence."

31

Trevor gave a short laugh. "Evidence of what? I beg your pardon, Lark, but I think you're imagining things."

"Possibly." I was still shivering, though no longer from cold. "Let's go into the living room."

Ann led the way. At the arch, she stopped short. Daphne bumped into her. "Uh-oh."

Trevor craned. "Strewth. You were right."

I said through my teeth, "Don't just stand there blocking the way."

The living room had been tossed. The Hide-a-Bed had been pulled down and the bedclothes churned. The drawers of the chest lay upended on the heap of sheets. Beyond, I could see that the cupboard and refrigerator doors hung open. Drawer holes gaped.

Ann was moaning. She moved to the couch-cum-bed and reached toward the tumbled pile of clothing.

I backed into the hallway. "We shouldn't disturb the evidence. They'll want to photograph it. . . ."

The others were picking their way through the room. Daphne had gotten as far as the kitchen.

"Come out of there!" I heard my voice sharpen. "Come out into the hall."

With backward glances and much clucking, they complied.

"I daresay I should take you ladies back upstairs to Auntie." Trevor's eyes darkened with earnestness. "I apologize for doubting you, Lark."

I took a long breath. My shivering had eased. "It doesn't matter. We'd better wait here, though, until the police come. You could run up and let your aunt know what happened, Trevor."

"She'll be most concerned for you."

I nodded. And for her real estate. That was natural. "Is there any point in disturbing her tonight?"

Daphne said, "She'll be walking Rollo very soon, anyway. I'll go up, too, shall I?"

When neither of us objected, she went to the door. After a moment, her brother followed her out. We heard their voices fade.

Ann and I looked at each other. Ann's lip was trembling.

"I know," I said wearily. "Me and my stupid photocopies."

She gave a damp sniff. "I'm scared."

"I am, too."

"It's not your fault, Lark. As soon as I put the originals in my handbag, as soon as poor Milos was stabbed, this was in the cards. They didn't find the papers tonight, so they'll guess the police have them. I reckon that means we're out of danger."

"But if they'd found the copies . . ." I leaned against the wall. If they'd found the copies, they would have assumed we knew what was in them. "I'm glad you made me get rid of them." That was an understatement. I was also glad Ann was still capable of reasoning. *I* was too tired to think. "What do we do now?"

She took a shaky breath. "Wait. Explain about this afternoon. I don't see why we have to mention the photocopies. The thief was after the originals."

"Probably."

"All the same, I wish you'd tell *me* why you copied them." Her voice was plaintive.

More guilt. God knew, she deserved an explanation. I tried to formulate a dignified rationale for my impulse and gave up. My brain felt like wet sludge. "It was just curiosity," I admitted. "I guessed that the papers had to do with the stabbing. If so, they're important to somebody besides Milos, someone unscrupulous. I wanted to know why—and what I'd got myself mixed up in. Then there's Milos."

"I'm going to the hospital first thing tomorrow."

"I'll go with you. Do you trust Milos?"

She cocked her head and thought, then gave a single, decisive nod.

I sighed. "I do, too. He's a decent man. The police were bound to confiscate those papers as soon as we mentioned them, and I knew we had to mention them. I started to wonder when Milos would see them again. Evidence can gather dust for years. If we're wrong and the papers aren't connected with the stabbing, then they're probably something Milos is working on, maybe even his translation of *Macbeth*. I don't think he should have to wit around for the police to release his work."

Ann was smiling a little. "Won't your daddy be surprised."

I groaned. I would have to call my parents—and Jay. But there were five hours between London and New York and eight between London and California—and what times should I call them? My head spun, though addition and subtraction are not ordinarily beyond me.

Within minutes, Constable Ryan arrived, followed by Miss Beale, with the Worths and Rollo in tow. Rollo took exception to Ryan and a minor scene ensued. Miss Beale wrung her hands, Daphne departed into the gale with the poodle in the lead, and our second interrogation of the day began.

Trevor hung around, looking distressed and ornamental. When the evidence crew, the Scene-of-the-Crime team in British usage,

33

appeared and began sifting through the mess, Miss Beale sent her nephew home. He made a token protest, but he was yawning.

Daphne returned sans Rollo, whom she had taken upstairs. The ladies left at midnight, Miss Beale still emitting anguished chirps and Daphne still scowling. Inspector Thorne, who looked as if he had pulled a sweater and trousers over his pajamas, arrived ten minutes later. Sergeant Wilberforce did not appear at all.

5

♦ ♦ ♦ ♦ ♦ ♦

At half past six that morning, I went running.

Our session with the police had lasted until nearly 2:00 A.M. When it was over at last, Ann and I cleared off our beds (my room had been trashed, too) and collapsed.

I was so tired, I thought I'd sleep around the clock, but I came wide awake at a quarter of six and knew at once there was no hope of going back to sleep. I stared at the smooth plaster ceiling for a few minutes, thinking about Milos, Milos's papers, and the trouble they had caused.

Then I got up, used the loo, and changed into warm-ups. They were the most comfortable clothes I owned. I had no intention of doing anything strenuous. I needed comfort. My body ached all over and my right elbow had turned purple where I cracked it falling under Milos.

I thought of brewing a pot of coffee, but Ann was making deep noises, not quite snores, that suggested she would sleep for the next six hours if undisturbed. I am not a dog in the manger. I found my key to the flat, zipped it and my coin purse into the pocket of my jacket, and let myself out the door.

It was chilly out but clear. The storm had blown the usual pall of smog away. London has filthy air, almost as bad as Los Angeles, and I had decided to avoid running while I was there. Sucking in all that carbon monoxide had to be dangerous. Still, that morning, the air was like crystal.

I took in the blue sky and the sleep-sodden neighborhood in one comprehensive glance. The English are not early risers. Sight of the phone booth on the corner reminded me that I had to call my husband. Six in the morning minus eight hours. Ten at night at home. Jay would be at the house and wide awake.

I got through without delay by dialing the AT&T operator in New York and charging the call to my credit number. The phone rang twice and Jay picked it up before the third ring.

"Hello?" He sounded tired. I could hear instrumental jazz playing in the background.

"Hello, darling. Evening class?"

His voice warmed. "I just got home from the last session. Do you mind if I tape you?"

"What?"

"I miss your voice, Lark. Next time we do something insane like traveling separately, I'm going to make you tape me a bedtime story. I don't sleep worth a damn without you."

"Oh God, Jay." I gulped. Trevor Worth's unreal image went pop and disappeared. "I miss you, too. Can't you just get on the next plane and come?" That was a mere wish. Jay runs the law-enforcement training program at the junior college. I knew he had to wind down classes, turn in grades, and do other tedious end-of-semester chores, so I took a deep breath and launched into an account of the previous day's events.

Jay had spent ten years in the LAPD and two as head of the Monte County CID, but I've never heard him grill anybody. He's the best listener I know. Telling him what had happened helped me clarify my perceptions. I didn't leave anything out—not the Mormon missionary, not Rollo the dog, not Trevor Worth's gold hair and plummy voice.

When I ran out of steam, he said, "You sent the papers to your father? I wonder how long they'll take to get to New York."

"A week at least, probably longer. I've heard horror stories of airmail deliveries taking up to a month."

"Shall I call him for you?"

"Yes. Please. I didn't explain much in my note. Aren't you going to ask me why I meddled with evidence?"

"You didn't know it was evidence at the time, and I don't see

36

what harm you've done the originals, apart from adding to what are probably hundreds of fingerprints. I don't like the sound of that break-in, though. Move to a hotel."

"We can't toss away two weeks' rent. Besides, I like the flat. You will, too. It's central, only two blocks from the underground station, and the landlady is friendly. Ann can't afford a decent hotel."

He sighed. "I suppose you're right. I wish I could talk to the man in charge . . . what's his name, Thorne?"

"Cyril Thorne. He was thorough. I liked him." I hesitated. "What about your friend in Leicester, couldn't he call Inspector Thorne?" Jay had corresponded with the chief of detectives for Leicestershire for several years. They were going to attend a weekend conference on DNA fingerprinting.

"I should've thought of that. What time is it there?"

"Six-fifteen."

"In the morning? Ouch. I'll wait a couple of hours and call Harry at home. I wish you had a phone in that flat."

"Me, too. There's no place to plug one in, even. I asked. Miss Beale was nice about the burglary. She said nothing was missing but the one figurine." The small but very heavy Inuit soapstone carving had vanished from the flat.

"That and your twenty pounds."

Ann's money, safely in her purse, had escaped the thief, but the few bills I stashed in a drawer for safety's sake had vanished. "I'll have to go to the American Express office as soon as they open. The thief didn't take my travelers' checks or credit cards." The police had concluded there was only one burglar.

"Or your passport, or the radio, or the toaster . . . it sounds phony, Lark."

"The carving was worth two hundred pounds."

"I still smell fish. He was after the papers."

"Yes."

"They think he was a pro?"

"They seemed pretty sure of it, more so after Thorne showed up. The burglar picked the front door lock and left through the window in the bedroom . . . oops, somebody else wants to use the phone. I have to go, Jay."

A man had materialized behind me at some point in the conversation. I gave him a placatory smile. He looked at his watch. He wore a business suit and a gold Rolex. I wondered why he didn't have his own phone. "Good-bye, darling. I love you."

"I love you, too. Call me tomorrow."

"Okay." I made kissing noises and hung up. "Sorry," I said in my best bored-British voice and walked off with as much dignity as I could muster.

Nothing was open, no convenience stores, no coffee shops, no newsstands. So I went running.

I jogged a couple of blocks, then crossed on a zebra to the impassive brick presence of the French Institute and the Lycée Charles de Gaulle. Another long block took me in front of the Yemeni embassy, very seedy, with its spy cameras tracking my progress, and across the Cromwell Road to the Natural History Museum. I trotted along Queen's Gate, past the complex of museums and colleges that stretches to the Albert Hall and the entrance to Kensington Gardens.

The park gate wasn't open yet, so I jogged at the edge of the vast open area formed by Kensington Gardens and Hyde Park. By the time I reached the next gate, the keepers were opening it. I dodged through and began running. I was conscious of my aches, so I didn't push myself. I just loped along, thinking in small disconnected bursts and avoiding doggie spoor.

I headed west, skirting people up early to walk their pets, clusters of chattering schoolchildren, and the trim businessmen striding alone or in pairs toward the City. I left Kensington Gardens at the main gate and jogged in place until the light turned green. The traffic had thickened by then, along with the sweet scent of exhaust fumes.

Slowing to a walk, I retraced my path. My favorite sidewalk café had opened, also the news agent next door. Elbow-deep in uniformed schoolchildren buying sweets, I waded over to the spread of newspapers and chose a tabloid at random—the *Daily Mail,* also copies of the *Independent* and *The Times.* Ann liked to read about royalty.

I bought *caffe latte* and a croissant with the last of my change and settled down at a small white table just outside the door. A pleasant babble of French rose from a clutch of young matrons at the next table, two with babies in carriers. I sipped until the caffeine jump-started my brain, then I started looking for word of Milos's accident or our break-in or both.

There was nothing on the burglary. The *Independent* (PASSENGER ASSAULTED ON UNDERGROUND) gave Milos a paragraph on page three, a bare summary of fact. The *Daily Mail* was less restrained. COMMUTER STABBED! it shouted. TERROR ON THE TUBE! and, in smaller type, MP Calls for Guards on Public Transport. No One Safe in Thatcher's London Says Liberal Spokesman.

I read the *Daily Mail* item through twice. The prose was purple, the writer had embroidered, and the story boiled down to the same facts the *Independent* had reported. I deduced that the police had made a statement. There was no mention of my name or Ann's, but the *Daily Mail* investigator had tracked down Bert Hoskins, who said several colorful things about foreigners. His wife must have been unhappy when he showed up late.

At eight, I walked back to the flat. When I entered the hall, Ann made an interrogatory noise, so I answered her, low-voiced, and slipped into the bathroom. I was in dire need of a shower, but the flat didn't have a shower. There was a Victorian tub. It had separate taps for hot and cold water, so it wasn't even possible to attach a rubber hose with a shower head. Baths are for meditation. I had already meditated my way past the tulip beds in Hyde Park. Sighing, I turned on the taps.

I rummaged through the shambles of my bedroom and found black tailored pants, a gray blazer, and a fuchsia blouse that didn't look too crumpled.

While I bathed, I did an inventory of chores. I would have to take my raincoat to the dry-cleaning shop by the tube station, and tidy the flat, and cash travelers' checks, and go to the police station to sign my two statements, and visit Milos—where was St. Botolph's? I was leaning back in the tub trying to remember the cross street when I found myself drifting off to sleep. I sat up with a nasty start, climbed from the tub, and almost blacked out from the effect of the steaming water. A shower would not have done that to me.

Cross and groggy, I dried off and dressed. My face looked pallid in the fogged mirror. I dabbed on some lipstick, gave my hair a last damp fluff, and went out.

Ann was sitting at the table in her pink robe, staring at the coffeepot.

"Good morning."

"Lark, honey, will you press the damned lid down? Pouring hot water into that little old pot took all my strength."

I obliged, grinning. "I hope I didn't wake you."

She blinked. "You may have or you may not. Who knows? I had to face the day sooner or later."

I poured two cups. "I brought you a copy of *The Times*."

She looked around, still blinking.

"I left it in the bedroom. Don't move; I'll get it for you. Drink your coffee."

When I returned, she had drunk half a cup and was half-focused.

"Do you want me to find your glasses for you?"

"I'm nearsighted, Lark. I don't need glasses to read." She raised *The Times* between us in the universal "don't talk now" signal, so I picked up my *Independent* and began to read the other news stories, the ones I had skipped over in the café.

Princess Diana had indeed worn shorts to her son's nursery school, tailored shorts with knee socks. Inquiries continued into the Hillsborough football disaster. The transport workers' union was going to call a strike. Chinese students were demonstrating in Beijing. A British writers' association had petitioned the Czech government to release imprisoned playwright Vaclav Havel. Had I ever heard of Vaclav Havel? Vague recollections from a senior seminar on absurdist theater surfaced but nothing definite.

Salman Rushdie I had heard of. Speaking of the absurd, the Iranians were still determined to execute him for blasphemy. One of my more satirical basketball players had given me a copy of *The Satanic Verses* as a bon voyage present. I left it behind. I didn't fancy sashaying through Heathrow Airport with it. Life is full of small cowardices. At least I had displayed the novel in my shop window when it looked as if the chains were going to remove it from their shelves.

I brooded over my coffee. Ann rustled *The Times*. "Another cup?"

"No, thank you, Lark. I reckon I ought to take a bath."

"Plenty of hot water." I poured myself another cup and stared at the crossword puzzle. I like crossword puzzles, but this one didn't make any sense. I wished I was home reading the *Chronicle* or the *Examiner*. I wished I was home, tucked into my bed with my warm husband.

"I wish I was home," Ann muttered. "I don't care about Princess Di's knees." She dropped the paper on the cluttered floor and stood up. "I'm homesick."

"Me, too." I eyed her. She looked as if she was about to burst into tears. "Uh, it's just bad luck. And culture shock."

Ann sniffed. "I miss my kids." She had two sons, both in college. "And I'm paying out my life's savings to suffer. There's no justice."

I couldn't argue with that.

"Oh, well, bath time." She heaved a sigh and picked her way through the living room clutter.

I had tidied her bed out of the way and cleaned up the worst of the mess the thief had created in the kitchen by the time she returned.

"That looks better." She shoved her glasses on and inspected my work. She was wearing a blue shirtwaist dress and looked crisp and collected. "Didn't Miss Beale say something about sending a cleaning woman?"

"Yes, but we'd probably better reduce the chaos. I have to go to Knightsbridge in an hour."

"To the American Express office? I'll come with you. I don't want to hang around here by myself. We can visit the hospital afterward. I'll buy flowers at the tube station." She poured herself another half cup of coffee. "Meanwhile, I guess I'll straighten up my belongings. I feel as if I ought to wash everything, what with that man pawing through my clothes."

It was half past eleven before we found the hospital. The woman at the reception desk told us with grim satisfaction that we would have to leave, Mr. Flatkick's condition had improved but was still Grave. He was not permitted visitors. Ann thrust the flowers at her, with instructions to give them to Milos, and we trudged off, our inadequate tourist maps in hand, in search of the police station.

It was a discreet brick building at the high-priced end of the Fulham Road. The city fathers had tucked it into the corner of a cul-de-sac opposite a posh terrace of fake Victoriana. Some architect of the Prince Charles school had made up his mind to clone Thomas Carlisle's neighborhood in Cheyne Walk. The long row of redbrick town houses looked smug and expensive. The police station looked like solid 1955 Council Housing. Only the nifty blue lamp outside the entrance indicated the building's purpose.

The Crime Scene technicians had taken our fingerprints the night before, so our visit was a formality, as far as the desk sergeant was concerned—just another pair of tourists adding to the roll of forlorn crime victims.

We waited on a stiff bench by the central reception desk. Finally, Inspector Thorne emerged, greeted us, and ushered us into his spacious office. He presented us with typed transcripts of our statements, two apiece. Ann began reading hers. I scanned the account of the burglary and decided it was accurate, though it didn't sound quite like me. I signed it, then read through the second account, visualizing what had happened. When I surfaced, I found Ann and Thorne looking at me.

I lowered the stiff narrative to my lap and met Thorne's eyes. "There's one thing I'd like to add."

His eyes narrowed.

"On the way to our flat from the South Kensington Station, I had Milos's papers photocopied. I mailed the copies to my father last evening, before the burglary."

His mouth opened, then closed with a snap. He did not look pleased.

I said doggedly, "I don't suppose that makes any difference to your investigation, but I thought you ought to know."

His eyebrows knotted. "Why did you copy them?"

Good question. I paraphrased the disjointed rationalization I had given Ann the night before, adding, "I can't shake the feeling that the thief was after those papers."

"Where did you post them?"

"At that post office on the Old Brompton Road—near the tube station. I poked the parcel through the outgoing mail slot."

"Too late for us to retrieve it," he said, more to himself than to me.

"Why bother? You have the original document."

He hesitated. "Mr. Vlacek may feel you invaded his privacy."

"He may. I'll apologize when I can talk to him. If he wants me to tell my father to burn the papers unread, I'll do that, too. There's plenty of time. Of course, we invaded Milos's privacy when we gave the papers to *you.*"

That was logical. He shifted gears. "What other information have you withheld, Mrs. Dodge? Obstructing a police inquiry . . ."

"I had no intention of hampering your investigation, Inspector. I wasn't sure the papers were relevant. I'm still not sure."

"Happen we'll find out," he said.

Ann and I exchanged glances. She had listened to the dialogue without comment and I thought she looked worried. I gave her a weak smile, though I didn't feel wonderfully confident myself.

Thorne took my amended statement out to a typist, who redid the last page in short order. I signed. Thorne told us we should not leave town without letting him know. Though his tone was not menacing and he showed us out himself, I could see that my little confession had created doubts. I was sorry for that. I wished I could provide him with a clearer explanation. My impulses often bewilder me, and photocopying those papers had been one of my weirder moments.

By that time, I was starved as well as exhausted. I yearned to go home to the flat, fix a sandwich, and take a long, long nap, but Ann was determined not to waste the afternoon. She wanted to visit the National Gallery and stroll along Charing Cross Road to look at used bookstores. I had meant to browse in the bookstores, too.

One of my customers lusted after nineteenth-century travel diaries. Though I dealt in new books, I was slowly developing a book-search service. I had an appointment to talk to an antique map dealer in Knightsbridge the next day, but it wouldn't hurt me to look for diaries. I thought I might find some interesting oddities for my Christmas display, too. Besides, I had not been to the National Gallery since I was ten.

So we headed east. We had a quick lunch in the basement cafeteria and went on upstairs, galloping past the Spanish masters and dawdling over the Impressionists. Ann was awed, except by Van Gogh's *Sunflowers,* which she said was too brown. I wasn't unmoved myself.

When you're with a person who is experiencing something for the first time, there's a natural but not very nice tendency to want to come across as the bored sophisticate. Ann's undisguised wonder provoked that kind of snobbery in me.

I had been fortunate enough to visit England three times when I was a child, twice for extended stays during my father's sabbatical leaves. I had also dashed through London as a college student on my way to international basketball competitions. All the same, I didn't know the city well enough to pose as a jaded cosmopolite.

As we entered the souvenir shop on the main floor, I caught myself stifling a yawn that was part weariness, part pose. Ann rooted among the prints and the postcards and I gave myself a stern lecture. The consequent remorse made me introduce her to the National Portrait Gallery next door—that and nostalgia. All those wonderful English faces had enchanted me as a ten-year-old. I wanted to see whether the magic still operated.

It did. I left the gallery almost light-footed, and Ann left in a soft murmur of teacherly delight. She wished she could have brought her high school students—except that she no longer had students.

We paused for tea and rather dry scones in a little Shoppe that would have received Miss Beale's assent. Ann talked. When her divorce decree came through, she told me, she had wanted to start over, so she resigned her teaching post, took a temporary job as a clerk in an Atlanta bookstore, and began planning to use her settlement money to open a small store in a resort town on the Carolina coast. She had attended the booksellers' conference as part of the research into her new life. Mostly, though, she had just wanted to see Britain—three weeks in London and three weeks driving around the countryside. It was the dream of a lifetime. I hoped she'd be able to realize it.

We drifted through the bookshops, accreting purchases. I had the proprietor of one musty place ship two books of nineteenth-century engravings home for me. Then Ann dragged me to the half-price theater booth in Leicester Square that handles tickets to most of the plays. She tried for *Cats*. It was indeed expensive. A tour group had overbooked for *Hamlet,* however. When I agreed to go with her, she settled for two good seats the following night at the National Theatre.

Ann was delighted with her coup, Shakespeare-daft. I thought of Daphne Worth and wanted to laugh. There are worse vices.

By that time, my feet ached almost as much as my elbow and it was half past five. We took a taxi home at Ann's suggestion, an unprecedented extravagance, but I was grateful to her. I didn't think I could face the tube during rush hour—not yet.

When we entered the flat, it was obvious that the cleaning woman had come and gone. Everything looked as if it had been spit-shined. A neat stack of pounds sterling lay on the dining table along with a note in Miss Beale's elegant script.

Miss Beale was very sorry but we would have to vacate her flat Monday morning. She had had a visit from Inspector Thorne regarding an unfortunate incident on the underground. She was willing to forgive the burglary, but she had strong reservations about persons who associated themselves with Middle European waiters, especially the sort who got stabbed in public. She was refunding twenty-five pounds in lieu of notice. Would we leave our keys in an envelope in the mailbox by noon Monday? No further personal contact was called for. She was ours faithfully, Letitia Beale.

"Faithfully, my foot," I fumed when I had deciphered the message. "Where's the receipt she gave us?"

"I left it on the chest. . . ." Ann waved a vague hand.

"It's not there, but I suppose it will show up. The maid probably tidied it away." Gloom settled over me, dulling my anger. Getting Miss Beale to take the rent had been a forlorn hope.

Ann was counting the bills. "Oh what a tangled web we weave, when first we practice to deceive."

"That's not very helpful."

"No, honey, but it's comforting." Her voice sharpened. "I'd be willing to bet Miss Beale took the receipt. I left it right by the radio, in plain sight. Whatever are we going to do?"

I flung myself on her couch-bed. "Start hunting for a cheap hotel."

"We could go to Hay-on-Wye."

"What?"

"That town in Wales that's nothing but used bookshops."

I looked at my roommate with fresh respect. Ann was at least ten years older than I and she had been through an ordeal that had left me reeling, physically and emotionally. Since she knew Milos better than I did, she was probably even more shaken by the stabbing. Yet here she was improvising a course of action, suggesting that we abscond, debunk, scarper.

It was an excellent idea.

"Why not?" I stood up. There were road maps in the bedroom. "Who needs a London flophouse? Jay and I can camp at the airport, if necessary. Let's do it."

"We'll have to tell Inspector Thorne where we're going."

"And why," I said with relish. "Maybe there's a law against instant eviction."

6

♦ ♦ ♦ ♦ ♦ ♦

She evicted you, didn't she?"

I glanced up from my newspaper, to find Daphne Worth beside my sidewalk table, steely gray eyes glinting. She wore an unflattering brown suit and sensible shoes, and looked as if she was on her way to work, though it was only eight.

"Were you speaking to me?"

The French ladies at the next table paused in their domestic chatter to watch us. Daphne flushed scarlet but held her ground. "Did she?"

I lowered the *Independent* and took a sip of M. Roche's excellent coffee. "We have until Monday to leave. Did you hunt me down here to gloat?"

She perched on the spare chair. "I saw you, so I decided to ask. Why didn't you tell Auntie about the stabbing?"

"Miss Beale is a thoroughly conventional woman, the sort who imagines a rape victim must be asking for it."

She compressed her lips but didn't contradict me.

"I thought she would toss us out on our ears the minute she heard we were involved in a police investigation, however innocently. There was a small chance she wouldn't find out. We took the chance and lost."

"You should have told her at once."

I swallowed cooling coffee. "But we didn't. She found out. That's that. Go gloat somewhere else. I want to read the paper."

"If you'd been open with her—" She broke off, which was a good thing, because I might otherwise have committed a breach of the peace.

I raised the paper to shut her out.

She muttered something.

"I didn't hear you."

"I said there's a tenants' rights group."

I laid the paper down and gaped at her.

"You could register a complaint."

I felt the ground shifting under my assumptions. "You're suggesting I lay a complaint against your aunt? Why?"

"She's not being fair."

A silence followed, in which I tried to rearrange my perceptions. Daphne fumbled in her purse and came up with a pen and a small slip of paper. She scribbled something on it.

"There. That's the telephone number. They probably can't do anything for you. Flats let on a short lease are a legal anomaly, but they'll want to know. The president, Marge Perry, is a friend of mine."

"Uh, thanks."

She rose, said good-bye, and left as abruptly as she'd come, heading in the direction of her school. I stared after her. I had thought her completely subservient to her aunt, a real zero, but she hadn't even asked me not to tell Miss Beale what she'd suggested.

I was still puzzling over Daphne Worth's motives when I got back to the flat. Splashing noises indicated Ann was taking a bath. I had already bathed and put on a respectable hospital and cop—visiting dress before I went out for coffee, so we left for the Chelsea police station as soon as Ann emerged. She was rosy and cheerful and, when I told her, just as surprised by Daphne's suggestion as I had been.

The day was blustery but clear and we seemed to be walking in the opposite direction from everyone else.

I stepped onto a zebra. "It was generous of Daphne to seek me out."

Ann swung along beside me. When we gained the sidewalk, the Fulham Road traffic closed across our path. "Either she's generous or she wants to cause trouble for Miss Beale."

"Good heavens."

"Daphne may resent her aunt's preference for Trevor. It was as plain as the nose on your face that Daphne is not Miss Beale's favorite."

I hadn't thought Miss Beale's preference was all that obvious and I said so.

Ann shifted the heavy purse to her other shoulder. "She hung on Trevor's every word. Didn't you see the way she watched him? Our old spaniel used to watch Buford that way. Daphne must've noticed."

I digested the idea. "Do you want to call the rights group?"

"No. I don't like being manipulated."

I dodged a pram. "I thought Daphne was sincere."

"Even so, what would be the point? We aren't going to sue. I don't want to waste any more time."

Now that we knew where it was, it took us only ten minutes to walk to the station. We were shown directly to Inspector Thorne's office. He seemed surprised to see us and not best pleased that we were thinking of leaving London.

I explained Miss Beale's reaction to his visit. Though I took some pains not to lay blame were it was due, he looked distressed.

"Oh dear, oh dear, oh dear." He rubbed the bridge of his nose.

"My reaction exactly. My husband is flying in next Friday and we had planned to stay on in the flat for another week after that."

"We have a list of hotels and bed-and-breakfast houses in the area. Shall I ask the desk sergeant to call round for you?"

I could imagine the welcome we would receive if the police arranged housing for us.

Ann beamed at him. "That's sweet of you, Inspector. Why don't we see what we can find on our own, though? We don't want to be pests."

He smiled back, almost as if he was flirting with her. "It's no trouble, Mrs. Veryan."

I mentioned the name of Daphne's tenant group just to see his reaction.

"Daphne Worth," he repeated, eyebrows working. "Oh yes. She was quite the activist, always organizing protests until she moved to Chiswick last year. I didn't make the connection yesterday. You could take your case to the association, Mrs. Dodge, but I'm bound to tell you they can't do you much good. They're opposed to letting out flats on short leases, so they won't have much sympathy for you, either, and they'll go to the tabloids for support."

Ann blanched. Nor did the idea appeal to me.

Thorne continued. "If you're bent on making a point—"

"I'll write a letter of protest to the agency that gave us her address," I interrupted. Time to change the subject. "Have you found the woman whose trivet was stolen?"

"Not yet. We've put a notice in the evening papers, however, and made a short appeal on the telly. Do you think she could identify the assailant?"

"She said she could." I didn't place much reliance on the Thatcher clone's sense of public duty. However, she had been indignant over the trivet. I wished I had seen more than the man's shoulder and the back of his head. I was pretty sure I could identify the accomplice who had held the door, though, and I told Thorne that.

He sighed. "Your description fits half the old lags in the metropolitan area. Happen we'll be able to narrow the field with our computers. I wish you weren't leaving town."

Ann said, "We'll be back next Thursday, Mr. Thorne. I have only four and a half weeks left before my return flight. . . ."

"And you'd like to see more of England than the Chelsea police station." He gave her another semiflirtatious smile.

I began to feel like a duenna.

"Will you let me know of you arrangements as soon as you can?" He *was* flirting.

"We have to visit Milos before we do that," Ann murmured. Her eyelashes fluttered behind the pink lenses. "We could telephone you from the Tourist Information Office."

"Leave a message, if you please, Mrs. Veryan." He turned back to me and the cordiality evaporated. "I've had a call from Leicestershire, from Chief Inspector Harry Belknap."

"Ah, Jay must have got through. My husband, I mean." I mentioned that Jay and Harry Belknap shared an interest in DNA fingerprinting. Thorne managed to look both skeptical and faintly alarmed. Few police officers like interference from outsiders, and technophobia afflicts them as often as it does the general public. I refrained from detailed explanations and we took our leave. All the same, it was interesting to know that Belknap had taken our plight seriously.

A double-decker bus shuttled us along the Fulham Road to the vicinity of St. Botolph's Hospital.

The receptionist greeted us with startling warmth. We had been touched by Fame in the guise of the *Daily Mail*. She had read the account of Milos's stabbing and decided we must be the unnamed American women who had witnessed the event. She wanted to know all about it.

We wanted to know all about Milos's condition. It was a standoff.

She called the head nurse on Milos's floor. "Matron says he can't receive more than one visitor at a time, love. And for no more than ten minutes. He's very ill."

Ann and I looked at each other.

"You go," I said. "Give him my best and ask him what he wants my father to do with the papers." Ann went off and I submitted, in a spirit of pure altruism, to the receptionist's curiosity.

I didn't tell her much beyond what she had read in the paper. I did describe the trick the assailant and his accomplice had used to get away, and I gave her a little color about my earlier sensations when the train stopped in the tunnel.

"Oh, I know, dear. Isn't it dreadful?" Between answering the telephone and dealing with a trickle of other visitors, all of whom eavesdropped in passing, she retailed half a dozen anecdotes of Terror on the Tube.

I think Mrs. Philbrick, that was her name, almost forgot about the assault, so eager was she to confide to a sympathetic listener the hard lot of a daily commuter from the southern suburbs.

"It's a pity you can't find a place to live in that's closer to your work."

"I've asked to be transferred half a dozen times," she mourned. "Me mum has to watch the boys till I come home, and that's half eight some nights. What we need is rent controls and more council housing close in."

"Won't happen with this lot in office," an elderly visitor grumbled. "Not a hope. Out to destroy the working class, they are."

A lively three-way discussion followed when the young typist, who was also stationed behind the counter, pitched in with the rumor of a three-bedroom flat in Kensington that had sold for 2 million pounds. All of them exclaimed over that, the man turning rather red.

"Sinful, I call it." Mrs. Philbrick shook her head. Her stiff curls bobbed. "Where will it all end? London Transport are going out on strike, too." The union had just announced a series of work stoppages on selected weekdays. "I'll have to ride Tony's bike to work, won't I? Or roller-skate. I don't know what we're coming to."

Assenting murmurs. The term *poll tax* surfaced. I began to lose the thread of argument. Something about the Duke of Westminster, who owned most of Mayfair, paying lower rates than a Pakistani family of twelve crammed into two rooms. That sounded like tabloid fantasy to me. My thoughts drifted back to Milos. What was keeping Ann? Her ten minutes were up.

Three visitors with complicated requests came to the desk at that point and I made my escape to a vinyl-covered couch that overlooked the street. Between bits of office procedure, I caught further snatches of the poll-tax controversy.

I thumbed through a brochure on lung disorders and a dispirited copy of *Country Life* with ads for manor houses in Berks, castles in the Inner Hebrides, and posh modern establishments on the Thames within minutes of the main line. All, of course, with price tags in the millions—architectural porn.

I wondered what it would be like to live in the Inner Hebrides. I wondered what our soon-to-be-vacated flat would bring on the open market—with and without burglars.

"Lark?" Ann had materialized beside me.

I jumped up. "How is he?"

She shook her head. "Not looking good and doped to the eyebrows. Let's go have coffee somewhere. The disinfectant they use in those wards smells like a public washroom."

We headed for the door. The receptionist called a farewell after us and I waved. Outside, the street swarmed with shoppers. We found a café near the Earl's Court tube station.

We sat at an outside table amid EC émigrés drinking real coffee and English shop clerks having their elevenses. Ann inhaled the coffee aroma. "Ah, that's better." She took a sip. "Milos didn't recognize me at first. He kept mumbling in Czech."

"You said he was doped up."

"I talked to the head nurse—matron, I mean. She disapproved of me, but she did tell me he was on pain medication and something to keep him from moving around and ripping out the sutures. The combination must be potent."

"Did you ask Milos about the papers?" I nibbled my croissant.

Ann sipped, frowning. "Yes. Several times. At first, he just seemed confused. I kept repeating that you had sent a photocopy to your father, who was a college professor. The last time I asked what he wanted us to do about the papers, he said something that sounded like *publish* or maybe *punish*."

Publish? So the papers were his translation of *Macbeth*, after all. I felt a twinge of unreasonable disappointment. "You're sure he didn't want the document shredded?"

"Honey, he mumbled a whole lot of stuff in Czech. I picked out

52

an English word here and there—*Lock,* for instance. I couldn't tell whether he meant lock as in lock of hair or loch as in Loch Ness. Maybe he was saying *locket* or even a Czech homonym."

"Maybe he was telling you to lock up the papers." I crumbled the croissant.

Ann took a reflective sip. "Possibly. He did repeat *lock,* but he didn't say *shred* at all, or, for that matter, *translate,* and his pronunciation was blurred. I'm pretty sure he said *publish,* not *punish,* but the matron was shooing me out by then."

I sighed. "We'll just have to ask him again tomorrow, and hope he's more coherent. What now?"

"I thought you had an appointment with the map dealer."

"God, you're right." I looked at my watch. "I have to be in Knightsbridge in half an hour."

"That shop near Harrods?"

I rose. "Yes. Do I have to change at South Kensington?"

Ann stood, too. She took out her wallet-sized map of the underground and squinted at it. "Yes. Knightsbridge is on the Piccadilly Line. Do you want me to come with you?"

"You don't have to." But I gulped. Mrs. Philbrick's horror stories were fresh in my mind. "Uh, one of us will have go to the main tourist office today if you're serious about Hay-on-Wye."

"I'll do it. They have a reservation service, don't they?" She took my arm and stopped me, looking up at my face. Behind the pink lenses, her eyes looked worried and kind. "Are you sure you'll be okay alone on the tube?"

I forced a smile. "I may freak out, Ann, but it's a short ride and I ought to deal with this little aversion now, before it gets worse. If I start hyperventilating, I'll get off at South Ken and walk to Knightsbridge."

She gave my arm a light pat. "That's a good idea. I'll see you at the flat. Want me to cook supper?"

"Dinner."

"Whatever." She was smiling. We had a north-south split on meal terminology. "I'll fix us some down-home food."

"You won't find hush puppies at that market near the flat."

"I was thinking of a tofu stir-fry, honey. Isn't that California comfort food?"

In Knightsbridge, I ordered two eighteenth-century charts of the California coast. I got home before Ann did and took a nap that probably would have lasted eight hours if she hadn't shaken me awake at five. My internal clock was thoroughly confused.

She broiled lamb chops—English lamb has to be the best in the world—and served them with a side dish of fresh pasta and an honest American-style green salad.

I ate every morsel she set before me and felt much better. "My compliments to the chef."

Ann grinned. "I couldn't find tofu."

While I did the dishes, she reported her adventures at the tourist office. We debated whether to hire a car at Heathrow and drive west or take Britrail to Cardiff and pick up a car there. She had collected a sheaf of brochures. Escape from London began to seem possible and my spirits rose. Ann was downright exuberant.

She consulted her watch and beamed at me. "Ready for the play?"

"Oh God, *Hamlet.* Do we have to?"

"Absolutely. It'll be a high point of the trip."

"And there have been so many low points." I made a face. "Okay. Let's take the underground. I think I'm over my funk."

"We can buy something sweet and sinful for dessert during the interval."

"Brilliant idea." I wasn't really over my tube phobia—I had almost had to walk to Knightsbridge—but I wasn't sure how many prodigal taxi rides Ann could afford.

The National Theatre is a glass and concrete structure of the sort that provoked Prince Charles to his famous outburst against contemporary architecture. I rather liked it myself. The terraces in front of the complex and the theater balconies gave an incomparable view across the Thames, with the Houses of Parliament and, downstream, St. Paul's Cathedral, floating on the river.

When the play let out, we drifted back toward the Hungerford Footbridge, taking our time. The historical buildings across the Thames were floodlit by then and their reflections shimmered on the water. We strolled, soaking in the postcard-perfect view.

Ann said dreamily, " 'London, thou art the flower of cities all.' "

"Who's that? Wordsworth?"

"Dunbar. A Scottish poet. Much earlier than Wordsworth."

We climbed to the bridge and started across. It was misting a little and chilly. Ann stopped midway and stood staring at the pinkly lit dome of St. Paul's as the last of the chattering playgoers streamed by us, bound for Charing Cross.

I glanced at her and saw that her cheeks were wet, whether from tears or mist, I couldn't be sure. I cleared my throat. "It was a thought-provoking production."

"Mm."

"I'm in love with Polonius."

Ann laughed and mopped her glasses with a tissue. "What a glorious Hamlet he must have been. He played Hamlet, you know, just before World War Two. The Ophelia was wonderful, too."

"You haven't said anything about the leading man."

"He surely did put an antic disposition on. I think I liked it—an antidote to the melancholy Dane cliché. Oh, look." A brightly lit launch pulled out from the Embankment and headed downriver. We watched it out of sight.

Ann heaved a sigh. "I guess we'd better head for home. Shall we take the tube?"

"Sure," I said bravely. "No sweat."

Tube trains stop running after midnight and it was half past eleven by then. I could see why the other playgoers hadn't stopped to admire the view. Charing Cross was almost deserted and several of the exits had been chained off. We descended to the right platform, our shoes clacking in the empty corridors. On the platform, two shadowy figures lurked beside a pillar. Ann and I drew together.

The wait dragged on. Finally, we felt the rush of stale air and heard the rumble as the train approached. A bunch of punk kids occupied the car that stopped in front of us. They stared out with cultivated sullenness.

"Next car." Ann dragged me down the platform.

The two men who had stood together near the pillar were already seated in the car we boarded. Ann and I hunched together by an elderly Jamaican woman. There was no one else in the carriage.

I was gritting my teeth. I stared at the underground map and checked off the stations as we passed them—Westminster, St. James. At Victoria, the elderly woman got off. No one entered.

Beside me, Ann clutched her purse and swayed with the rocking motion. Neither of us said a word. As the train pulled into Sloane Square, the site of the assault, the two lurkers moved toward us.

I almost leapt from my seat and ran off the train. My heart thumped. Then the men stepped off the car, a woman with a shopping bag got on, and the doors closed.

I looked at Ann. "No suitable quotes?"

She rolled her eyes. " 'Or in the night, imagining some fear / How easy is a bush supposed a bear!' "

"That's not *Hamlet*."

"No, but it's apt." She smiled. "I do get pedantic, honey. It's the English teacher habit."

"I like it. All I can ever remember are irrelevant bits that sound funny."

" 'I'll lug the guts into the neighbour room'?"

"Like that."

South Kensington station was just as empty as Charing Cross had been and the arcade was spooky without the flower vendors and newspaper stands. We jaywalked, London-style, to the south side of the street and moved past the shuttered shops at a good clip. A pub spilled comforting light and noise at the first corner and a police car, blue light revolving, passed us as we walked. I saw it turn down our side street.

An empty bus rumbled by, and a taxi full of well-dressed revelers. Still, it was quiet for a weeknight in a city.

As we turned the corner, Ann stopped dead. "Look. Isn't that our house?" The question was not rhetorical. Ours was only one of a long row of nearly identical Regency-style town houses, and both of us had tried to enter the wrong areaway at different times.

The police car sat by the front steps and the main door to the building stood open. It did not take genius to realize that something was wrong. We walked, feet dragging, toward the blue-lit scene. I think both of us were afraid to find out what had happened. My stomach had tied itself in a knot.

"That's Daphne Worth talking to the officer," Ann murmured.

"Another break-in?"

"Lord, I hope not."

We reached the wrought-iron railing and Constable Ryan moved toward us from the gate. His face looked menacing in the inconstant blue light. "Move along . . . oh. You live here."

"Until Monday," I said. "What's going on?"

"There's been an accident."

Accident? Ann and I stared at him.

"Your landlady, Miss Beale, has had a fall."

Ann clucked her tongue. "Those awful rubber strips on the stairs were a disaster waiting to happen. I hope she's not badly injured."

"She's dead, madam."

Silence. My heart paused, then thudded into danger mode. I heard Ann draw a long breath.

"You'd best go down to your flat," Constable Ryan said. "We'll send someone down to question you."

I swallowed hard. "Question us? We've been gone all evening."

"Even so, Mrs. Dodge."

Ann had fished out her keys. She undid the gate with a minimum of fumbling and I went down the concrete steps after her. The front door lock, the one the burglars had picked the night before, opened smoothly.

Ann entered the flat. As I followed her, I heard Daphne Worth's voice from above, shrill with strain and anger.

"But why did they have to kill Rollo, too?"

I shut the door and leaned against it.

7

◆ ◆ ◆ ◆ ◆ ◆

He's here, Lark. Wake up!"

"Mm . . . who?" I blinked awake. I had been dreaming of Jay, such is the power of positive wishing.

Ann turned on the bedside light. "Inspector Thorne."

I squinched my eyes shut, opened them, and sat up. "Okay, I'll be with you in a minute."

Ann was still fully dressed in the lavender suit she had worn to the play. As she whisked from the room, I glanced blearily at my watch, saw it was half past two, and decided the constabulary would have to suffer the sight of me in the jeans and sweatshirt I had changed into earlier.

I had meant to nap and was lying atop the duvet, but I had fallen into heavy sleep in spite of my good intentions. My limbs felt like overcooked pasta.

Ann had brewed coffee. Thorne, who looked as tired as I felt, though he wore a rumpled suit rather than jeans, was warming his hands on a flowered mug. A woman in her thirties sat on the couch beside him, also nursing a mug. Both of them rose, unsmiling, and set their cups aside.

"Mrs. Dodge," Thorne murmured. "Detective Sergeant Baylor."

The woman, who was about Ann's age and plumply pretty in a glen plaid suit, extended her hand. I shook it.

I took the mug of coffee Ann held out to me and sank onto the armchair. The two detectives resumed their places on the couch.

"This is a bad business," Thorne rumbled. "Poor lady, her neck was broken." Sergeant Baylor watched me with bright brown eyes.

"Do you have a suspect?"

Thorne's eyes narrowed and I heard Sergeant Baylor take a sharp breath. "An odd question, Mrs. Dodge. Very odd indeed. That's an ill-lit stairwell and the stairs themselves are in poor condition. What leads you to think Miss Beale did not meet with an accident?"

I took a sip of scalding coffee to ease my suddenly dry mouth. "Miss Worth, something I heard her say . . ." I quoted Daphne's anguished question. "So I thought, if the dog was killed . . ."

"I see." Thorne didn't look as if he saw anything and his tone was skeptical. Sergeant Baylor had taken out her notebook.

I suppressed a yawn—nervous not sleepy. I was wide awake.

Ann covered the awkwardness with sad exclamations about Rollo and Miss Beale and the horrors of climbing the staircase with those feeble little lights winking on and off. I think all three of us ignored her, but she set a warmer tone.

At last, Thorne took up his cup again. When Ann wound down, he said, "Do either of you own a pair of short white cotton stockings? Anklets, I believe they're called."

Ann shook her head. Behind the pink lenses of her glasses, her eyes widened.

I stared at Thorne, baffled, too, but apprehensive. My stomach was doing unpleasant things. "I brought half a dozen pairs of cotton socks. I wear them with running shoes."

Thorne took another swallow of coffee. "Will you ascertain whether one of those stockings is missing, Mrs. Dodge? Sergeant Baylor will accompany you."

"I don't understand. . . ."

Thorne interrupted me. "Understanding is not necessary, madam. Your cooperation is. I can send for a search warrant. . . ."

I rose. "Sergeant Baylor may look through my laundry bag as long as she likes, Inspector. I have nothing to hide, not even dirty linen."

The mild witticism drew not the ghost of a smile from either of the detectives. Sergeant Baylor stood and brushed her skirt straight.

When I had tidied up after the burglary, I had stuffed much of what was lying on the floor, whether it was clean or dirty, into my laundry bag. The bag looked like a lumpy sausage. I upended it on the duvet and started sorting.

I was wearing a lot of intense blue and fuchsia that spring, and my undies lean in the direction of lace and pastel colors. The white socks were easy to spot. There were five of them. I laid them next to one another on the bed and poked everything else back in the bag.

Baylor didn't say anything. I moved to the dresser, hoping the stray sock had found its way into the top drawer. Three neatly rolled pairs lay in a corner, like sandbags holding back the froth of panty hose and pastel briefs. I searched grimly. I opened the other drawers and rummaged without success.

"A sock is missing." I cleared my throat. "In addition to the Inuit carving and the twenty-odd pounds we reported."

Baylor nodded. I followed her back to the living room and said nothing as she told Thorne the results of the search.

When she finished, Ann said, "I think you'd better explain, Inspector."

I drank cold coffee and didn't look at anyone.

After a silence that may or may not have been pregnant, Thorne said heavily, "We found the Eskimo carving in the mop pail. It was hidden in the toe of the missing stocking and there are stains on the fabric, possibly hair, as well."

My pulse thrummed. When neither Ann nor I commented, Thorne went on, "We're fairly sure the dog was coshed—skull fractured. It's also possible that certain of Miss Beale's head injuries were inflicted by the same weapon. Mind you, we're not sure. We'll have to await the forensic analysis."

"Before you arrest Lark for murder? That's crazy," Ann said in the tone of voice she would use to calm a dangerous lunatic. "She was with me all evening."

Thorne leaned forward. "And all afternoon?"

Sergeant Baylor's pen poised above her notebook.

I said from the depths of my funk, "Ann was out shopping for food when I came in around three. I napped—from about three until five. When . . ." I cleared my throat again. It felt tight. "When did Miss Beale's accident occur?"

Thorne's voice was as cool as his eyes, but I noticed an odd

61

thing. While his vocabulary had grown statelier than in our earlier sessions, his vowels had slid back in his throat and his *r*'s rolled like the River Tyne. "We don't know. She lay in the main entryway, head down, with her feet still on the stairs. As far as we can tell, no one saw her today. . . ." He glanced at his wristwatch. "Yesterday."

"That's hard to believe." Ann leaned forward. Her hair had begun to wilt. A blond strand hung over her forehead. She brushed it aside. "There are other tenants, tenants with access to the foyer and stairs. We have no key to the main building."

"According to her niece, Miss Beale often left the door unlatched in daytime."

That was news to me—bad news. Ann grimaced.

Thorne continued in the same heavy northern voice. "The ground-floor flat is leased by a French chemical firm as a pied-à-terre for their commercial travelers. We believe no one is in residence at the moment. The first-floor tenants are on holiday. The gentleman who lives above has not yet returned. A householder across the street saw his auto leave at half nine in the morning."

"So she . . . Miss Beale might have lain there all day." I swallowed hard. "Could . . . did she live long after the fall?" Could we have done anything for her? was what I meant to ask, though my guilt was unwarranted. Neither Ann nor I would have tried to enter the main door. Miss Beale's note had specified no further personal contact. I wondered whether we still had the note.

"We have no way of knowing until the autopsy, Mrs. Dodge, and even then . . ." Thorne's voice trailed, as if finishing the sentence required more energy than he summon. He rose. "I shall have to ask both of you to remain in London until further notice."

"We were supposed to leave the flat Monday morning." I took some pleasure in reminding him of that.

"I've spoken to Miss Worth. She has no objection to your stopping on at the same rent if your presence will assist me in my inquiries."

"Oh, and how about Mr. Worth?"

"She says he'll agree. *She* was most cooperative." There was a definite stress on the pronoun.

Ann heaved a sigh. She had spent a lot of thought and energy arranging our excursion to Wales. However, she made no objections. I didn't, either, God knows. Thorne hadn't arrested me. I supposed I should be grateful. I wondered whether Jay was home yet.

As we saw the police to the door, I decided it was time to state the obvious. "It's a little hard to believe in rampant coincidence, Inspector. Surely there's a connection between Milos's stabbing, the burglary, and Miss Beale's accident." Once more, I forced out the euphemism. Thorne wasn't going to hear the word *murder* from my lips.

"If there was a burglary."

A hot wave of anger energized me. "What the hell does that mean?"

He stood in the tiny hallway, flat-footed, regarding me from tired, unsmiling eyes. "Happen 'twas faked, Mrs. Dodge. Nowt was taken save the murder weapon. And the white stocking."

I translated, fuming. What about my twenty pounds? Of course, he had only my word that there had been twenty pounds.

Ann leapt into the breach. "Now, Inspector, honey, you're letting your imagination run away with you. Milos was stabbed, and some lowlife broke in here looking for his papers. When he couldn't find them, he came back. If the scoundrel took the sock and the carving and used them to whop Miss Beale upside the head, why I reckon he just had a purpose we don't know about yet."

Thorne had shrugged into his raincoat. Ann gave his lapel a small pat. "You go home and get some rest now, hear? When you look at the situation in the morning, I just know you'll find a solution."

Thorne smiled the ghost of a smile. "Happen you're right, lass."

I wished I could speak Georgia—or Geordie. Sergeant Baylor's bright brown eyes shifted from Ann to her boss, but she didn't comment on the flowering of dialects.

It was three in the morning. When the two detectives had gone, I stomped back into the living room. Fright and frustration drove me to the coffeepot. I poured a reckless cup and gulped it without cream. "He has to be out of his mind. Does he really believe I'd kill Miss Beale over possession of this ghastly cave? The man is nuts, loony, bonkers. . . ."

"Now, honey."

I rounded on her. "If you dump the butter boat over me, Ann, I swear I will commit murder. Inspectah, sugah, ah jest know yoah gonna solve this little old crahm any minute now." My imitation was neither accurate nor kind, but I was fed up. I am not fond of the stereotype of Southern Womanhood under the best of circumstances. Ann was an intelligent adult. I saw no reason why she should do a bad imitation of Scarlett O'Hara.

Ann sank onto the couch-cum-bed. "Lord, Lark, what's the use of antagonizing the man?"

I said through my teeth, "There has to be a middle ground between antagonizing Thorne and covering him with praline syrup. What is with you, anyway?"

She stared at me through the pink-tinted lenses, opened her mouth, closed it. Finally, she said, "I do conciliate, don't I?"

I gave a short, sharp nod.

She sighed. "Buford—my ex-husband, that is—was apt be a trifle irascible." She wrinkled her nose, as if the word tasted bad. "Hell, he was a loudmouthed bully and as notional as a mule in a hurricane. I got so I placated him without thinking. I'm sorry, Lark. It's a terrible habit. I did't mean to say anything inappropriate. I guess I'm a little tired."

"It's okay." I felt two inches high. "In fact, it probably helped. Just don't feel as if you have to seduce the man on my behalf."

She gave a crooked smile. "Have a little dignity?"

I squirmed.

"I admire you, Lark. You're so independent-minded."

"Like a mule in a hurricane?"

The smile turned into a grin. "You said it, honey. What're we going to do?"

I shook my head. "Hide? When the press finds out I'm a suspect, I'll have to hide. You may not have noticed, but the British press is largely composed of gossip mongers and paparazzi. Thank God there's no phone."

Ann had gone pensive. "I'm going to visit Milos. I'm sure there's a connection between his stabbing and Miss Beale's murder. I want to find out what it is, starting with those papers."

"Do you think he'll be able to talk?"

"Or willing? That's the real question. I thought he was just a simple refugee, but if he's smuggling state secrets . . ." Her voice trailed.

I wasn't liking the idea, either.

My understanding of international espionage was drawn entirely from spy thrillers. Since I detest spying of any kind, I had not read many. I'd stopped halfway through one best-seller when the so-called hero blew away the villain and a dozen assorted bystanders in front of the Louvre, and left on a plane for New York the next morning without so much as a mild *hélas* from the *Sûreté*. As fiction, the story lacked verisimilitude, and if it was reality, I wanted no part of it. The thought of being caught up in such shenanigans was even more appalling than being held prisoner by British tabloids. There had to be a tamer alternative, but Inspector Thorne's alternative featured me as the goat.

Ann had pulled out the Hide-a-Bed and disappeared into the bathroom with her robe and slippers. Tactful. I rinsed my cup, turned off the burner, and drifted to the bedroom.

Needless to say, I slept badly and briefly, my dreams full of bloody images. Milos, eyes twinkling, flitted among the corpses chanting snatches of Shakespeare. Rollo yipped pitifully. When I finally admitted to myself that I was awake, it was six and my body felt as if it was in a mid-Pacific time zone. I slid into sweats and running shoes and oozed out the door. I didn't even think about lurking reporters.

Fortunately, the press was not yet on the loose, though Thorne had posted a constable by the front entrance. The man—it was not Ryan—gave me an unsmiling nod as I walked past him.

I tried to reach Jay from the pay phone and got our answering tape. I left word that I'd call later, thinking as I spoke that the recorded message Jay and I had concocted the previous winter was too cute for words and would have to be replaced. No shops were open, nor did I think the gates of the park would be, so I headed toward the river and jogged along the Embankment as far as the Chelsea Hospital. The weather was as gray as my mood.

I swung by the newspaper stands in the tube station on my way back and bought *The Times* and the *Independent*. I didn't even allow myself to focus on the tabloids. I tried Jay again without success and remembered that he had been scheduled to attend an obligatory end-of-semester gathering, the kind administrators imagine will delight their staff, who are so exhausted from grading term papers they want only to collapse. I didn't record a message.

I was visualizing Jay on the dean's redwood sun deck when I bumped into the reporter.

"Sorry," I muttered.

"Mrs. Dodge?" She was young and dressed in punk black, with her hair sheared off asymmetrically in the style fashionable that season. She used red eye shadow. She pulled out a notebook.

I kept walking. I could see the constable watching us from the pavement in front of the house.

"Will you tell our readers your sensations when you were informed of your landlady's death?"

"What paper?"

"Pardon?"

"What newspaper do you represent?"

"Ah. Wendy Wills, *Daily Blatt.*" The *Blatt* was two shades yellower than the *Daily Mail.*

"Miss Beale's death is a great tragedy, Ms. Wills. Mrs. Veryan and I extend our condolences to her family. I have no further comment." I kept my voice as pleasant as possible. The constable was still watching, but he made no move to intervene.

I unlatched the gate that led down to our areaway. A flashbulb popped. Ms. Wills had a photographer with her. Enterprising.

I turned and made sure the gate had locked behind me.

"Why did you come to London, Mrs. Dodge?"

Why indeed. Another flash. I blinked.

"I'm told you had a grievance against Miss Beale."

I didn't respond.

"Was she going to evict you? Did you kill her? Did you kill the dog? What of poor little Rollo, Mrs. Dodge?"

I was wrestling with the door lock by then and my newspapers slid to the pavement. I opened the door, gathered up the papers, and entered. The reporter's shouted questions pursued me.

I made sure the door would hold, then went into the bedroom to check the window. It opened on a private park with high iron railings. The railings hadn't slowed our burglar. They'd be duck soup to a reporter of Ms. Wills's stripe. After I had secured the latch and closed the curtain tightly, I tossed the papers on the bed, stripped off my sweats, and ran a bath. When I no longer felt smirched and slimy, I dressed in jeans and a pullover and went back to the papers. Ann hadn't stirred, as far as I could tell. At least the flat was soundproofed.

The *Independent* story, though it made a lower corner of page one, was short, restrained, and reasonably factual. "A confidential source" had leaked the tale of our eviction. Probably not the police. Daphne? Trevor? Daphne's friends in the tenants' league? The report mentioned our burglary but drew no connection to Milos's stabbing. Apparently, Thorne had not yet identified us to the press as the unnamed witnesses. I wondered how long it would take for the journalists to figure that one out. Perhaps they had forgotten Milos.

I also wondered when I would be able to sneak out and telephone Jay. It was 11:00 P.M. at home, and if I didn't call soon, he would worry. If I did call, he would also worry, of course.

I stewed for half an hour. Then I dug out my sunglasses and the blue beret I had bought as a souvenir for Jay's secretary. Not much of a disguise. Nothing could camouflage my height. I nosed out the door. There were no reporters in sight, though the constable regarded me with interest from his perch on the steps that led up to the front door.

I said good morning to him and scurried down the street to the telephone kiosk. Two householders were walking leashed dogs. Otherwise, the area was deserted. The Old Brompton Road was livelier—cars, buses, some early shoppers on the sidewalk. No one seemed to notice me, though. I got through to Jay on the first ring.

I poured out my story to my silent husband, not excluding Rollo's demise and my encounter with the press vanguard.

When I wound down, he said grimly, "That does it. I'm coming tomorrow."

"But what about finals?"

"I'll do the grades I can tonight and give the rest of the students Incompletes. Kayla can monitor the tests for me." Kayla was his secretary.

"But we're already in debt. . . ."

"Old Mason in the music department has a couple of cheap excursion fares available. His wife broke her leg last week and they won't be able to use the tickets. I told him I might want one of them. . . ."

"At the dean's soiree last night?"

"Yeah. I'll have a two-hour layover in LA and four hours in Dallas, so I won't get in until eleven Sunday morning London time."

"Oh, darling." I knew he hated to fly. Guilt washed over me. "I'll meet you at Heathrow."

"Gatwick," he corrected. "If you're not arrested."

We talked for another twenty minutes—big spenders—and I took down the flight number. When we hung up, I felt better and worse. I wanted Jay with me, but bankruptcy stared us in the face. Also, it sounded as if Mason had booked a flight from hell. Taken with the inevitable jet lag, the ordeal was bound to flatten Jay. At least I had flown nonstop from San Francisco. However, a flat spouse is better than none.

On that philosophical conclusion, I started back. Then it occurred to me that Ann and I would need to escape sooner or later, if only to lay in supplies. I returned to the kiosk, dialed the taxi dispatcher, and asked for a cab at eleven o'clock. She wanted me to name a destination. I said Harrods. If reporters pursued us, we could surely lose them there. It's the most confusing store I've ever been in.

Ann was sitting in the kitchen staring at *The Times* as if she had forgotten how to read.

"Jay's coming."

She focused on me. "How nice."

"I mean soon. Sunday."

She blinked and readjusted visibly. "Why that's wonderful, Lark, honey. I'm sure he'll straighten everything out in no time at all."

"Now, cut it out."

She took a gulp of coffee and said with dignity, "You may reproach me for my style of discourse after ten-thirty, not before."

I told her about the press siege and the taxi. I was beginning to feel almost cheerful.

Ann liked the taxi idea, but she intended to make for the tourist information bureau as soon as the cab set her down in front of Harrods, then go on to the hospital. I didn't object to that and we concocted plans. They did not include a visit to the Chelsea police station.

8

♦ ♦ ♦ ♦ ♦ ♦

At eleven o'clock, we leapt up the steps, dived through the reporters, and escaped into our waiting taxi amid a chorus of shouted questions, most of them unanswerable. By that time, a dozen representatives of the Fourth Estate and their auxiliaries, plus an ITV camera unit, had assembled in front of the house. Flashbulbs strobed as the taxi pulled out.

"Harrods?" the driver asked in a bored voice, as if he was accustomed to abetting notorious fugitives. Perhaps he was. When I said yes, he made no further attempt at conversation—just flipped his meter on and drove. I love London taxi drivers. Not only do they know every obscure side street in Central London, they are tactful.

Ann and I sank back in the huge seat and looked at each other.

"Do you think they'll follow us?" she asked.

"The police or the press?"

Our taxi turned a corner and she clutched at the convenient door grip. "Whatever."

The driver pulled onto the Cromwell Road. Traffic was thick. I craned around and spotted half a dozen other shiny black taxis, their ENGAGED signs lighted, on the wide street behind us. Any one of them might hold a reporter. "Plan B."

"Right."

The light changed and we sailed majestically past the Victoria and Albert Museum, then obscured by billboards the canny director had let out for an enormous sum to replace funds the Thatcher government had cut from his budget. Beyond the V and A and the ultramodern Ismaili Center, past the Brompton Oratory with its demure dome, lay the posh shopping district of Knightsbridge and the arrogant gray bulk of Harrods department store.

When the cabbie wheeled grandly around and pulled in behind a Jaguar, I already had the fare and a suitable tip in my hand. We climbed out and I thrust the money through his open window. It's possible he touched his cap, but we didn't dally to thank him.

I made a path through a coachload of tourists—German or Scandinavian, I thought—who were milling about the main doors. Inside, Ann and I split up. I squirmed and elbowed my way through clumps of chic English shoppers and bewildered foreigners toward the back of the store. Ann headed west for the escalator.

When I passed the mouth-watering array of goodies in the food section, I hung a left. Then I veered around into men's shirts and slipped out the east doors into the horde pouring from the adjacent tube station. I didn't spot anyone following me.

For once, the crossing light was with me. I surged across the street and cut back to the American Express office. The queue inside gave me fifteen sweaty minutes. I scrunched down and tried to look shorter, but the line moved with reasonable speed. There were three tellers on duty. I had cashed the last of my travelers' checks, zipped back to the tube station, and thrown myself on a Piccadilly Line train within half an hour. I didn't pause long enough to work into a good phobia.

I spent the morning the way untold thousands of London housewives did—grocery shopping. Ann's purchases the day before had been limited because we thought we were leaving for Wales. Also, we had not anticipated Jay's presence. I laid in enough for a siege.

I bought a pasty at one of the delis near the Lycée and ate it as I walked along, London-style. At about half past two, I retrieved my raincoat from the dry cleaners. It would be some time before Ann returned. She had intended to undo our Welsh travel arrangements and visit Milos at the hospital. I thought about walking to Waterstone's Bookstore on the Old Brompton Road, but I was laden with loot and my arms ached. Reluctantly, I headed back to the flat.

The reporters had dispersed. Perhaps they had pursued us and been bamboozled. More likely, they had grown bored waiting. The constable's eyes widened when he saw me and he reached for his radio, but I had the key routine down pat. I managed to slip into the flat with a minimum of delay. I was stowing the last of my booty in the kitchen cupboard when the gate buzzer sounded.

Inspector Thorne was not pleased with me for disappearing. I played innocent and offered to show him the groceries, but he and Sergeant Wilberforce, who was back on duty, hauled me off to the Chelsea police station, anyway.

I suppose all police interrogations have common elements. Thorne remained massively courteous, but he and the sergeant took me through my statement so many times, I lost count. They did a Mutt and Jeff on me, though it was hard to tell which of them was supposed to be the nice guy and which the intimidator. Behind their masks, Thorne seemed angry, Wilberforce cool. Neither was amused.

Around 4:30, they took a tea break. A uniformed woman brought mugs of horrible sweet tea with milk. The infusion was strong enough to dissolve teaspoons, but sugar and milk disguised the tannin. I drank four swallows of the awful stuff and came wide awake.

"Now, Mrs. Dodge, let's go over your decision to attend the theater one more time."

"Promise?"

Thorne blinked. "Eh?"

"Do you promise this is the last time?"

He sighed. "No promises." Wilberforce looked bored.

I summoned patience. "There was no decision involved. Ann wanted to see *Cats* before she left London, but the tickets cost too much, so she found cheap seats for *Hamlet* instead. That they were for Thursday night was purely fortuitous." I had already paraphrased the same information umpteen times.

He nodded. "Now, in the afternoon, you returned alone around three. Did you ring the bell for Miss Beale?"

"I went straight down to our flat and straight to bed. I saw nothing suspicious. I didn't hear the dog. I slept until Ann came home, because my internal clock was haywire."

"You woke around five." He no longer pretended to sound skeptical about my two-hour nap. Progress. He led me through the rest of the evening, from the lamb chops to our return on the tube, and this time, when I wound down, he rose from his chair. "All right, Mrs. Dodge. That's all for now. I must ask you to leave your passport with us."

That was a blow—not as heavy as being booked into jail, but a blow, nonetheless.

"How am I supposed to cash checks?" I had no traveler's checks left, but he didn't need to know that.

He was unmoved by my possible fiscal plight and added that I was not to leave London without notifying him.

Caffeine from the tea jangled in my bloodstream. I was damned well going to meet Jay at Gatwick on Sunday. I thought about telling Thorne, but it was none of his business. I rose and brushed my skirt straight.

"Sergeant Wilberforce will drive you to your flat."

"I'll walk," I said coldly. "I need the exercise."

Ann met me at the door. "Where have you been? Milos has disappeared!"

"What?"

She took my pristine raincoat and hung it in the hall closet. "I went to the hospital. When I asked to see Milos, I got a runaround from the receptionist."

I followed her into the living room and sat in the armchair. "Maybe they moved him to another hospital."

She hunched on the love seat/bed. "I don't think so. When I asked to talk to the sister in charge of that ward, the receptionist hemmed and hawed and allowed as how I'd have to see Matron. That took a while. Finally, I was sent up to the third floor to a glassed-in office and this dragon lady just stonewalled me."

I had a brief flash of Stonewall Jackson charging through the hospital.

She leaned forward. "That woman would shame a clam. She said Mr. Vlacek was no longer in hospital and she was not authorized to give out information about patients to strangers. I said I was no stranger. I did the whole act, Lark, honey. I begged, I pleaded, I cajoled. I did everything but claim Milos was the father of my unborn child. It didn't do a particle of good. She told me zip."

"I wonder if Inspector Thorne knew about Milos's disappearance?" When Ann frowned, I explained my little sojourn at the police station.

"They took your passport? Oh, honey . . ."

"I won't need it for a couple of days. Unless Daphne tosses us

72

out on our ears. Why don't you think Milos was transferred to another hospital?"

"Matron would have had no reason to withhold that from me. Telling me would have gotten me out of her hair. She was hiding something."

I said slowly, "I hope he hasn't taken a turn for the worse."

"What if the assassin made another attempt on his life? I reckon the police moved Milos for his own protection and told the hospital to cover up."

That seemed farfetched to me. Perhaps my doubt showed on my face.

She continued, hands clenched on her knees. "The only other explanation I can think of is that Milos died and they're waiting to notify whoever is next of kin before they admit their incompetence to anybody else." She teared up. "God, Lark, what if he's dead?"

"He's not dead." I got up and went to the kitchen. "They probably just moved him to another hospital."

"Then why did Matron . . ."

"Maybe she wouldn't tell you anything because she hates Americans. Matron hasn't seen me and neither has the ward sister. Shall I go over during visiting hours tomorrow and tell them I'm Milos's sister from Canada, eh? I do a great Toronto accent. They'll tell me everything."

That provoked a small smile.

"I hope you like fish. I bought plaice for dinner."

Ann had no objection to plaice. We comforted ourselves with cookery and settled down for a quiet evening. Ann had collected a bundle of maps and brochures from the tourist office. She pored over them as if they provided mental escape. I was listening to a string quartet, but my mind kept puzzling over Milos's disappearance. I had pooh-poohed the idea that he was dead, but I was by no means sure he wasn't. The knife had punctured his lung.

Around 8:30, the bell rang, and Ann went to the door. Daphne Worth entered, looking rumpled and forlorn.

Ann showed her into the living room. I felt awkward at first, and I think Daphne did, too. We paid her a week's rent from the stash Miss Beale had returned, and I poured a round of wine from the carton I had opened for dinner. Ann murmured baroque condolences and tut-tutted about the press and all three of us had another glass of plonk. I mentioned that Jay was arriving early. By the time we finished off the carton we were on first-name terms and Daphne was telling us her troubles.

Miss Beale's will named Daphne and her brother as coheirs. While proving the will would take some time, the lawyers saw no reason the flat should remain unoccupied. Daphne had moved in. She would be able to walk to work in five minutes instead of commuting for an hour from Chiswick—and someone had to dust the knickknacks, after all. The problem was that Trevor had just announced his intention of moving in, too.

"Don't y'all get along, honey?" Ann was pink from the effects of too much wine and her accent had thickened.

Daphne blinked at her like an owl.

"You and your brother?"

Daphne gave a small shrug. "Oh, we go on well enough these days, though we fought like cat and dog when we were children. I'll fetch up darning his bloody socks and cooking his meals, and I can't abide his posh friends."

Ann and I made universal female noises. Men.

Emboldened, Daphne went on, "And he'll stick me with the housekeeping tab. Brother Trevor is not precisely scrupulous about money." She glanced at us and made a moue. "I don't mean he's dishonest, but he did borrow from Auntie. As far as I know, he never repaid her. Trevor went to public school. He picked up the accent and a lordly attitude toward debt."

The term *public school* triggered off Ann's teacher persona and she launched into a series of questions about the differences between the British and American educational systems, which Daphne answered with relish and less prejudice than I expected. After all, Daphne was a teacher, too. I poured a round of bad Burgundy from a half-empty bottle that had sat in the cupboard for a week.

Burgundy induced melancholy. Daphne began to reminisce about her aunt. According to her, Miss Beale was a saint. She had nursed Daphne's grandparents through the cantankerous ailments of old age, devoting herself to them, while Daphne's Mum married a wastrel car salesman and bore two kiddies. When the car salesman scarpered, Miss Beale came to the rescue.

"I was eleven," Daphne enunciated, holding her glass out. I poured the last of the Burgundy. "Trevor was thirteen and set to leave for his posh school. Auntie paid the fees. I'll never forget Mum's relief."

"Couldn't Trevor have applied for a scholarship?" Ann was interested—also pinker.

Daphne wrinkled her nose. "Trevor's not a scholar. He was always good at games—tennis, you know, and cricket. He's a stylish cricketer. He left school when his A-level passes weren't good enough for university."

"What does he do for a living?" I asked. I had imagined Trevor in the wig of a barrister.

Again she shrugged. "Sells posh automobiles. Like father, like son."

"Rolls-Royces?" Ann took a ladylike sip of Burgundy.

"And Mercedeses. The odd Maserati." Daphne hiccupped and patted her acetate blouse. "Sorry. I'm tiddly. Do you know that showroom on the Old Brompton Road, the one with the red Porsche in the display window?"

Ann and I nodded.

"Trevor works there," she said dispassionately, "but he never could persuade Auntie to buy a car. She walked or took a taxi or rode the tube. Poor Auntie."

"I suppose your aunt lived here all her life," Ann murmured.

"In this house? Yes, except for the time she spent studying in Europe. Auntie was a linguist. She worked as an au pair in France when she was a young woman, but her real love was the Slavic languages, not French. She worked as a translator until last year." Daphne's face darkened. "She said she wanted to savor early retirement. . . ."

"Uh, did your aunt speak Czech?" I interposed, ideas shifting beneath the haze of booze.

Daphne blinked at me. "To be sure. Czech and Slovak and Polish. And Russian. She worked as a translator for the BBC, off and on. Grandpapa taught at Imperial College, you know. He was deep in the Moral Re-Armament movement, and he despised Stalin. Still, he made Mum and Auntie learn Russian, just in case."

I tried to square this account with my perception of Miss Beale as the insular type. If she was a student of Middle European languages, why had Ann's association with Milos bothered her to the point of evicting us? Perhaps she had objected to Milos not because he was Czech and a foreigner but because he was a waiter. The British, I reflected solemnly, had thought *Lady Chatterley's Lover* pornographic not because of the sex, not even because of the four-letter words, but because it portrayed a lady falling in love with a gamekeeper. There *was* a Tory grandfather.

I could see Ann's eyes gleaming behind her pink lenses and I had no doubt she was digesting the possible ramifications of Miss Beale's Czech connections.

Daphne gave a melancholy giggle. "My mother forgot her Russian as soon as she learned it. Auntie used to try to persuade her to keep up her languages, but Mum couldn't be bothered. Auntie said it was a great waste of talent. I'm rotten at languages myself, and Trevor's not much better." The brooding look settled again on her squarish face. "Poor Auntie." She dashed off the last of the Burgundy as if she was toasting Miss Beale.

"Poor lady—and poor Rollo, too," Ann murmured with tipsy sincerity.

Daphne's rather protuberant gray eyes glittered with unshed tears. "Poor old Rollo." She sniffed. "Auntie was a tough old bird. I'm sorry she's dead, God knows, but at least she could try to defend herself. Whoever killed Rollo ought to be hanged." British law had abandoned the death penalty many years before.

I made a ponderous philosophical foray into the murk of British ethics, and Daphne responded with a passionate defense of dumb animals. I said I didn't think Rollo was all that dumb.

Daphne withered me with a look. "You Americans, you're so violent."

I was about to protest when sanity intervened. I was drunk. Daphne was drunk. There was no point in arguing. Perhaps she came to the same conclusion, for she rose, wobbled, regained her balance, and stuck out her hand.

"Mussay g'night. Thanks awfly for the wine. An the lolly." She waved the twenty-pound notes in her left hand.

I shook her free hand. I thought about curtseying but concluded I would fall to the floor if I bent my knees. Ann shook hands, too, murmuring southern nothings, and Daphne departed.

When we had closed the door on Daphne, Ann took my elbow. "Wasn't that interesting?"

"Miss B's knowledge of Czech? You bet your booties. But I'm sorry 'bout Rollo." My tongue blurred the last sentence. "Godda goda bed."

"Weren't you supposed to call your husband?"

I stared at my wristwatch. "No' forn hour."

I heard Ann sigh. "Well, that leaves an hour for you to sober up in. My goodness, Lark, you didn't have to match the woman drink for drink."

"I thought I saw you chugalugging along with us."

She considered that. "You're right. I did."

We had a fit of drunken giggles, repaired to the coffeepot, and sobered sufficiently so that I could negotiate the distance to the phone booth without falling in the gutter. Ann went with me for safety's sake.

Jay was tired and rather cross and seemed not to notice my exaggerated clarity of speech. I took down the information on his flight and assured him I would meet him at the airport. He said he would call my parents before he left. We made ritual good-bye noises. The call took about ten minutes.

Ann and I sloshed back, ducked down our stairs, under the constable's suspicious eye, and went to bed. In spite of my potations, I slept like a baby and woke without the least trace of headache at eight o'clock. Ann was being sick in the bathroom, so I pulled on my sweats and went out for papers.

By ten, Ann was on the road to recovery and I was deep into the *Independent*. Much discussion of Britain's role in the upcoming European Economic Union. The latest on the investigation into Miss Beale's death featured a photo of Ann, glasses gleaming maniacally as she looked over her shoulder at the photographer. There was no word at all on Milos, certainly no mention of his disappearance from St. Botolph's.

Ann was drinking weak tea and leafing through the *Times*. I don't think she focused. Flipping pages was just a way of avoiding conversation.

I turned to the opinion pages. An excellent article detailed the progress to date on three disaster investigations: the King's Cross fire, the train crash at Clapham Junction, and the Lockerbie airplane crash. The article alluded to but didn't analyze the recent Hillsborough football disaster in which more than a hundred Liverpool fans had been crushed to death by the drunken crowd.

There is something about disasters of that magnitude that fascinates while it repels. I read the section dealing with Lockerbie carefully. One of my father's favorite students had transferred to Syracuse University expressly to take part in its overseas studies program—and been killed at Lockerbie—so I had followed the story from the beginning with almost obsessive interest.

The investigation was being conducted with great thoroughness by the Scottish lord advocate, by the chief constable of Galloway and Dumfries—and by the FBI, the CIA, and half a dozen other agencies associated with aviation or foreign governments. Shocking allegations had been made in the world press—of CIA foreknowledge; of information passed on to the airline at Frankfurt—where

77

the flight originated—and ignored; of possible security laxness at Heathrow.

At that point, it seemed clear that the plane had been destroyed by a terrorist bomb hidden in a cassette tape player. The assumption was that the terrorists were tools of Iran, taking vengeance for the shooting down of an Iranian airliner by an American military jet. Many dark hints were circulating about the involvement of other governments, but the *Independent*'s reporter separated fact from rumor. It was good journalism and I appreciated it. I also began to brood about Jay's long flight to Gatwick.

To distract myself from visions of my husband being blown to bits somewhere over Hudson Bay, I turned to the bitchiest of the gossip columns. The writer, a woman, had clearly cut her teeth on the tabloids. Her air of snickering tittle-tattle was unpleasant, but she could turn a phrase. I was admiring her snide innuendos about a minor royal and his hairdresser when my eye caught the phrase "murder investigation in Chelsea." My stomach knotted.

Across the table from me, Ann moaned gently.

"What's wrong?"

"Nothing, honey. Just thinking about my sins."

"Try meditating on this." I began reading. " 'Two rich American women living in pricey West End digs are helping the police in their enquiry into the brutal murder of Letitia Beale Friday evening. Miss Beale had the bad luck to let a flat to the Americans. And very bad luck it was for Miss Beale's doggy, too. Little Rollo's skull was smashed by a single blow from a cosh. The weapon, my dears, was improvised from a rare Esquimaux statue stolen from the flat and an intimate item of apparel peculiar to Americans.' "

"Socks." Ann snorted.

" 'The Hon. Patricia Windom, Secretary of the Chelsea Dog Lovers' League, expressed the sentiments of Britons everywhere. "It's bad enough," said Winsome Pat, "that undesirables are buying their way into our most exclusive neighbourhoods. Tell them to leave our dogs alone, I say." Hear, hear.' "

Ann said through her teeth, "That's actionable."

"I doubt it. There's more. This, mind you, is the *Independent*. Shall I run out for the *Daily Blatt*?"

Ann groaned. "I'm a sick woman."

I was merciless. " 'Americans are not as me and thee. When a dog is killed on the motorway, they make jokes about road pizza. They are tenderer of their own safety. After the Lockerbie airplane crash in December, bookings on flights from America to Britain

78

took a nosedive. Hotels and restaurants all over Chelsea filed for bankruptcy. Of course, the odds of dying in an air disaster are rather less than of being coshed with an Inuit statue. Unless you're an innocent poodle.' "

"There's something lacking in the logic there," Ann opined after a heavy silence.

"It would seem so, but probably only to me and thee." I tossed the paper at the wastebasket and missed. "The *Daily Blatt* articles will have that flavor, but they're probably shorter. I think tabloids have a four-paragraph limit."

"You're saying the business with the press can only get worse?"

"Seems likely. We can hope for a distraction."

"Prince Edward running off with a taxidermist?"

"Or Thatcher invading Vanuatu." I retrieved the article, smoothing the crumpled newsprint and smearing my hand with ink. "What we need is a clipping service."

"Good God, why?"

"After this is over and we're safe at home, we'll want to appreciate the full horror of British journalism. Your grandchildren will be able to read all about Granny's famous vacation."

Ann got up. "We don't need a clipping service. We need action."

"*I* need breakfast," I announced. "Then I'll put on my articles of intimate apparel and my running shoes and lead the press off for a trot through the park."

"You cannot run today, Lark." Ann reached into the kitchen cupboard and pulled out a box of Weetabix. "This is no time to be dillydallying. Eat and get dressed."

"You don't like my apparel?"

"Wear the wool suit. It looks Canadian."

"Thanks a lot. Canadian?"

"You are going to impersonate Milos's long-lost sister, remember?"

"I was joking, Ann."

"It's a long shot, but we're desperate. Inspector Thorne needs our help."

I thought of my interrogation. "He'll have to get along without mine."

"Don't be petulant." She poured a bowl of cereal and sloshed cream on it—real cream. The English do not believe in cholesterol.

I ate my Weetabix like a woman—with banana.

Ann was serious. She wanted me to go to the hospital and find out what I could. I must admit my urgency about Milos had receded in my concern for myself. I did not wish to study conditions in Brixton Prison for Women firsthand. I was willing to take Dorothy Sayers's word that they had been deplorable even in the 1920s.

We argued and expostulated. I had almost reached the point of putting on the Canadian suit when the gate buzzer sounded. The whites of Ann's eyes showed, and I imagine mine did, too. I went to the door.

My mother's ancient friend, Elizabeth Stonehouse, climbed down our steps despite her arthritis. She came in. We gave her coffee and she gave me the name of her solicitor. Her kindness and concern blunted my exasperation with the *Independent*'s gossip columnist. Dame Elizabeth was eighty if she was a day, and I didn't deserve her attention. It's true she made it plain her concern was for my mother's child, but I was beyond being picky. I thanked her and tried to ease her agitation.

Ann was agog over Dame Elizabeth's visit. "I read her books in graduate school."

"She's a genius," I said glumly. "And a real scholar. Lady Margaret Hall. She reads the *Daily Blatt,* though."

"No!"

"Or the equivalent. How else would she know I was in trouble? Our names weren't mentioned in *The Times*." I cleaned the over-worked *cafetière* pot. "Obviously, we ought to do something. I'll go to the damned hospital, if you think I can do any good."

"Of course you can." Ann cleared *The Times* and *Independent* from the breakfast area. "Visiting hours are one to three. If you dress now and walk to the hospital, you'll be just in time."

I dressed. I would have preferred to spend the day in sweats, but I tugged on panty hose and the wool suit. We did not have to look out to know that the press was lurking. At 12:30, Trevor Worth came down and verified the fact.

"By Jove, it's war out there." He ran a hand through his red-gold hair.

"No fun," I agreed.

Ann poured him a cup of tea.

He sipped and looked around as if seeing the apartment for the first time. "What a small place this is for the two of you. But you're welcome to stay as long as you like."

"I'll remember that as I'm hauled off to the Old Bailey," I murmured. "Do have a biscuit, Trevor."

"The Old Bailey!"

"Trial by press." I showed him the column. "I *like* dogs."

"Lord, don't take it seriously." He munched a wafer.

I didn't respond. Members of the Chelsea Dog Lovers' League would be picketing the flat at any moment.

Trevor made soothing noises through the crumbs and Ann flirted with him halfheartedly. Presently, he left. I geared up to visit St. Botolph's Hospital. Ann geared up to divert the press.

As I slipped away, I heard her telling the assembled reporters all about her springer spaniel, Pattycake, and how Pattycake had saved the infant Ann from a nasty copperhead. She was explaining the differences between copperheads and timber rattlers when I moved out of earshot.

It would be idle to suppose I wasn't followed. A sharp-eyed reporter saw me slinking off and trailed me to the South Kensington station. I took the tube to Victoria and caught a taxi back to St. Botolph's. I don't know whether my game plan worked, but I was alone when I walked into the hospital.

The receptionist was a blue-haired woman I had never seen before. Nor was the child laborer behind the desk familiar.

I drew a deep breath. "I wish to see Milos Vlacek immediately. I am his sister. From Toronto." I don't know whether I sounded Canadian. I'm pretty sure I didn't sound Czech.

The woman regarded me for a moment without speaking, then fiddled with the control board. "Mr. Vlacek's sister is here," she said inclear BBC English. She listened. "Very well."

She nodded to me. "Matron will see you in a few minutes. Why don't you wait over there?" At that point, her sense of humor must have overcome her, for she added, "With your other brother."

I turned to the reception area. The young man who had given Milos the papers at the Barbican Centre was sitting on one of the vinyl couches, flipping through a magazine.

My adrenaline started to flow. I stalked over to him. "Hello there. Where's Milos?"

He gaped at me. He had dark eyes, a faint mustache, and a slight overbite.

"Milos Vlacek," I said through gritted teeth. "Don't play dumb. I know you know him."

He stood up. "I beg your pardon, madame?"

"I saw you give Milos the papers. What have you done with him?"

"Papers?" His eyes darted around the reception area. "We can't talk here."

81

"No? Why not?"

He started toward the exit. I followed, mentally cursing the high heels I had worn to bolster my Canadian image. I was half a head taller than he was, though, so I stayed right behind him, heels or no heels.

Outside, it was drizzling and the traffic hummed along the Fulham Road.

"Where is Milos Vlacek?" I took his arm. He was wearing a leather bomber jacket of the sort then fashionable among younger men. The leather felt cold and slimy under my fingers.

"Where?" I repeated.

"Hambly," he muttered, or something like that. His eyes darted. "Who are you?"

"That's unimportant. All you need to know is that I can identify you to the police."

"I do not know what you are talking about."

"Milos has disappeared from the hospital and the staff won't say what happened. I want to know where he is."

"Hambly," he repeated. He was breathing unevenly and his eyes still darted around. "The papers. You mentioned the . . . the document."

"You know very well the police have it. Now stop evading me. Milos is a sick man. He needs proper medical care. I want to know where you've taken him."

He was gaping at me. "The police have our document? Oh, no! That cannot be!"

I was going to explain about the copy—probably an unwise impulse—when he whirled and hopped on the rear platform of a passing bus.

I stepped into the street to follow him and was almost run over by a taxi. The driver was so agitated, he actually tapped his horn, and I could see the elderly passenger waving a furled umbrella at me in the rear window. I began to sprint after the red double-decker bus, heels and all, but it turned north as I watched. The man in the bomber jacket jumped down. He was gone before I reached the corner.

9

◆ ◆ ◆ ◆ ◆ ◆

I started back toward the hospital, feeling like the fool I was. Milos had disappeared and I had just chased off our only lead to his whereabouts. If I returned to the hospital, Ann's Dragon Matron would give me a scolding or, worse, hail me off to the police station for perpetrating a fraud. The only logical course was to do what Jay would have told me to do from the first—go to the police of my own accord and take my humiliation neat.

I caught a bus to the other end of the Fulham Road, because my respectable pumps hurt like hell, and walked down Lucan Place to the police station. I asked to see Inspector Thorne. Then I waited. Finally, Sergeant Wilberforce, cool as always, came for me and sat me down in Thorne's office.

"Detective Inspector Thorne is not here at the moment, madam. Do you wish to add to your statement?" He sat behind Thorne's desk.

The question threw me. I stared at his impassive features and discovered he did not like me. The silence between us stretched. "I have nothing further to say about Miss Beale's death. I came about Milos Vlacek."

"Yes?"

"Do you know that he disappeared from St. Botolph's yesterday?"

Something flickered in Wilberforce's eyes, but I couldn't read what it meant. "We know Mr. Vlacek was discharged from hospital, yes."

"The man has a punctured lung. He can't have been told to go home and take it easy. Be real, Sergeant. Either Milos is in another hospital or he's dead. If he was transferred by police order, I wish you'd say so and put our minds at ease. Mrs. Veryan and I are afraid he may have been abducted."

"What makes you say that?" Cagey. He fiddled with a silver cuff link.

I threw up my hands. "I give up. I suppose you don't think I'm trustworthy, but you ought to know that I just spotted the younger foreigner we told you about, the one who handed Milos the Harrods bag Wednesday at the Barbican."

His eyes narrowed. "Where?"

"Waiting in the hospital lobby to speak to the matron. When I confronted him, he ran off. I lost him a couple of blocks from the Earl's Court tube station."

Another long silence ensued. "Did you think to ask his name?"

"No. He told the receptionist he was Milos's brother." I didn't mention my own imposture.

Sergeant Wilberforce seemed to make up his mind. Slam. His shapely hands came down flat on the surface of the desk. The cuff links flashed. "May I suggest that you go back to your flat and stop interfering in police business? Things may be different in the States, what with lynch mobs and Guardian Angels and so on, but in Britain, we frown on vigilantism. You are a material witness, Mrs. Dodge, a suspect in a murder case. We're asking very serious questions about your background. . . ."

I tried to hold on to my temper, out of recognition that he was at least partly right, but the "Americans are not as me and thee" echo was too much. I stood up. "Ask away. I'll go back to my flat and sit there. Meanwhile, think about this. Milos bled all over my raincoat. That makes a difference to me. I care what happens to him. He may be just a waiter, a nonentity by English standards, but he's a decent human being and he doesn't deserve to be written off because he's an alien. 'Wogs begin at Calais.' Is that the premise here?"

He drew a sharp breath.

I looked him right in the eye. "Something has happened to Milos. I can't ignore that and neither can Ann, whatever you and Inspector Thorne may do or think, and whatever political expedience may dictate."

I was glad of my Canadian suit and beastly pumps. I stalked out, looking respectable. Wilberforce made no attempt to stop me.

Walking back to the flat, I began to cool down. With every step, my gloom deepened. Wilberforce probably thought I was a CIA agent, and I had just laid a mouthful of rhetoric on him that was bound to feed that suspicion. I'm a bookseller, I thought, making a mental speech. I am a former Olympic athlete. I am wholesome, for God's sake. My mother is a poet and my father is a history professor, and I come from a long line of Quakers. I would no more kill Miss Beale than I would kill a poodle. Bad thought. Road pizza.

I strode onto a zebra and brought traffic to a screeching halt. I'm innocent, I wanted to shout, but there is a sense in which no modern person is innocent. We make jokes about spooks and moles, but we continue to pay the taxes that support them. We do not inquire too closely into our investment portfolios. We accept government policies that violate our principles because a majority agrees with the policies. We imagine that the terrorist's bomb will blow up someone else's airplane.

Philosophy is poor company. By the time I reached my street, I was looking at the situation from the police viewpoint. Maybe I had come on like a vigilante.

I no-commented my way through the diminished but alert cordon of reporters and entered the flat.

Ann was poring over maps. "Do you know that it's only four hours by train to Edinburgh?"

"No kidding."

She laid down the AA atlas, which was the size of a small pillowcase. "What happened?"

I told her of my encounter with Milos's delivery boy, omitting nothing, and did a terse summary of my session with Wilberforce, too.

Ann wasn't interested in police procedure. "Hambly?"

"He said that twice, but his accent was pretty thick. I may have misheard. Is Hambly a town?"

She consulted the index of cities in the atlas. "I don't see it."

"Brum." I poured myself a glass of water from a plastic bottle. London tap water suggests something out of Milton, so we were experimenting with salubrious *eaux* from Scotland and the Massif Central.

"Brum?"

"That is how native speakers refer to the city of Birmingham."

"Well, imagine that. I have a cousin in Birmingham. Alabama." She rooted through the index. "Hammersley? Hampton Court? Hammersmith?"

I brooded over my springwater.

Ann was mumbling her way through the index. "Hamble. Hamsterly. Hanbury. Hanley . . . Henley. How about Henley? That's not far."

"He said Hambly—as far as I could tell. Maybe it's an ancient Czech curse."

"Could he have been saying Wembley?"

"As in football? No."

She set the atlas down. "What was his tone of voice?"

I considered. "Impatient, as if anyone would know what he meant. He wasn't interested in Milos's location. When I mentioned the papers, he almost hyperventilated. He wanted to know where they were."

"Did you tell him your father had a copy?"

"I just told him the police had the papers, and he moaned and said, 'Oh, no!' Then he jumped on the bus."

Ann got up and started pacing, which was difficult in the limited space available. "Hambly, Hamble, Henley."

"I think they're going to arrest me for murder. Pin it on the nearest American. Just like the journalists."

That caught her attention. "Now, Lark, honey . . ."

The doorbell, as opposed to the gate buzzer, rang. One of the Worths—or the police, coming to take me into custody. The gate lock kept the reporters at bay.

It was my turn to play butler. Trevor and Daphne Worth were standing in the areaway, Daphne glancing up at the reporters by the railing.

Trevor gave me a winsome smile. "May we come in?"

"Of course. How are you?" I was not in the right frame of mind for company, but Ann positively beamed. She cleared her maps and guides off the love seat and installed the Worths there, offering coffee, tea, or sherry. We didn't even have sherry. They agreed to tea.

I sat on one of the kitchen chairs and tucked my legs under. "My husband's flying in tomorrow."

"Splendid!" Trevor favored me with one of those charming smiles that had to be useful selling Porsches.

"So you said yesterday." Daphne gave a short, sharp nod. "Apropos of your husband's arrival, would you and Ann object to moving to the ground-floor flat? We'd charge the same rent," she added, as if one of us had squawked. In fact, both of us were gaping at her.

Ann recovered first. "I thought that flat was let to a French company."

Trevor cleared his throat. "It was. The *directeur* called, however, very agitated over the scandal. He gave us a month's notice."

"I don't think you'll have difficulty disposing of a two-bedroom flat in this area," I murmured.

"In the long run, no. Meanwhile, though, we could arrange for you to sublet."

Ann said, "I beg your pardon, Trevor, Daphne, but I don't quite understand why you want us to move." She shot a glance at her almost-felonious roommate and added, "That is, I could understand your kicking us out because of the press, but that's not what you're suggesting, is it?"

Daphne had flushed red. "No! Good grief. The thing is—"

"The thing is," Trevor intervened, amused, "Daph and I get on better at a distance. I'll take over this flat and leave her to Auntie's bric-a-brac. We thought you might not object to moving upstairs. There are two bedrooms and a telly."

"And a telephone," Daphne chimed in.

I said slowly, "If you want the same rent, I don't see why not. What do you think, Ann?"

"My land, it sounds like paradise. How soon can we move?"

Daphne heaved a relieved sigh that fluttered a loose strand of hair. "Now, if you like. Trevor and I will be happy to help you carry your traps."

We drank tea. Daphne gave us a small lecture on proper brewing methods.

Two hours later, we were installed in the pied-à-terre and Ann was on the telephone, giving the elder of her two sons a blow-by-blow account of his mother's adventures.

The flat was quite a change from our basement cave. For one thing, the windows let in light. For another, Ann had a room to retreat to. It had been a slight strain for me to have to step over her recumbent form if I wanted a glass of milk at night, but it must have been a large strain for her.

87

While I waited for her to finish her call, I sat in the living room and admired the French firm's taste. The furniture was upholstered in what looked like, but (thank God) was not, the hides of zebras. Pillows in burnt orange and ocher took the curse off the black and white. The carpet, a businesslike clay color, matched the heavy drapes, but cheerful gauze day curtains blocked the stares of the curious. A black granite mantel served as foil for the tiny artificial log in the fireplace, and someone had selected handsomely mounted prints of African animals for the flat-white walls. One glass-topped end table bore what I hoped was a reproduction of a Benin bronze. The faint scent of Gauloises under the odor of furniture polish lent a suitable atmosphere to the hypermasculine decor. We had moved from a cave to a lair. The only thing lacking was the head of an eland over the mantel.

The bedroom was going to tickle Jay, whose taste runs to futons and austere Japanese screens. I disposed my clothes in the armoire before falling in a fit of giggles on the lush velvet coverlet of the double bed. Everything was done in shades of plum velvet, and a strategic mirror in one corner of the carved plaster ceiling suggested what a peek in the bedside table confirmed: a well-supplied pit of seduction. The thought of all those latex condoms was wonderfully cheering.

Ann's bedroom, with its pale blue walls, dark blue carpet, and Renoir prints, was pleasant but much more businesslike. The small kitchen sported blond wood and white tiles and appliances that had clearly never known the touch of human hands. We had been a little disappointed to discover that the fixtures in the bathroom were Best British, rather than French. Thee was, of course, no shower.

According to Daphne, the firm manufactured ultramodern explosives. For mining and construction, she had assured me with great earnestness. We were to pay her the rent if we had to stay on another week, but we'd have to keep a log of our telephone calls. She would deal with the French.

When Ann finally hung up, it was still only half past seven. There was no point in trying to reach Jay. He was somewhere between Los Angeles and Dallas, so I subtracted five hours instead of eight and called my parents. Dad hadn't yet received the parcel, but he promised to have the document translated as soon as it arrived.

I could tell my mother was not best pleased that Dame Elizabeth had felt obliged to trudge down the stairs to the basement flat. Without exactly reproaching me, Ma indicated that she meant to call her friend and atone.

Both parents were relieved I had not been arrested. Possibly, they hadn't believed I would be. I told them they should have sat through the interrogation. They noted our new telephone number and promised to call again later in the week.

When I hung up, Ann was heating steak and kidney pies in the tiny Krupp oven and puzzling over the directions, which were translated from the German. I made a salad.

"I'm a trial to my parents," I announced, rinsing lettuce.

"All children are a trial to their parents, honey." She took two futuristic black plates from the dish cupboard. "Beau is thinking of marrying an ichthyologist."

"You don't like fish?" I whirled the lettuce in the dryer.

"I like fish fine, and little Amy would be a nice child if she didn't wear three pairs of earrings at once, but neither of them has any money, and Beau is only a junior. I refuse to support a grandchild."

"Amy's pregnant?"

"Heavens, how you do go on. However, they'll probably decide having a baby and going to school at the same time is a fun thing to do. I had Beau my second year in graduate school, so I don't favor the idea. Besides, I'm too young to be a grandmother." She clattered the cutlery.

I portioned the salad makings between two bowls and topped them with oil and vinegar dressing. "How's your other son?"

"Tommy's too caught up in the perils of being a freshman to cause trouble now. Give him six months."

We chatted amicably about her offspring and my parents, ate, and watched the telly for an hour. Fortunately, the news didn't feature us. I went in to my plum velvet bed early because I meant to take off for Gatwick by nine. The trains ran from Victoria every fifteen minutes, but the trip took an hour and Jay was due in at 11:15. I wanted to be in place, waiting for him.

As I left the flat the next morning, I heard Ann's alarm going off. She planned to spend the day in and around the British Museum, she had said, and not to wait dinner for her. I think she was being tactful, though there was less need now that we had so much luxurious room in the flat.

I dressed in black tailored pants and a teal sweater with a crocheted collar because Jay had told me the sweater deepened the color of my eyes. It was raining a little, so I also wore the tan raincoat and the garish scarf—and flats. My feet still felt the effects of wearing pumps.

Victoria swarmed with commuters, but most of them seemed

to be heading in the opposite direction. The handful of passengers in my Gatwick-bound car were silent, engrossed in their newspapers. I had bought an *Independent* and the *Telegraph*. Once we crossed the Thames, there was nothing to see, unless Clapham Junction may be considered scenic. I had plowed through the *Independent* and was searching for the *Telegraph*'s report on the murder of Miss Beale when we pulled into Gatwick station. Since the *Independent* article was a perfunctory update, I abandoned both huge Sunday newspapers. No news is good news.

I took the elevator up to the airport—the train runs beneath it—and strolled to the airline ticketing section to look at the monitors that showed arrivals and departures.

All airports are interchangeable, and Gatwick was more generic than most. Passengers, with their luggage heaped on metal carts, stood in long lines for each airline's security check. Large white signs with heavy black print advised passengers to keep their bags and parcels with them at all times and to report unattended parcels at once.

I wondered whether the signs and security checks had been posted before the Lockerbie disaster. This was my first trip abroad since my marriage. The usual X-ray routine was in place near Departures, but I didn't remember the signs, or the brisk airline personnel inspecting passports and opening bags as passengers checked in, from my earlier experiences. When I had left San Francisco International, however, the airlines had taken similar precautions with overseas passengers. Travel was getting more and more paranoid.

No one at Gatwick seemed to object to the checking process, but the stark signs made me edgy. I verified that Jay's flight was due five minutes early and drifted through to the reception area. I had come nearly an hour before the plane would land, so I took my time inspecting the layout.

The huge tiled room where friends and relatives awaited incoming passengers had almost no amenities except loos and a shop selling newspapers and magazines. The amplified announcements on the PA system echoed unpleasantly. There was no place to sit. I decided to ride the escalator up and buy a cup of coffee.

The second floor was a zoo. Magazine concessions, the large duty-free store, and shops selling the doodads passengers forget to pack surrounded a dull lobby. Passengers waiting to board hunkered in the dull seats. Back the other way, the cafeteria was clearly too small for the volume of customers. The lines for breakfast snaked along by steam tables and liquid dispensers. There was no restaurant in the usual sense of the word.

I chugged through the shortest cafeteria line and bought a pot of tea on the theory that the tea couldn't be as awful as the coffee looked. I wandered around the no-smoking section and finally perched on a stool by a high counter with five other people sitting in a row like birds on a telephone wire. The Formica-covered tables were either occupied or littered with trays, dirty dishes, and cups.

School-leavers in maroon and gold uniforms moved among the crud, working without urgency. Children howled or romped, depending on their temperaments. Parents growled. Businessmen snapped newspapers open and gulped tea. Everywhere, bags and baggage carts and parcels sat on the sticky floor. Nobody was going to leave a bag unattended, even for a minute.

Wishing I'd kept my copy of the *Telegraph,* I drank tea and waited. The PA rattled out announcements in English, French, and German. In San Francisco, the alternate languages were Japanese and Spanish. I felt very far from home and my edginess moved rapidly toward impatience. I wanted to see Jay.

After a last acrid sip, I rose, bussed my teapot and cup on the nearest debris-laden table, and went back down to the waiting area.

A brass rail at chest height topped the glass partition that separated incoming passengers from the people meeting them. I positioned myself about halfway down, between a Pakistani family and a couple of men waiting for a cousin. My station gave me a clear view of the arrival corridor.

It was easy to tell when one of the jumbo jets unloaded. The passengers' luggage all bore the same airport tags and people carried the same kinds of souvenirs and sporting gear. It was early in the season for large groups of touring families but the right time for seniors. Some of the elderly passengers looked as if they might collapse in the gangway, though I thought the distance from plane to reception area had to be less grueling than the endless tiled corridors at Heathrow. Gatwick was a much smaller airport.

Jay's flight was announced. My heartbeat quickened, then smoothed for the long wait. He had to go through customs. After what seemed like an hour but was more like twenty minutes, I saw a clump of mixed businessmen and tourists straggling out with DFW or LAX, the connecting flight, on their luggage tags.

I saw Jay well before he saw me, and I waved and called his name, modulating my voice so as not to annoy my British compeers at the rail. They don't like outbursts of public emotion. Jay didn't hear me, of course. He plodded on. He was frowning a little and his shoulder sagged under the weight of his battered gray garment bag. He wore jeans, a sage green pullover, and the tweed jacket I had bought him as a joke when he became a professor. He looked so American, a lump rose to my throat. I waved again. This time, he saw me.

His eyes widened a little but his expression didn't change. He veered toward me without pausing and almost careened into a family of English tourists with Disneyland balloons tied to their luggage cart. Jay is inclined to come straight to the point. When he reached the rail, he dropped the bag on the floor. I suppose I was babbling greetings. He didn't say anything. He took my head in both hands and gave me a long un-English kiss on the mouth, and I made a discovery.

"You have the shakes."

"Right. Get me out of here."

I pointed toward the end of the rail. "I'll meet you there."

I dashed through the waiting crowd. I had seen Jay in that state only once before and the circumstances had been unpleasant. I elbowed my way past a woman with an artificial smile. She was holding up a sign identifying her to a tour group.

I hugged Jay again. "When did it hit you?"

"After customs." He was speaking through clenched teeth.

At least he hadn't shaken all the way from Dallas to London. I took the garment bag from him, slung it over my left shoulder, and put my right arm around his waist. "Come on."

As we threaded through the crowd and made our way past Departures to the main exit, I reflected on what Jay had just gone through. I could feel his body trembling against my arm. He didn't say anything. Neither did I. There was nothing to say.

We slithered through the patient lines of departing passengers and made for the exit to the train depot. I had not thought to buy him a ticket when I arrived.

"Wait right here," I muttered as we reached the ticket queue. I dropped the bag.

"Okay."

I forged into the line behind a kid with a monumental backpack and bought Jay a ticket. That done, I led him through the turnstile and down the elevator to the train level. We boarded a waiting train and sat quietly for five minutes until the train gave a small lurch and set into motion. I could feel Jay trembling beside me, but the shaking was less violent than in the airport.

Once the train left Gatwick for open country, I said, "Better?"

"Yes. I'm tired." He wriggled his shoulders against the back of the seat.

I let out a long sigh. "Then lean against me and nap. We're an hour from Victoria. Are you okay?"

"Yeah."

"I'm sorry."

He squeezed my hand. "I think I may see my thirty-ninth birthday, after all." Jay would turn thirty-nine in May. For some reason, thirty-nine was bothering him more than thirty-eight.

"I'm relieved to hear it."

We sat. The shaking eased. A Britrail employee pushed a cart through, flogging crisps and fish-paste sandwiches. Jay gave a drowsy snort of laughter. "Jesus, what a trip. Remind me to tell you what it's like to spend four hours at Dallas airport. G'night, Lark." It was broad daylight.

"I love you," I said. He fell asleep as I spoke. At a guess—what with final exams, flying, worrying about flying, and worrying about me—he hadn't slept in thirty-six hours.

When the conductor came to check tickets, I handed him mine and Jay's. The man, rosy and just this side of plump, gave me a beaming smile. Jay didn't stir. The other passengers regarded me with smiling benevolence, as if I had kept him up with nonstop sex all weekend. I wished that had been the case.

When we pulled into Victoria Station, I shook Jay awake. It took awhile. Everyone had left the car by the time I got him on his feet and retrieved the bag. We queued for a taxi.

"You're not under arrest." He yawned.

The woman standing beside me gave me a startled glance and looked away. I felt my face go hot. "Not yet."

Jay stretched and peered past the double lineup of waiting taxis. "Holy shit, they do use those red buses."

I smiled. "And the black taxis, too."

"And it's raining."

"All the time."

"I expect we'll get used to it after a year or so."

"Year!"

"It'll take at least that long to get me back on a plane."

"That's okay. I'll abandon you," I said lightly. The woman beside me climbed into a taxi. I could see her peering back at us as her cab pulled away.

I explained to the waiting driver where we wanted to go and

we got in. The cab pulled out into the stream of traffic heading for the roundabout in front of Buckingham Palace. Traffic was heavy but no more so than usual. I settled back and began giving Jay a recap of the past day and a half, notably our new flat, my interrogation, and Milos's disappearance.

Jay made a small choking sound.

I stared.

He was grinning. "Look at those damned cars. The ones in front of us."

I looked. "What about them?"

"They're booming along with a neatly strapped-in passenger and no driver."

I sighed. British cars, naturally, reverse the position of driver and front-seat passenger. Until they get used to the idea, the illusion of driverless vehicles causes Americans and other right-minded people to do a double take.

"Just watch out when you cross the street," I muttered. "You'll look the wrong way and step out in front of a taxi." As I had almost done on Sunday in my pursuit of Milos's courier.

Jay settled comfortably against me. The trembling was gone and his eyelids hung at half-staff. He was going to fall asleep on me again if I didn't do something. I pointed out the palace guards, the statue of Queen Victoria on her little traffic island, and other scenic wonders and was describing the amenities of the plum-colored bedroom when we pulled up in front of the house.

I paid the cabdriver. He did a U-turn in front of the constable on duty as I dragged my groggy husband and his bag up the steps. I introduced Jay to Constable Ryan and let us in the door.

The ghastly foyer appeared to make no impression whatsoever on Jay. He was beyond rational thought, but he did appreciate the bedroom—for about two minutes while he flung off his clothes and burrowed under the plum-hued duvet.

"G'night," he said again, and zonked out.

I retired to the living room and watched the telly.

I also thought uncomfortable thoughts. Had I been waiting for a rescue? Jay must have thought so or he would not have subjected himself to that hideously prolonged flight when he had a ticket for a direct flight from San Francisco in four days. If I had come across to him as that desperate, I deserved to be kicked. Even if I had been arrested, what could Jay have done? He was not a magician—or even a member of the British bar. And I *hadn't* been arrested. False alarm, with the stress on alarm.

10

♦ ♦ ♦ ♦ ♦ ♦

I woke Jay at five, thinking he shouldn't sleep too long if he
wanted to set his internal clock straight. He claimed he felt considerably friskier, and we tested that theory out on the plum bed.
Satisfaction made *me* sleepy, so we took a long walk in the park
afterward, followed by early dinner at a bistro on the Old Brompton Road. When we got back to the flat, Jay made a brief call to
Harry Belknap, just touching base. We were twining together on
the faux zebra sofa and puzzling over Miss Beale's murder when
Ann showed up.

I thought she looked tired and preoccupied, but when I introduced her, she went into her graciousness mode at once. She was so
animated as she told Jay about the mummies in the museum, I
thought I must have been mistaken.

I wanted Jay to like Ann—and vice versa, of course, though it
rarely occurs to me that any sane person can dislike Jay. I saw the
satirical gleam in his eyes as she launched into ritual effusion, but he
was smiling at her by the time she described the fifty-two uniformed
schoolchildren she had once counted trying to fill in their notebooks
in the Egyptian gallery.

"And, my word, didn't those shrill little voices echo off the pillars and tombs and things?" She rolled her eyes. "It sounded just like a food fight in the cafeteria back home. I was so nostalgic, I almost burst into tears."

Jay laughed.

"Did you see the Elgin Marbles today?" I snuggled back down beside him. He put his arm across my shoulders.

Ann sighed. "They were disappointing. The Portland Vase, too. I don't understand why Keats got so worked up. However, there was this nice little temple reconstruction next door, with a nice little bench in front of it. I sat there a good half hour, resting my feet and thinking Greek thoughts. It was a whole lot quieter than the tombs of the pharaohs, even on Sunday."

"No lie."

Ann gave Jay a rueful grin. "I keep trying to see the things a good tourist is supposed to see in London, but what with this awful business of Milos and poor Miss Beale's murder, I reckon I've been lucky to catch a glimpse of Big Ben, let alone the Elgin Marbles."

"Frustrating," Jay murmured, stroking my back. "What do you think happened to Vlacek?"

Ann set her wineglass beside the bronze on the end table. "I think he was kidnapped by the same scum who had him stabbed." Behind the rose-colored lenses, tears glazed her eyes. "I'm afraid for his life, and the police don't care! It's not right. They may be torturing him."

I straightened and scooted sideways on the couch, the better to see Jay's face. "They wouldn't have to torture Milos. He's a very sick man."

Jay smoothed his mustache. "Who are 'they'?"

Ann and I exchanged glances. She said, "The Czech secret police?" It was hard to tell whether her words were a statement or a question. They didn't sound convincing.

Cold suddenly, I rubbed my sweater-clad arms. "Or British Intelligence trying to cover up some inconvenient fact." I groped in the murk of my ignorance of international espionage. "Or even trying to protect Milos from the Czech police."

"From the Czechs?" Jay's eyebrows twitched. He took a skeptical sip of bitter. Ann and I had been trying an assortment of English beers from the local equivalent of a bottle store. Jay seemed to approve.

"Or from the KGB," Ann said darkly. "If the police are trying to protect Milos, why don't they just say so? They're hiding Salman Rushdie from the Ayatollah, after all, and they've let the media know all about that. They've even permitted reporters to interview Rushdie."

"Your friend Milos was the victim of an assault," Jay murmured, watching both of us over the rim of his glass. "Sounds to me as if he's in protective custody."

"Then why doesn't Thorne just say so!" I burst out.

"Or that matron at the hospital," Ann added, indignation burning spots of color on her cheekbones. "She knew I was worried."

"They may not trust you." Jay's voice was mild.

Ann made an indignant noise.

"Thorne thinks we faked the burglary," I conceded. "And he took my passport."

Jay put his hands behind his head and gazed at the plasterwork ceiling. "I've been trying to think it through since you called me, Lark, and it doesn't make sense, but I can't come up with a scenario that ties everything together, either."

"Surely you don't believe I faked the burglary and coshed Miss Beale's poodle?"

He lowered his gaze to my indignant face and smiled at me. "No, darling, I do not, but I'm trying to follow Thorne's thought processes. Is there any possibility Milos was stabbed by accident?"

"Huh?"

Ann was staring at him, too, her lenses glittering.

Jay brought his arms down and picked up his beer glass again. "This woman whose bag was stolen on the subway, how close was she to Vlacek?"

"Standing right beside him," I said.

"Was she carrying a purse with a shoulder strap?"

I frowned, trying to remember.

"Yes," Ann said decisively. "A brown calf handbag with a strap. I noticed her because she blocked my view of Milos and Lark. I was trying to keep them in sight. I didn't want to lose them in the crowd when we got off the train."

Jay brooded. "Then isn't it possible the man meant to steal her Harrods bag all along, and that he had his knife out to slash the strap of the purse?"

I rubbed my forehead. A headache was forming between my eyebrows. "Are you saying he meant to slash the strap, and that he stabbed Milos accidentally?"

"When the train lurched." Jay smiled at me. "Something like that."

I turned the idea over in my mind.

"What about the man who held the doors open?" Ann asked.

"That's an old pattern on subways and commuter trains," Jay explained. "The purse snatchers work in pairs."

We sat there in silence. I was trying hard to make my impressions fit Jay's theory, because I disliked the idea of espionage.

"I don't believe it." Ann shook her head. She was pink with agitation. "Those papers of Milos's mean something."

"And the man in the doorway was staring at Milos." I had to agree with Ann, though I was reluctant to let the accident idea go. "The train didn't lurch, either. It was standing dead still in the Sloane Square station when Milos was stabbed. And what about the burglary?"

"Coincidence?"

"I suppose you're going to say Miss Beale's murder was a coincidence, too."

"Mmm."

"And the fact that she spoke fluent Czech is another coincidence?"

"Did she?" He sat up and put the beer glass aside. "You didn't mention that. How do you know she spoke Czech?"

Shamefaced, I confessed to our drunken session with Daphne.

He got up and began prowling the room. "Czech. That's weird. Are you sure your meeting with Milos was an accident, Ann? At the pub, I mean."

Ann's jaw dropped.

"Was it?"

"I think so. The Green Lion is near the Hanover, and Milos came in with another waiter. I ate at that pub on impulse because it looked like something out of an English movie. And he didn't . . . doesn't know where I live."

My head was spinning from Jay's abrupt reversal. "What are you saying, Jay? Do you think Milos was trying to get to Miss Beale, that he found out where Ann was staying? . . ."

"From the hotel?" Ann interjected doubtfully. "I did leave the basement flat as a forwarding address."

"He discovered Ann was going to rent Miss Beale's flat, and he cozied up to Ann in order to make contact with Miss Beale? No, that's too complicated, Jay. Milos didn't even intend to walk us home after the matinee. He said he was going to get off at Gloucester Road."

Jay was peering at a drawing of a wildebeest. He turned. "You're probably right. Chelsea is a fairly international part of London, isn't it?"

"I showed you the Lycée and the Yemeni embassy," I said. "And the Greek deli and the Chinese restaurant."

"And so on. So it's not all that odd to bump into another Czech speaker. No wonder Thorne is confused, poor bastard. I don't envy him."

I said, "Don't overdo the empathy. That man would be as happy as a cat with three tails if he could charge me with murder. What's more, the press would love him for it. DEPRAVED AMERICAN BASHES BRITISH DOG."

Jay grinned. "Come on, Lark."

"He doesn't believe me, Ann." I stood up and went over to the pile of newspapers beside the fireplace. "Did we save that column from the *Independent?*"

Ann said in small voice, "I'm sorry. I put it out with the trash this morning. I saved *The Times.*"

I straightened. My right hand was smeared with printer's ink. "It doesn't matter. I'll buy a couple of tabloids tomorrow. There are bound to be fresher examples of the 'lynch Lark' school of journalism." I trotted into the bathroom and washed my hands.

When I came back, Ann was explaining the tenor of the article to Jay. "And the woman was so snide, almost gloating."

Jay pulled me down beside him on the sofa and began kneading my shoulder muscles with one hand. "Sounds unappetizing."

"And we've been besieged by reporters." Ann frowned. "Or we were yesterday and the day before. They seem to have taken today off."

I nestled against Jay. He was working on the other shoulder. Great hands. "Maybe there's an international crisis or something else has happened to distract them. Did you buy the *Evening Standard?*"

"No, and I suppose it's too late to get one now." She looked at her watch. "Lordy, it's eleven-thirty. I have an appointment in the morning." She began gathering up her purse and the small paper sacks she had brought in with her. Souvenir postcards and slides, I supposed, and more paperback books. Ann was going to have to pay an excess luggage charge when she flew home. Books weigh a ton.

She said good night, shaking Jay's hand warmly and giving me a hug as we, too, rose to go in to bed.

The plum bedroom throbbed with uxorious lust—and whatever the wifely equivalent may be. I felt sorry for Ann, alone with her cool Renoirs.

"Nice woman." Jay watched me pull off the teal sweater.

"Do you like her? I'm glad." I kicked off my flats and wriggled out of my jeans.

"She tells a great story." He spoke absently and his eyes were gleaming. Marriage is a splendid institution.

I slept until half past seven without so much as twitching, and I woke happy. I looked at Jay hopefully, but he was out of it. He didn't even stir when I kissed him on the forehead. I didn't have the heart to wake him, though I should have. It would take him that much longer to overcome his jet lag.

I slid out of bed, took a quick bath, and dressed in sweats. A strange constable patrolled the sidewalk near the house—tag end of the night shift, probably. I nodded to him and went on to the corner and across the zebra. I bought an *Independent,* coffee, and croissants for three, then performed a juggling act as I carried the supplies several blocks home. Ann was up when I reentered the flat.

She fell on the coffee without speaking.

"I didn't buy *The Times.* Sorry. You can have a piece of my *Independent.*"

She took a long pull at the coffee. "That's okay, honey. I'm going to take a bath and go off to the hospital. I want to try Matron one more time. I have a ten-thirty appointment in Bloomsbury, so I'll have to get in gear."

"All right." I sat at the blond table in the kitchen and pulled the plastic lid off my coffee. "Any preferences for dinner? My turn to cook."

"Anything," she said absently.

I shook the paper open. "Okay."

"I think I'm in love."

I stared at her over the top of the newspaper.

She smiled. "With your husband."

"I'm forewarned." But I was pleased. "He likes you, too—said you tell a great story."

"Well!" She took a gulp of coffee and set the paper cup on the counter. "Need the bathroom?"

I waved a croissant. "Feel free."

Ann left at half past eight. No signs of life from the bedroom. I drank the third cup of coffee, which was tepid but good. Jay doesn't drink coffee. Then I tidied the kitchen and living room and poked through the stack of tour guides Ann had left on one of the end tables. Hereford and South Wales, Yorkshire, the Scottish border. She wanted to get out of London, and I didn't blame her.

Jay was scheduled to attend his DNA fingerprinting seminar on

Saturday and Sunday in Yorkshire. It was the May Day bank holiday, and he was supposed to stay at a hostelry near Thirsk provided by the sponsors, an international police association. I found Ann's guide to Yorkshire and looked up Thirsk. It sounded pleasant. Perhaps we could rent a car and I could tootle around the Yorkshire countryside while Jay considered the forensic analysis of bodily fluids. Thirsk. Castle Howard? York? I had visited York as a child and loved it. I began reading.

The door buzzer sounded. I leapt up and tried to forestall a second buzz, but the caller rang again before I could reach the door and press the button that would admit him.

It was Thorne, looking cross and accompanied this time by Sergeant Baylor. He seemed to alternate between Baylor and Wilberforce. I wondered whether that was usual. I had gathered the vague impression from British detective stories that it wasn't, but fiction is fiction.

I led the police into the living room and offered them coffee. They declined. Thorne sat on the zebra-patterned sofa. Baylor perched on an armchair and took out her notebook. She seemed fascinated by my sweats.

I stood by the fireplace. "Welcome to our new flat. What can I do for you?"

"Follow my instructions," Inspector Thorne snapped.

"I beg your pardon?"

"You left London yesterday without notifying me."

I sighed. "I beg your pardon, Inspector. I went straight to Gatwick Airport to meet my husband and came straight back."

He grunted. "I thought Mr. Dodge was scheduled to arrive on Friday."

"He was. When you lifted my passport, he changed his mind."

"I see. Well—" He broke off. Sergeant Baylor was gaping.

I turned. Jay, wearing a pair of jeans and nothing else, was standing in the bedroom doorway, blinking. "Lark, where's my . . . oops." He ducked across to the bathroom and shut the door.

I bit back a grin. Sergeant Baylor had been treated to the sight of a California-brown torso of collectible quality. I hoped she appreciated it. I did.

Thorne was blushing.

I said blandly, "I don't want to waste your valuable time, Inspector. I'm sure you had something to tell me. Or did you want to speak to Ann? Unfortunately, she's out for the day. Won't be back until dinnertime."

He cleared his throat. "I meant to tell you that the woman whose bag was stolen on the tube has come forward."

"About time. She was shouting to all and sundry that she could identify Milos's assailant. Did she?" I heard the battery-operated razor I had bought Jay kick in.

"Mrs. Watt has provided us with a detailed description." Thorne favored me with a constrained smile. "She has also agreed to look through our rogue's gallery to see if she can identify the man. Once Mrs. Watt has narrowed the possibilities, I shall have to ask you and Mrs. Veryan to look through them."

"Certainly. Any time." I took in the implications. "Does that mean you're no longer claiming I faked the burglary?"

He heaved a sigh. "It never seemed likely, lass."

Lass? Progress. Should I press my advantage? "It would be a relief to have my passport back."

He reached into his breast pocket, drew out the slim blue passport, and handed it to me without comment.

"Thanks," I murmured, playing it cool, though the relief I felt surprised me. Was I so dependent on external validation of my identity that I couldn't be without my passport for forty-eight hours? A depressing thought.

I caught a glimpse in the corner of my eye of Jay sneaking back to the bedroom. "Uh, would you like a cup of tea or coffee? I have the feeling my husband will want something soon."

"I wouldn't say no to a cup of tea."

"Coming up." I slipped out to the kitchen and put the kettle on. I had laid in a supply of herbal tea for Jay. I was fairly sure Thorne would find that insulting, so I filled the regular teapot with hot water from the tap to warm it properly and tried to remember Daphne's lecture on tea making. Ann's packet of Twining's would have to do.

By the time I readied the tray, Jay had gotten himself dressed. He emerged as I carried the refreshments into the living room. Thorne rose.

I set the tray down and made introductions. Jay shook hands with Thorne and Sergeant Baylor, and I creamed and sugared according to everyone's preference. I even took a cup of Twining's breakfast blend myself. I thought it tasted all right.

The two men had begun those skirmishes of professional courtesy men have to go through before they can deal with one another without reaching for their swords. Sergeant Baylor and I listened, like good hinds. She was not taking notes.

"I hear you're a policeman yourself, Mr. Dodge," Thorne said heavily.

Jay shot me a glance. "I was, sir, for some years. Now I run a training program."

"An academy, eh?"

"I suppose that would be the equivalent term. I still do some consulting work for the county CID."

"You're a friend of Chief Detective Inspector Belknap, I believe."

"We've corresponded. Harry invited me to deliver a paper at a conference he organized up north. I don't know the fine points of British procedure, so when the assault occurred on the subway, I called him to see what Lark's obligations as a witness may be—whether she'll be required to return for a trial, that sort of thing."

"Happen she'll be called," said Inspector Thorne, "if we make an arrest." He took a hearty swallow of tea.

That I'd have to testify in court hadn't occurred to me. More travel expenses. I squirmed in my chair.

"So Harry said. He was very helpful."

"He called me." Thorne spoke in neutral tones, but the reproach was evident. Invasion of territory.

"I'm sure he thought he owed you the courtesy, sir. He wouldn't want you to think he was interfering with your witness." Jay sipped at the brew he favors.

"Hrrmph. Well, I don't mind admitting I was taken aback by Mrs. Dodge's proximity to murder, as well as assault and burglary. However, I've done some checking. . . ." Thorne cocked an eyebrow.

Jay smiled slightly. "Normal procedure."

"Aye." Thorne took a final gulp of tea and set his cup down. "Both ladies came up clean, and a new witness has come forward in the assault case. Her evidence tallies with what Mrs. Veryan and Mrs. Dodge reported. I've returned Mrs. Dodge's passport, and I trust there's no ill feeling, but I'll have to ask her to notify me if she leaves London." He turned to me, adding with heavy good humor, "Even for Gatwick Airport."

Jay's eyebrows shot up. "Good God, Lark."

I said, "I realize now I should have called Inspector Thorne. I'm sorry." I did my best to look meek and repentant. It's possible that I fooled Thorne. In any case, he let the matter drop.

"I believe you were with the Los Angeles police at one time, Mr. Dodge."

"For ten years." Jay looked wary. He had left the LAPD after he was caught in a cross fire between a sniper and the SWAT team. Technically, he had retired on a disability pension. The Los Angeles experience was a sore point. "I'm from L.A. I trained there."

Thorne's eyes gleamed. It turned out he was a devotee of all the ancient cop shows filmed in Los Angeles. He was full of questions, but most of them involved gross violations of normal police procedure in TV's version of reality—starting with "Dragnet."

Jay answered him patiently. Pretty soon, they were sharing a laugh at the absurdities of Hollywood, and Jay asked several flattering questions about Scotland Yard. I thought that was all to the good. It was obvious that I was not going to do any bonding with Thorne myself. Jay might as well. I'm in favor of male bonding. I poured everyone more tea.

However, when they got to "Rumpole of the Bailey," I decided it was time to rescue Sergeant Baylor.

I let the last anecdote run its course. When the chuckles died down, I said, "I hope Sergeant Wilberforce relayed my concern about Milos Vlacek's disappearance, Inspector."

Thorne turned to me, his features reassembling in the professional mask. "Ah."

"I saw the man who handed Milos the papers at the Barbican."

"Oh, aye. So Wilberforce said."

"He told me to butt out," I said bluntly. "I presume that means you have no interest in what the man said to me."

Thorne's eyes narrowed. "You spoke to him?" He jerked his head at Sergeant Baylor.

When she had set her cup down and taken her notebook from her purse, I gave Thorne as thorough an account as I could of what the man in the bomber jacket had said before he hopped on the bus. Thorne was noncommittal. He asked one or two questions about the man's appearance but didn't seem very interested in what he had said about the papers.

"Is Hambly a town?" I asked.

"I don't recall a town of that name," Thorne replied. "Do you, Sergeant?"

"No, sir, but if the man spoke with a foreign accent . . ." Her voice trailed.

Frustrated, I got up and started collecting cups and saucers. "Is Milos in protective custody, Inspector Thorne? Ann is terribly upset about his disappearance. I'm worried, too."

"Mr. Vlacek was released from hospital at his own request," Thorne said. "He's not in custody."

"Do you know where he is?"

He was silent for a moment, frowning down at his hands. Finally, he met my eyes. "No, I do not, Mrs. Dodge. He left St. Botolph's in a private ambulance."

"That's a relief! Where was he taken?"

Thorne shook his head. "I don't know, and if the hospital staff know, they aren't saying. I sent a constable to question his landlady, but she's seen nowt of Mr. Vlacek since before the accident. She's, er, concerned about the rent. His mates at the Hanover haven't heard from him, either."

"Has a missing-person report been filed?"

"Mr. Vlacek is an adult, lass, and he's not wanted for any crime. He is probably at a private nursing home, or in the care of friends. I have questions for him, to be sure. Whoever is caring for him is bound to make contact with the hospital in a day or two about his National Health benefits. If not, I'll put out the word that he's wanted for questioning."

"He's still very ill."

"He was in a recovery ward when he, er, discharged himself. His surgeon and Matron advised him not to leave, but he insisted. And he was moved in an ambulance." Thorne rose. "Sergeant Baylor and I must be off. . . ."

I thanked Thorne for what he had told me of Milos. I was relieved but not completely satisfied. I had the feeling that Thorne was holding something back, but I could think of no way to persuade him to tell me anything he didn't want to tell me.

We shook hands all around and Thorne offered to take Jay out for beer with the boys when the investigation was over. They didn't clap each other on the back, but they might as well have.

Jay gave me a mild scold for not reporting my Gatwick excursion to Thorne, but his heart wasn't in it. I didn't take umbrage. When I had fed us breakfast, we walked over to the Victoria and Albert, by way of doing our touristly duty. I thought he'd probably run out of steam when his body reminded him it was the wee small hours at home, and I was right. He yawned his way around the V and A, though the marvelous rooms that look like an architectural rummage sale tickled him. We looked at the Mogul paintings and that was enough of that for the time being.

He revived briefly in the open air, so I made him go shopping with me. I thought he ought to meet Daphne and Trevor, and we were out of wine. I dragged him down the Old Brompton Road to a wine specialty shop. Daphne, I knew, would drink anything short of hair tonic, but Trevor's tastes were probably more finicky. I bought a good Burgundy and a white Bordeaux, which Jay carried for me, and we both browsed among the paperbacks at Waterstone's. We stopped at the grocery store, and at the butcher shop for lamb chops, and I laid in cheese and water biscuits at the deli. By that time, Jay was a zombie, so I took him home and tucked him in.

I wrote Daphne a note, explaining that Jay had come and inviting her and Trevor for a glass of wine after dinner. Then I went back to my *Independent* to see whether I could figure out where the press had gone. The president of Nigeria was making a state visit, which meant the queen and royal carriages and a parade. I felt a twinge of regret that I wouldn't get to see the fun, but it was nice to know the press had some sense of proportion.

I woke Jay at 2:30. He grumbled but got up and we had sandwiches. Ann came in about an hour later with more pamphlets and booklets. She looked so discouraged, I was glad I could at least assure her that Milos's abductors had carried him off in an ambulance.

I ought to have prepared her for the news. She collapsed on the zebra couch, her face as pale as milk. I thought she was going to faint.

I leapt up and hurried over to her. "Are you all right?"

"Hush. Let me think." She took off her glasses and rubbed her face with both hands. "Oh, Lord, I wish I could think."

Jay had gotten up and gone to the kitchen. He returned with a glass of water and another of the Burgundy I had opened to breathe before dinner.

Ann took the wineglass and drained half of it at a gulp. Gradually, her color came back. In fact, she began to look flushed.

"I thought you'd be glad about the ambulance," I said, bewildered.

"Oh, honey, I am. Believe me. It's just that I don't know what to do now."

"Why don't you tell us what's on your mind, Ann?" Jay is trained to negotiate with hostage takers, distraught snipers, and would-be suicides. I recognized the warm, unthreatening tone of voice.

Ann responded like a rose in a spring rain. "You'll think I'm a fool, I reckon, but I've been so worried. Yesterday, I was having lunch in the British Museum cafeteria and talking with this nice Englishman who happened to sit at my table. He was doing research on the medieval manuscripts at the museum."

"I'll bet that was interesting." Jay, still soothing, was watching her intently.

"Well, I was interested, and we talked, and one thing led to another. I ended up telling him about Milos and asking whether he knew the address of Amnesty International."

"Zow," I said. "The human-rights people."

"I thought maybe they could do something." Ann took another, less drastic swallow of wine. "He said they had an office nearby but that I'd be better off talking to this organization he knew about that dealt with British civil-rights violations, and he helped me set up an appointment for this morning."

"The Henning Institute," Jay murmured.

She looked at him, wide-eyed. "What do you know about them? Are they reputable?"

"Yes. They're a watchdog group, tend to focus on Ulster. That business in Birmingham with the alleged IRA bombers—the claim is that the evidence was rigged by the police and the courts." Jay's voice was neutral now.

Jay is interested in the problem police forces have of working within the limits of constitutional protections. Since my mother shares the interest from a strong civil-libertarian viewpoint, they had exchanged a lot of information since my marriage. Neither of them is hard-nosed, so the interchange had done both a lot of good. When Jay wrote his paper on DNA fingerprinting, he dealt with the potential for violations of the Fourth Amendment. He dedicated the article to Ma.

"Well, that's a relief." Ann finished the wine. "Because I just reported Milos as a possible human-rights violation."

11

◆ ◆ ◆ ◆ ◆ ◆

Jay and I sank onto our chairs like well-rehearsed puppets. Ann watched us. She was flushed with wine and, quite possibly, embarrassment.

I was thinking how ingenious it was of her to have come up with a lever. I had not heard of the Henning Institute, but I should have thought of Amnesty International or, given my family associations, of the American Friends Field Service Committee.

My feelings were an odd mixture of admiration, chagrin, and mild hurt that Ann hadn't confided in me. After what Thorne had told me earlier, I thought it possible that Ann's rescue effort was unnecessary, but she hadn't known of the ambulance, and Thorne—or, to be fair, Wilberforce—*had* been stonewalling us. But was Milos in good hands? I wasn't sure, and I didn't think Thorne was, either.

I looked at Jay. His eyes were bright with what looked like suppressed amusement. I glared at him, daring him to laugh.

He didn't. "By this time next week, Thorne's ass will really be in the wringer."

Ann made a distressed noise. "Oh, no! Why? That's not fair!

I didn't suggest that Mr. Thorne was at fault. I don't think he is."

"He's the officer in charge of the investigation." Jay smoothed his mustache. "Where the buck—or the pound—stops. He has the press on his back already because of the murder. When the Henning people start investigating, he'll be fielding calls about Vlacek from *important persons*."

"Questions on the floor of the House of Commons?" I was trying to imagine a sequence of events.

Jay considered. "Probably, and when the politicians take up the cry, the press will catch on very fast. I don't envy Thorne."

"Should I warn him?" Ann put her glasses back on and peered at Jay.

"It might be kind. Of course, the Institute may decide not to do anything. As I said, they tend to specialize in Irish cases."

Ann sat for a long, silent moment, frowning. "The woman I talked to promised they'd make inquiries. Maybe I should call them off, but I can't help wondering who ordered that ambulance. And how voluntary Milos's discharge was." She stood up. "I wish Mr. Thorne and those people at the hospital had been open with us. If they'd been frank, I would have waited a day or two. Well, what's done is done. I'll call Inspector Thorne tomorrow morning. Now I'm going to lie down and read for a while."

"Dinner at seven-thirty," I murmured. Then I remembered I hadn't told her Daphne and Trevor were coming after dinner. She agreed, without enthusiasm, that we owed them hospitality—and a look at my husband.

"Good God, you mean they have to approve of me?"

I laughed. "Don't let it get to you, Jay. When they're well oiled with that wine, they'll think you're wonderful."

"Especially Daphne." Ann shot an impish grin over her shoulder. She shut the bedroom door with a neat click.

"Does that mean," Jay asked in bemused tones, "that I'm going to bowl Daphne over with my natural charms or that Daphne oils easily?"

I refused to answer.

But when the Worths joined us, Daphne was back to being Miss Starch. Perhaps she was shy; perhaps Trevor brought out the worst in her. She kept her knees together, sipped like a lady, and sat up very straight in one of the armchairs. Trevor, by contrast, was expansive and genial on the zebra-striped sofa.

While Ann and Daphne talked over the pros and cons of herding fifty ten-year-olds through a museum, I sat on the hassock and watched Jay and Trevor go through the same ritual Jay had played out with Inspector Thorne that morning. In that case, the disputed territory had been professional. This time, I expected the arena to be sexual—a touch of guilt on my part—but, to my surprise, it was literally territory: the house.

Jay said, "I believe I ought to thank you and your sister for making the larger apartment available to us."

Trevor took a sip of the Bordeaux. "Not at all. I've had my eye on the basement flat since Auntie refurbished it. It's ideal for one, cramped for two, but until this flat was free, Daph and I didn't feel we could ask the ladies to move. My dear sister has strong feelings about eviction."

"And you don't?"

Trevor smiled. "I'm no crusader. Daphne is. A difference of temperament."

"I'd like to see the basement flat sometime—just for curiosity's sake. Lark's description of it after the burglary was, uh, vivid."

"I say, do you fancy a look at the scene of the crime?"

"I've seen that already," Jay murmured.

Trevor looked blank for only an instant, but Jay pressed his advantage.

"Tell me, Mr. Worth, why did your aunt leave the foyer and stairs in such a dangerous state of disrepair? You said she refurbished the basement flat. This flat is modern, too, and, uh, handsome. The hallway is a real puzzle." He had spent more than an hour before dinner poking around the fatal stairwell.

"But my dear man, Auntie didn't own the building. Just the three flats—hers, this one, and the basement. The chap above you, Carruthers, owns his, and Mr. and Mrs. Givens own the other. All of the houses in this terrace belong to the earl of Rotherhithe."

"I'm damned." Jay let out a low whistle. I was surprised, too. I had assumed Miss Beale was erratically parsimonious.

"Rotherhithe is second cousin to the duke of Westminster." Trevor added in fake Cockney, " 'im as owns Mayfair."

Jay picked up the wineglass I knew he was going to nurse all evening and took a cautious sip. "We call that sort of arrangement a condominium. That is, people buy apartments in a larger building, but they also pay for the upkeep of the common areas—stairs, hallways, landscaping, and so on."

"Things are rather different here." Trevor flashed the famous smile and took a gulp of Bordeaux.

"So it seems. Do you and your sister plan to sue the landlord?"

"Heavens, no. That isn't done. Besides, Auntie was murdered. His Lordship can scarcely be blamed for that."

Jay chuckled. "I never thought I'd have a good word to say for ambulance chasers, but any American lawyer worth his salt would poke your argument full of holes in five minutes. That stairway is a death trap, with or without a murderer on the fourth-floor landing. It's a tort waiting to happen."

"You must have a legal background, James."

"You might say so." Jay shot me a sardonic look. I hadn't mentioned Jay's police connections to the Worths. The subject had not arisen. "Fear of personal-injury suits would force American landlords in a wealthy neighborhood like this to keep the buildings in decent repair. Their insurance companies would insist."

"Americans must be a litigious lot." Trevor sipped his wine.

"American lawyers sure are."

"Will you pass those munchies, Lark?"

I rose and retrieved the tray from the end table. "Sorry, Ann. Do try the Stilton, Daphne. The man at the deli assured me it was ripe."

"Oh, thanks." Daphne cut a wedge of the blue cheese and laid it on a water biscuit. "Mmm, very nice."

Ann helped herself to the Brie. "Daphne says we should go to Hampton Court before the tulips fade."

"Good idea. That's near Windsor, isn't it?"

Daphne made a face. "Close. Stay clear of Windsor. It's crammed with tourists." She blushed at her own tactlessness.

Before she tangled herself in "I don't mean tourists like you" apologies, I stepped into the breach. "I'd probably better stick to London for the time being. Inspector Thorne might toss me in the clink if I try to leave town."

"He held Lark's passport over the weekend," Ann explained.

Daphne's eyes went round. " 'Strewth. I thought he suspected Trevor and me. He grilled me for hours Friday, and he's been interviewing all of our friends."

"I'm sure that's just routine, honey. They always suspect next of kin." Ann cut another bit of Brie. "Trevor would like more of the white wine, Lark."

"Right," I said meekly. I left the tray with the ladies and carried the bottle to Trevor. He and Jay were discussing the rival merits of Ferrari and Maserati. I filled Trevor's glass. He gave me another absent smile, but I don't think he noticed me. I faded back into the decor and listened.

It was obvious that Trevor's employment was not just a means of making a living. He was passionate about automobiles. Jay isn't, but he can talk car if he has to. In this case, he didn't have to. Trevor was singing a solo.

I decided to leave him to it and edged back to Ann and Daphne.

"Will there be a memorial service for Miss Beale?" Ann was asking.

Daphne grimaced. "Auntie has been cremated. Her solicitors said it was what she wanted. I daresay I ought to arrange something with the vicar for her friends."

"Are you and Trevor her only family?"

"There's Mum." She sipped. "My mother is in a nursing home. A stroke."

"Oh, I am sorry, my dear."

Daphne sighed. "Don't be. I visit her every week, of course, but she's a difficult woman. I can't cope with her tantrums." She reached for the Stilton. "And Trevor's no help. The nursing home is the best solution all around."

It was hard to think of an appropriate response to that. Ann tried. "I remember when Buford's old granddaddy had a stroke, Nana wasn't strong enough to care for him, and all the children were working. A nursing home was the only logical solution." She took a breath and shifted to a less perilous topic. "I imagine you must find it easier to get to your school from here, Daphne. You had a flat in Chiswick, didn't you? Where's Chiswick?"

"West. I shared digs with two other teachers. One bedroom, one bath. It was ghastly." Perhaps Daphne thought she had been revealing too much, for she finished her wine and rose. "Thanks awfully for the wine. We must be off. Tomorrow's a working day, you know. Come along, Trevor."

It took Trevor perhaps ten minutes to wind down, but Daphne was determined to leave. All three of us saw them to the door amid polite shaking of hands. When they had gone at last, Ann said, "Whew. There's a family feud going on there."

I blinked at her. "Really?"

Jay yawned. "Maybe they're like Midwesterners. You know, at a cocktail party, the men congregate in one corner, women in the other."

Ann smiled. "Southerners are like that, too, but it doesn't seem to be the pattern here. I don't think Daphne and Trevor exchanged two words this evening—beyond necessary politeness, I mean. And Daphne really resents her brother. No wonder he wanted our flat."

"Maybe he bored her to death talking about cars," Jay suggested.

Ann laughed but stuck to her guns. "No, there's something else going on."

"Did you find Trevor boring, Jay?" I picked up the demolished cheese platter and carried it toward the kitchen. "I thought you encouraged the car talk."

"It seemed like his topic." Men can be bitchy.

"Why, my goodness, Jay, Trevor was just trying to *relate*."

Jay grinned at Ann. "Touché. Good night, ladies. I'm beat."

I glanced at the wall clock. It was only ten. "We could boogie all night at the Hard Rock Cafe."

"Fat chance," he said amiably, kissed me, and went off to bed.

Ann and I tidied the kitchen.

I ran a dishpan of hot, soapy water and set the wineglasses in it. "Tell me about the Henning Institute."

"Their headquarters are near Bloomsbury Square, and someone called Lord Henning is the major sponsor. I wish I knew more about those papers of Milos's." Ann picked up a dish towel. "I did my best to convince the woman to do something, but I don't think she took me very seriously."

"Jay called Dad from Dallas. The papers hadn't come. It really is too soon, Ann. My mother's always complaining about the length of time it takes for a letter to reach her from England. And that was a parcel."

Ann sighed. "Our suspicions are too nebulous. Mrs. Burke— that was her name—said the Czech embassy is riddled with secret police. They're called St. B's, after the street in Prague where they're headquartered, and they play rough. She said it was unlikely that the British government would bother Milos unless the information he had was extremely embarrassing."

"Like that ex-spy in Australia whose memoirs Mrs. Thatcher tried to ban?"

"Like that." She wiped the last glass and set it in the cupboard.

I shut the cupboard door. "What if Jay was right and the stabbing was a goofy accident?"

"Followed by burglary and murder?"

I ran a damp cloth over the counter. "I keep hoping we'll turn out to be a pair of hysterical women, but I don't think so."

"I feel like a real fool for embroiling you in this mess, Lark. I like Milos, but goodness knows, I was just looking for a little adventure. I didn't bargain on a Robert Ludlum novel."

I laughed. "I like Milos, too, you know. I think you did what you had to do, going to this rights organization. In fact, you were darned clever. I'm with you."

She gave me a quick hug. "That means a lot. Good night, Lark."

After Ann deserted me, I sat in the living room watching the news. The state visit had gone off without a hitch. Princess Di and Prince Charles would be spending the holiday at Sandringham. An outbreak of salmonella in the north had been traced to a batch of hazelnut-flavored yogurt. The commentator called it *yoggurt*. For some reason, the irony of health-food aficionados being felled by their favorite nosh gave me the giggles.

I decided to turn off the telly before my snickering woke Ann and go to bed. Jay was sound asleep. I snuggled in beside him. When I woke at half past six, he was already up.

I drifted out to the kitchen and found him reaching Ann's old *Times*.

"Hi." I stretched and yawned, then put the kettle on. "What time did you wake up?"

"Four."

"Great stuff, jet lag." I looked closer. His face had a grayish tinge and his eyes were shadowed. I felt a clutch of dismay. "Uh-oh. Nightmare?"

He set the paper down. "It's okay, Lark. I brought the Walkman. And I took a hot bath about an hour ago."

"But it's been more than a year. . . ."

He sighed. "Yeah, I'm a little depressed. I thought the plane flight would probably trigger off a doozy, but it's no damn comfort knowing I was right. I wonder how long it takes to row across the Atlantic?"

The kettle shrieked. I removed it with numb fingers and poured boiling water into the *cafetière* pot.

Jay's nightmares were a legacy of posttraumatic stress disorder Twenty years before, the year Jay turned nineteen, he had had a tour as an army medic in Vietnam. The day he was scheduled to return to the real world, he boarded a Pan American charter at Tan Son Nhut just as the air base came under a rocket attack. After nearly a year of combat, he had not expected to make it home alive. The rocket attack lasted two hours. Then the plane took off. He claimed he held it together and in the air all the way across the Pacific Ocean. Jay does not like to fly.

I had found out these interesting facts only when I proposed our trip to England, and then only after prodding. I had taken a cool, rational view of the situation. He should not be debarred from normal interaction with the world because the world had been insane when he was a kid. He agreed—reluctantly and after considerable thought. He flew at home, short hops, and he had medication to take if he suffered an anxiety attack before the flight or halfway through it. Nobody had said anything about anxiety attacks afterward.

For the most part, Jay was fortunate. He did not suffer flash-backs or ungovernable rages or other debilitating symptoms, and he had long ago worked out routines, such as the hot bath and jazz on the Walkman, for dealing with nightmares. They had decreased in frequency since our marriage, but they were appalling when they did happen. From my viewpoint, the worst thing about them was my inability to do much that helped.

I pressed the lid of the coffeepot down viciously and poured a cup of cloudy liquid. It was far too weak.

"Damn. Damn me for thinking up this self-indulgent expedi-tion, and damn Ann for getting caught up in Milos's melodrama, and damn Thorne for taking my passport. . . ." I was beginning to cry. I bit my lip hard and sat down at the table.

Jay touched my face. "Hey, cut it out. Go for a run with me." Running was another remedy, an effective one when it was possible.

I sniffed. "In the park?"

"Sure, in the park. Then we can come back and spend the morning canoodling on that weird bed."

I gave a watery laugh. "Okay. Ten minutes."

"Make it five." He was wearing sweats and running shoes, and he was wound up like an overworked spring.

We were out the door and trotting toward the zebra in ten minutes flat.

We zipped all the way around Hyde Park and most of Kensing-ton Gardens. I was ready to do it again, but Jay pulled me down on a bench.

"Hey! Enough." He was panting and laughing.

I said between gasps. "You're sure?"

"Yes." His breathing steadied. "Lead me back, Lark. I want breakfast, and I'm damned if I know where we are. What's that?" He pointed at Kensington Palace.

"Princess Di's little town house. Come on." I jogged him home via the news agent's. I would have bought croissants, but I didn't have enough change in my zip pocket.

116

We took a bath together. Showers are better, but the bath was not bad.

We had spilled quite a lot of water on the floor. I made toast while Jay mopped, and we were both feeling a lot better by the time Ann got up. All the same, I was worried. I wondered how much it cost to take the *QE II* to New York.

Jay and I were lying on the plum bed—fully clothed, we are not sexual athletes—and reading the *Independent* together when the phone rang. I heard Ann answer. After a few minutes, a timid knock on the door sounded.

"Come in," I caroled.

Jay sat up and swung his legs off the duvet.

Ann's head poked around the edge of the door. "Inspector Thorne wants us to look at those mug shots this morning, Lark." She blushed. "Shall I tell him you're otherwise engaged?"

Jay pulled me to my feet. "Tell him Mrs. Dodge will cooperate fully with the authorities. She's coming. I'm going to take a nap."

I kissed him. "Okay?"

"Okay."

Ann cleared her throat. "He'll send a car, he says. Fifteen minutes?"

"Fine."

I spotted ferret-face halfway through the second page of photographs Sergeant Wilberforce showed me. Ann had already had her turn and was waiting for me in Thorne's office.

"That's the one."

"Are you quite sure, Mrs. Dodge?"

"Quite," I said coldly. I hadn't forgiven Wilberforce for Sunday, and I don't think he'd forgiven me, either.

"And you can't identify the other man, the assailant?"

"I saw his shoulder and the back of his head as he left the train. I might be able to pick out his suit fabric but not his face."

He closed the book and I rose.

"Mrs. Dodge?"

"What is it?"

"If I spoke too heatedly on Saturday, I beg your pardon."

I stared at him. He did not look or sound penitent, but neither was I. "I think you meant what you said, Sergeant, and anyway, I gave as good as I got."

At that, he smiled slightly. "True."

I nodded. "It's okay. Is there anything else you'd like me to look at?"

"No. Inspector Thorne wants to speak to you."

"Certainly."

Sergeant Wilberforce cleared his throat. "Were you really an Olympic basketball player?" Ah, the background investigation. They *had* been thorough.

"I was chosen for the 1980 team. If you recall, the U. S. team wasn't allowed to go to Moscow that year, so I didn't make it to the games."

"That must have been disappointing."

I gave a rueful grin. "You can say that again."

He laughed. "I can but I won't." He showed me into Thorne's office, seated me beside Ann, and reported that I had identified the same man Ann had also recognized.

Thorne rubbed his hands, beaming. "Thank you very much indeed, ladies. Happen we'll have chummy in custody this time tomorrow."

"Who is he?" Ann asked, taking the words out of my mouth.

"An old lag, name of Albert Parks. 'Sparks,' he's called. Pickpocket, burglar, failed con man, general handyman to the big boys when he isn't behind bars. I wouldn't have thought of Sparks in this case. He's an old-fashioned crook, not violent by nature. I shall have words with Master Parks."

I said, "The woman on the tube, er, Mrs. Watt, did she identify him, too?"

"She wasn't sure. He was one of three she thought were possible. She also gave us a possible on the knife artist."

"Milos's assailant?" Ann asked, breathless.

"Yes. Do you think you might be able to pick that one from a lineup?"

"I only saw his profile." She lifted her huge purse to her lap. "I'll try, certainly. Inspector?"

"What is it, lass?"

Ann was pink with embarrassment, but she spoke steadily. "I was so worried over Milos's disappearance, I reported it to the people at the Henning Institute."

Thorne's smile faded. "Eh?"

She lifted her chin. "The Henning Institute. They have offices in Blooms—"

"I know who they are. Why, Mrs. Veryan?"

I could see Ann swallow, but her grave voice didn't falter. "I still think Milos was spirited away from that hospital against his will. I told the woman I contacted all the circumstances and explained what I knew of the papers. I think the Czech secret police may have abducted him to keep him from revealing information their government wants to hide. You've had Milos's papers for a week now. Have they been translated?"

"They have." He spoke without expression. "I'm not at liberty to tell you the contents, but they are not germane to my investigation."

Ann returned his gaze. "Very well, Inspector. I thought I ought to let you know what I'd done. I'll apologize—when I've seen Milos and talked to him."

I thought Ann might add a flurry of soothing phrases, but she rose with great dignity, shook hands with Inspector Thorne, and smiled at Wilberforce.

I said, "Congratulations, Inspector. We'll sleep easier when Parks and his partner are in custody." I, too, shook hands.

Thorne said heavily, "In the matter of Miss Beale's murder, I trust neither of you will leave town without notifying me."

"I've learned my lesson." I looked at Ann.

"I'm just sure you'll find him and that he'll spill the beans right off." Ann was gushing a little. "He looked like a weak personality."

I shook hands with Wilberforce. "You're an inch or two too short to play professional basketball, Sergeant, but I hope you'll try the game for fun. It's an exciting sport at any level of skill."

Wilberforce inclined his head. "I think there's a court in Chelsea."

"Good morning, ladies," said Thorne in tones of dismissal. We left.

12

♦ ♦ ♦ ♦ ♦ ♦

When we got home, I rousted Jay out and we ate lunch while I told him about our identification of Parks. I think all three of us were relieved to put a name to one of the criminals. I know I was.

After lunch, Ann and I took Jay off for a look at Parliament (Ann's idea of the minimum a tourist should see in London) and a nice walk along the Embankment to the Tate Gallery (mine).

Jay was being biddable. He gawked obediently at Westminster Hall, deplored the fact that we would have had to wait until Wednesday evening to see a session of the House of Commons, and strolled with us through the hordes at Westminster Abbey. Outside, we made him admire the statues of Churchill and Emmeline Pankhurst. He said good things about Rodin's *Burgers of Calais,* too, but I think he preferred the equestrian statue of Richard I riding loftily off in the direction of Pimlico. At the Tate, I was merciful. We drank in the Turners and left the rest for later.

The three of us dined at a pub off Sloane Square and took the tube home. We had to show Jay exactly where the assailants had gotten off, and he scouted their possible escape routes. It was nearly ten when we climbed on a westbound car. He made us wait for a

Circle Line train, in case its carriages were different from those on the District Line. I think they were, marginally. Something to do with the doors. He stopped just short of making Ann and me reenact Milos's stabbing.

It was early for theatergoers and late for everybody else, so the carriage was almost empty. I nearly overbalanced showing Jay how I had caught Milos. He wanted to know my angle of vision and Ann's. The handful of passengers watched us, wide-eyed, as we got off at South Kensington.

Jay wasn't particularly interested in the South Ken station, though the scene there, where we had waited for the paramedics to come for Milos, evoked the experience more vividly for me than Sloane Square. The last of the news vendors was packing it in as we left the station. Ann bought the *Evening Standard*.

It seemed strange, approaching the house in the dark, not to find the constable standing on the steps and a reporter or two lurking. The press had definitely gone on to better things. I missed the policeman.

I almost tried to unlock the gate to the areaway. Trevor's light was on in the basement flat.

We entered the murky foyer, I batted the light on, and Ann sprinted for the door of our flat, key at the ready. Jay didn't follow us in immediately, and when he did enter, he was carrying a filthy light bulb.

"What's that for?"

"I'm going to replace it." He began rummaging in the kitchen cupboards.

"Won't the landlord object?" Ann asked.

"His Exalted Lordship clearly hasn't seen the place since 1928." Jay found the light-bulb stash and extracted a hundred-watt bulb.

"Yeah, but the janitor mops once a week," I said. "And collects the garbage."

"Then he's in for an illuminating surprise."

"He'll replace the bulb."

"You can keep substituting stronger bulbs. Maybe he'll get the point. Show some initiative, Lark. I don't want you and Ann coming into a dark foyer while I'm off in Yorkshire."

Ann was heating water for tea. The kettle shrieked. "When do you go north, Jay? Friday morning?"

"Yes, around ten. Harry Belknap will meet me at the York railroad station and drive me to Thirsk."

"I want to come, too," I blurted.

He frowned. "There are no facilities for families where we're staying, and the sessions will run late."

"I could hire a car and stay at a b and b near Thirsk. It's supposed to be pretty country."

"Hmm. That's a thought." He took the light bulb out into the foyer, leaving the door ajar, and returned almost at once. "No sign of neighbors." He was covered with dust. He headed into the bathroom.

Ann was rattling teacups. She fixed Jay's herbal stuff in one of them and carried the laden tray into the living room. "Maybe you and I should hire a car in London and drive north to Thirsk, Lark. That is, if you don't mind company."

"Good idea."

Ann poured two cups of real tea and removed the bag of wet herbs from Jay's cup. "Inspector Thorne just wants us to let him know when we leave and where we're going. He didn't say we couldn't leave."

Jay reentered and sat in one of the armchairs. Ann handed him his cup and tried the idea out on him.

He smoothed his mustache. "If Thorne makes an arrest, he'll want you to identify his suspect."

I said, "We can't sit around waiting for that forever. If we had a car, Ann and I could drive back when he needs us."

"Well, let's see what happens in the next couple of days."

Ann gave me a cup of properly creamed and sugared tea. "I have to stay in London until the Henning people contact me."

"Surely they'll act soon." I sipped, burned my tongue, and set the cup on the end table. "Won't they?"

Ann sighed. "Let's hope so, honey. Hanging around London indefinitely could get expensive."

We batted the idea of going to Yorkshire around for a while, then Ann went off to bed, her newspaper under one arm.

Jay came over and sat on the couch beside me. "Do you want to come north?"

"I want out of London." I wriggled against him. "And I want to be with you. Why don't you stay overnight with me at the b and b? Ann can rent a separate room, and I can drive you to the conference and pick you up in the evening."

"And you and Ann can spend Saturday and Sunday exploring. Sounds good to me." He gave me a hug. "Time for bed, woman."

"All you do is sleep."

He gave me an exaggerated leer. "Not *all*."

I think he had another nightmare that night. At least I dimly remember him getting up around two and coming back several hours later. I tried not to wake him when I got up at seven. He came out at 8:30, yawning and looking reasonably rested. Since Ann was up and in the kitchen, too, drinking coffee and reading the paper, I didn't question him.

Ann was going to the public library, she said, and then meant to ramble around the Earl's Court area. I volunteered to call Thorne to see what he thought of our leaving for York.

I reached him around ten. He didn't want us to leave London altogether but said he thought a weekend in Yorkshire would do us good. He could contact us via Jay's police conference. He even suggested that Ann and I travel up with Jay by train because of the horrors of driving through London. We could rent a car in York. I thanked him for the idea and hung up.

Jay and I stared at each other.

"Well, here we are," I muttered.

"Undeniably. Are you going to show me Scotland Yard and the Old Bailey?"

The thought didn't fill me with enthusiasm, but it was something to do.

Jay found the area around Scotland Yard disappointing. I think he wanted something hung with gargoyles and flying buttresses, but the Metropolitan Police have existed less than two hundred years, and that part of the city was heavily bombed during World War II, anyway. Except for St. Paul's, the architecture is nineteenth and twentieth century.

Since we were so close to the Barbican Centre, I took Jay to see the fateful cafeteria. He thought the complex looked like a second-rate suburban mall. I thought it looked like a first-rate suburban mall. We settled our difference of opinion amicably by visiting the Museum of London, which is unlike anything in any suburban mall, being one of the most human museums anywhere. Jay fell in love with the fire engines. We looked but did not eat at the cafeteria.

In fact, we hopped on the tube during the rush hour—at roughly the same time Ann and Milos and I had boarded the carriage the week before. I was feeling phobic by the time we reached Charing Cross, but I gritted my teeth and didn't say anything, because I owed Jay a panic attack. At least the train didn't halt in the tunnel.

Beside me, Jay was doing a very un-English survey of our fellow passengers. I almost asked him not to stare. The train lurched and swayed, passengers swarmed on and off the car, and I recited my mantra under my breath. When we decanted onto the South Kensington platform, I pulled Jay over to the bench Ann and I had sat on.

"Hey, you showed me this last night."

I said through clenched teeth, "Let me breathe for a minute."

He sat beside me. "What is it . . . oh. I'm sorry, Lark."

"It's the rush-hour crowd. It was like this when Milos was stabbed." I closed my eyes, wondering whether I'd have to put my head between my knees.

Jay took my hand and sat with me as the commuter tide ebbed and flowed. He didn't say anything. The PA system crackled out its garble. A train pulled in on a gust of stale air.

I opened my eyes. "Okay. Let's go."

With three or four trainloads of commuters surging like spawning salmon up the grimy staircase and through the tollgates, there was no point in sprinting. We flowed upstream at their speed, but I was half-running by the time we reached street level and the open air. We dashed across the traffic island to the far side of the Old Brompton Road.

Jay touched my arm. "Slow down, ace."

I was gulping air. "Okay."

"Show me the famous car dealership."

I reversed course in front of the post office and we inspected shop windows. My stationer/copyist, the pharmacy, a travel agent, a tiny bureau de change. The car broker's window displayed a glowing BMW in metallic blue-grey and a carmine Porsche. A salesman was showing the Porsche to an upscale couple in matching tan Burberrys. There was no sign of Trevor— unsurprising, given the late hour. The dealership would close at six.

We strolled on. I rarely approached the flat from that side. Jay found the gardens interesting—the burglar's egress. The wrought-iron fencing and elaborate gate looked impenetrable to me, but he suggested half a dozen ways to get in. Getting out was easy. We walked all the way around the cul-de-sac on which the terrace of houses was arranged and came in from the opposite direction.

Ann was cooking southern: fried chicken, mashed potatoes, coleslaw. The only things missing were okra and peach pie. We contented ourselves with a peach sorbet she had found in one of the shops—and we didn't miss the okra. Ann and Jay settled down for a look at the news and I took the telephone into our bedroom to call my father. No dice—no package.

Thursday, the weather finally broke. The day dawned clear and

125

almost balmy. A few fat, puffy clouds sailed across the sky and the wind was light. It was ideal touristing weather. Unfortunately, we had to do laundry and pack. A tiny laundromat, which I had learned to call a launderette, was only four blocks away, near the Lycée Charles de Gaulle. It opened at half past eight, so Jay and I headed for it while Ann held down the fort. She was still waiting for the telephone call from the Henning people and she had also volunteered to make train and b and b reservations for the northern jaunt. In return, I would wash her clothes and we could all sightsee in the afternoon. That was the deal.

I let Jay haul the duffel bag full of dirty laundry the four blocks while I toted the change. English coins are heavy and English laundromats expensive, so the burden was not as unequal as it sounds. I did carry the detergent.

Jay and I sat on the stiff wooden benches and read our morning papers—for some reason he had decided to patronize the *Telegraph*—while the four loads, two white and two colored, whirled and sloshed. He had made it through the night without bad dreams and was full of energy. He wanted to see the British Museum in the afternoon. That seemed reasonable. I intended to poke through the Bloomsbury bookshops.

Five other people, one the attendant, filled the tiny establishment to capacity. None of the four customers spoke English. That gave Jay and me status with the attendant and she actually changed a pound coin for us. The others pantomimed their desire to change assorted bills, but the woman just compressed her lips and shook her head. Another bewildering example of London retailing.

In all likelihood, three-fourths of the launderette's customers would lack the right change, yet there was neither a coin machine nor a till. I knew from sad experience that none of the surrounding shops would make change, either. A greengrocer had ticked me off so rudely when I asked to change a pound coin that I had since boycotted him, though his produce looked luscious. He probably lost a lot of customers that way. So did the launderette. By nine, all but one of the other patrons had wandered disconsolately off, dirty clothes bags trailing, in search of the right change.

Jay watched them go and gave me a grin that showed he was on to the situation. The attendant poked a batch of clothes into one of the dryers, humming cheerfully to herself. Maybe she was xenophobic. The machines whirled and spun. I had finished the *Independent,* and Jay and I were loading the communal wash into two dryers when Ann entered.

"What's up?" I asked. She looked pink and rather pleased.

She glanced at the attendant, who was watching us with bright-eyed curiosity. "Uh, we had a call. Parks has been picked up. Mr. Thorne wants to see us right away."

I looked at Jay over a load of wet sweats.

"Go ahead, Lark. I'll bring the stuff home when it's dry."

"Thanks." I handed him the remaining coin hoard and gave him a hug. "See you at the flat in an hour or so."

"No problem."

Ann and I caught a cab at the taxi rack in front of the Norfolk Hotel. We were being ushered into Thorne's office within ten minutes, me in jeans, T-shirt, and sneakers, Ann looking proper in her flowered dress.

Thorne entered, beaming. "Well, ladies, we finally nicked Sparks. I trust you'll pick him out of the lineup."

I had been trying to visualize the tout all the way to the station. "I hope so."

"We will," Ann said confidently. "However did you find him so fast, Inspector?"

Thorne made a gesture of modest deprecation. "Routine inquiries, Mrs. Veryan. He was bound to turn up at his local sooner or later."

It was amusing to think of plainclothes detectives hanging out at Parks's favorite pub, blending into the paneling. That was a lot of beer and bangers.

Thorne took Ann off first, so I stood by his office window and watched the passersby in Lucan Place and thought about the next day. With Parks in custody, I felt easier about leaving London over the bank holiday weekend. It would be great to get out into the countryside, to see a bit of the real England again. I remembered incredible flower gardens, neat village squares and greens, and the way daffodils and bluebells grew wild in the meadowlands. Funny what kids notice. On the southwest coast, fuchsias grew wild, too, like weeds, but probably not in Yorkshire.

My thoughts drifted to Milos and I shivered. He had been removed from St. Botolph's in a private ambulance. What exactly did that mean? The British health-care system had a bad press in the United States, but at least it was a system. My impression was that elderly people and children in particular were well cared for, and that fewer people fell through the cracks than at home.

Parallel private facilities existed, though they were expensive. The best scenario had Milos in the care of a competent staff at a private nursing home, with some generous-minded plutocrat footing the bill. I hoped that was where Milos was, but it seemed unlikely. And private hospitals surely kept records. The police would have found him if he was receiving professional care.

When Ann and the inspector returned, I asked him whether there was word of Milos's whereabouts, but he just shook his head.

Ann's smile had faded as soon as I mentioned Milos's name.

"How did the lineup go?"

She shrugged. "I'm not supposed to comment."

"Come along, Mrs. Dodge." Thorne led me out and down a long corridor to an unlabeled door. He was explaining the lineup procedure.

Beyond the one-way glass, the room was dark, except for a low, brightly lit ramp at the front. The ramp adjoined a blank white wall. We sat on what felt like old theater seats, Thorne at my left hand. No one said anything.

Five men entered and spaced themselves along the wall at roughly arm's length from one another. They were wearing dark clothing and all five were short and slim. For a panicked moment, I thought they all looked alike, then someone in the darkened room dropped something, a book or notebook. At the sound, all five started slightly. One cupped a hand above his eyes. The others peered.

I said, "He's second from the left." My pulse thumped and I felt a choking sensation in my throat.

"Are you certain?"

"Yes." The tout's stare was unmistakable.

Thorne sighed. "Let's make sure." He picked up a microphone and asked the man to step forward a pace. Parks's shoulders slumped in the brown suit jacket. He obeyed and I repeated my identification.

"Right," Thorne said. "That's it, then. Thank you, gentlemen." The other four men shuffled back the way they had come, and ferret-face waited, head bent, while a uniformed guard entered and led him out the opposite door.

Thorne rose. "That's the ticket." He took my elbow as we went out, guiding me through the door. In the hall, I could see that he was pleased with himself—and presumably with Ann and me. Wilberforce and Ann were chatting in Thorne's office when we entered.

It took us less than fifteen minutes to finish the formalities, though Ann prolonged leave-taking with a variety of exclamations to the effect that we were all terribly clever, especially Thorne. She did prod him about Milos before we left and he admitted that a police bulletin had gone out. At least they were now looking for Milos.

We departed, having shaken hands. Parks would be charged as an accomplice to the assault on Milos. Thorne had seemed confident that forensic evidence would also tie Parks to the burglary, at which point that charge would also be entered. Parks was in for some heavy questioning. I felt mildly sorry for him until I thought of Miss Beale and Rollo.

We walked home, both of us sunk in reflection. Jay was just crossing the zebra as we reached the post office.

"Did you finger the perp?" He swung the laden duffel to his left hand.

"Right off the bat."

"It was definitely the man who held the door." Ann smiled at him.

"Good. Then we're all set for Yorkshire."

Ann said, "I found a b and b about five miles from Thirsk, but I haven't arranged the car yet. Hertz is booked for the bank holiday."

"We'd better reserve seats on the train." I pulled out my key and opened the front door. So far, the reporters had not returned, but I had the feeling they would once Thorne announced the arrest.

Jay and I sorted clothes into neat piles while Ann did the rest of the phoning. She managed to reserve a Ford Escort from a northern car-hire outfit I had never heard of. By that time, it was almost eleven, so she decided to nag the Henning people. She took the phone into her bedroom, and Jay and I carried our belongings into our bedroom and began to pack. I don't know how long Ann's conversation lasted. When we finally came out, she was sitting in the living room, staring into space.

"What is it?" I asked. Jay had ducked into the kitchen to make sandwiches.

Ann started and focused on me. She looked strained. "I'm not going with you."

"Oh, Ann."

"They're giving me the runaround."

"They've been doing that for two days—and you can bet they won't work over the holiday. You know what those volunteer outfits are like. Come on, Ann, you need a break."

"So does Milos."

I sat on the zebra couch. "Do you honestly believe staying here will help him?"

She began to cry. "I wish I knew what to do."

"Come north with us and get a fresh viewpoint on the problem. You're running in circles."

She took her glasses off and wiped her eyes. "I guess you're right, honey, but I'll feel like a deserter."

"We'll be back Monday afternoon."

"I just don't know, Lark."

"Well, pack for the weekend and come to Bloomsbury with us this afternoon. Stick your head in the institute's door and glower at them or something."

She gave a damp chuckle. "All right."

At that point, Jay brought in three workmanlike cheese and tomato sandwiches and three beers. Ann ate her share cheerily enough and joined us for the afternoon.

We agreed to rendezvous at five at the front gate to the British Museum. I pottered around the used bookstores and showed up five minutes early, laden with travel diaries and a nice edition of *The Pickwick Papers*. Jay was already there.

"Looking for your mummy?" I murmured.

"No, I am not, but about two hundred kiddies were. I fled the sarcophagi and hid in the tumuli."

"The Sutton Hoo treasure?"

"I was more taken by Bog Man. Skinny little fellow."

We stood by the gate, exchanging favorite oddities and watching the ebb and flow of the crowd. Visitors to the BM tend to come in clumps. One very large Spanish family clustered directly in front of the main entrance, blocking the sidewalk. A coach was gathering in fifty or so Japanese tourists with cameras. Most of the groups, though, were schoolchildren in uniform, or coachloads of seniors from remote British villages, all decked out in their best bibs and tuckers. Everyone seemed to be in a holiday mood and the sun continued to shine.

Jay ducked across the street to look at a shop that displayed tartans, most of them too garish to consider wearing. He returned sans purchases.

"Ann not here?"

"Not yet. I'm beginning to worry about her."

"Maybe she got fed up and went home."

"That's possible. I think there's a pay phone around the corner. Why don't you stand here like a beacon and eavesdrop on the Spanish tourists?"

130

"They're just arguing over which restaurant to eat dinner at."
Jay speaks both street Spanish of the kind common in the L.A.
barrios and the more genteel kind he learned in college.

"Well, watch for Ann. I'll be right back." I headed toward
Montague Street and one of those futuristic phone booths that take
charge cards.

This time, I had my card in my purse. I let the phone ring
twelve times—my mother's magic number of rings—but no one
answered. I had given up and was trudging back to the entrance to
the museum when Ann strode across the zebra, halting five taxis, a
tour bus, two vans, and a dozen assorted sedans. It is a tribute to
the patience of British drivers that no horn honked.

"What is it?" I asked. She looked wild-eyed and a bit breathless.

"I saw the kid with the bomber jacket."

Jay had spotted Ann, too. He broke free of the Spanish visitors
and joined us. "What kid? The one who gave Vlacek the papers?"

"The one I chased away from the hospital?" I ran my free hand
through my hair. "Did you talk to him, Ann?"

Ann had caught her breath. "No. It was the most exasperating
thing. I just don't know what to make of it, Lark. He was coming
out of the Henning Institute."

I stared at her.

Jay was frowning. "Out of the institute? Where were you?"

Ann took a gulp of air. "Catty-corner across the square. I went
straight to the institute when I left you all, and they were real polite
but still equivocal. So I got disgusted and left. I decided I might as
well look at the shops. I found a place that specializes in theatrical
books and old posters, and I lost track of time. They had a playbill
autographed by Sarah Bernhardt, and a cast list with Henry Irving
playing Hamlet, Lark. I almost bought it."

"No kidding?" I wondered how I had missed that shop.

Jay said, "Did you decide to go back to the Henning people?"

Ann shifted her purse, which overflowed with small parcels, to
her left shoulder. She had bought more books. "Yes. It was feeble
of me, but I decided to give it one more try before I came to meet
you. I was just entering the square when I saw Milos's friend coming
out the door. I called out to him and started to run, and this taxi just
came out of nowhere, so I had to jump back on the curb. I ran after
him, Lark, but he was already at Great Russell Street by the time I
got across the square. I lost him."

Jay said slowly, "I wonder why . . ."

Ann's eyes kindled. "I think we ought to go back there and ask
that woman in the office what's happening."

"Yes," Jay said. "I smell fish."

We could not have taken more than five minutes to reach the institute office, but when we tried the door, it was locked. Ann rang the buzzer—leaned on it. Nobody answered. I stood on the areaway curb and tried to peer in the single window, but a lace curtain obscured the room. I saw no lights. The bland neoclassic facade of the building revealed nothing.

It was closing-up time, of course. The terrace of town houses had been converted to offices, each with its own door, all with discreet signs. Building association offices, solicitors, a couple of academic institutes, the odd accounting firm—and the Henning Institute. Terribly respectable. One or two offices showed lights, but most looked as if the tenants had shut up shop. Two men in dark suits, umbrellas furled, walked past us in the direction of Russell Square.

"No sign of life," Jay muttered. Ann looked as if she might cry.

I said, "The kid is probably a student. We can walk toward the university library and keep our eyes peeled. Maybe we'll spot him again."

Jay was looking at Ann. "Did you catch his attention when you called out to him?"

She shook her head. "I don't know. He didn't run or anything. He was just walking fast, the way Londoners do." Her mouth trembled.

"It's a big university." Jay eyed her. "Even if he's not trying to avoid us, we're unlikely to run across him. Let's go home."

"I just knew something was wrong," Ann muttered. "They know more than they're telling me."

"Home." Jay gave me a glance. "We'll take a taxi this time around."

I would have walked all over the university in three-inch heels before I would have taken the tube at that hour. Jay was reading my mind; also, possibly, Ann's. She looked tired and defeated.

We went back to Great Russell Street and hailed one of the taxis that circle the huge museum complex like sharks. We didn't say much on the short ride home. I, for one, was thinking in circles. When the cab pulled up at our house, Trevor Worth was waiting on the steps.

13

◆　◆　◆　◆　◆　◆

Did he ever let you drive the Porsche?" Ann smiled over at Jay as the train slid out of King's Cross station. She was sitting opposite him.

Jay grimaced and eased his shoulders against the back of the seat. "For ten miles on the M Four. It was damned strange shifting gears with my left hand."

The previous evening, Trevor had taken Jay for a two-hour drive after dinner in one of his employer's sportier models.

The train entered a tunnel. A child shrieked and the young man across from me burrowed deeper into the paperback book he was reading. The train was chock-full of vacationers, some standing.

"I'll bet Trevor's a lousy driver." I squirmed closer to Jay. I had been the teensiest bit put out not to be asked to go on the test drive. How much male car bonding was necessary?

"Drove like a bat on the motorway." Jay gave my thigh a mild, husbandly squeeze as the train swayed out of the tunnel and past a battened-down suburban station. "But so did everybody else, especially the rigs with three trailers."

I stretched my legs, careful not to disturb the paperback reader. "No fifty-five-mile-an-hour speed limit."

"Really?" Ann looked alarmed. We were picking the car up in York.

"Not on the motorways."

"Are those the freeways?"

"Yes. We'll avoid them."

Jay said, "I had to admire the way Trevor slid through the roundabouts without smashing up. I kept looking in the wrong direction for oncoming traffic."

"How was the car?" Ann was watching the suburban villas flash by. The train had picked up speed.

"Okay. Smelled almost like a new car."

We had had an active evening. On top of calling the police and explaining Bomber Jacket's suspicious presence at the Henning Institute to Sergeant Baylor, who was on duty, we had had to entertain Daphne. Daphne had joined us for a glass of wine while the men went out skylarking—her word.

"Daphne thinks Trevor's going to buy the Porsche," I murmured. "She does not approve." Daphne had been full of her own plans for a walking tour in Dorset. Thorne had demanded a detailed itinerary. That had annoyed her. She'd showed us a copy.

Ann hefted her purse to her lap and began digging. "She's jealous. She doesn't even have a driver's license."

"Tickets, please." The conductor appeared at my elbow as if by magic.

When he had moved on down the aisle, Ann leaned toward us, her eyes earnest behind the pink lenses. "Do you all really think I was right to come?"

"Absolutely."

Jay added, "You called Thorne. There was nothing more you could do for the moment. And I'll feel better knowing you and Lark aren't trapped in that B-movie foyer with the light off."

Ann sighed.

"And look at that." I pointed out the window.

"My goodness, yes. Isn't it beautiful?"

She leaned back and all three of us fell silent as the countryside, intense green patched with the electric yellow of rapeseed fields in bloom, opened out on either side of the train. The landscape wasn't beautiful—*beautiful* was far too melodramatic a word for that mild, undramatic area—but after three weeks of London grime and noise, it was wonderfully pleasant to look at open fields. The sky was blue, and the world, or at least Yorkshire, lay all before us. I felt the muscles at the base of my neck unknot, one by one.

The journey from King's Cross to the city of York takes two hours by train. Ann and I had brought guidebooks and Jay the paper he was supposed to deliver at the conference. We read and gazed out the window and didn't talk much. The rolling green fields and the dreamy church spires—slightly out of focus in the moist air—created the illusion that we were traveling backward in time. When the stacks of the nuclear power plant south of York finally loomed into view, I flinched. We had not, after all, reached the kind, indefinite past.

Jay looked up from his paper. "I wonder what they thought about Chernobyl?"

Ann shivered.

Chernobyl, the Salman Rushdie case, the Hillsborough disaster, Lockerbie, the fire at King's Cross station; and, on an individual scale, Milos's injury and Miss Beale's murder—the joys of modern civilization. I wondered what a Victorian thinker—Harriet Martineau, perhaps, or John Stuart Mill—would have said of such events. I wondered what distressful lyric the sight of those cooling towers would have provoked my mother to. Not for the first time, I wished I had inherited her gift for words.

We eased into the York station shortly after noon. About half the passengers got off with us and an equal number waited to board—heading for Edinburgh. We strolled through the brightly lit station, out the main entrance, onto the sidewalk. There we stopped dead.

"Oh my land," Ann breathed.

Jay didn't say anything, but he was staring, too. There may be a more remarkable medieval city wall somewhere in the British Isles, but only in York do visitors step from a modern train station and gawk across four lanes of traffic at fairy-tale battlements.

The sun shone busily on elegant gray stone, and a few late daffodils starred the lush green of the supporting earthwork. The wall was sinuous, indifferent to the trivial comings and goings on the street below, and huge. It is not possible to view the wall of York without a feeling of deep respect for the builders. Now that was a civilization.

"You can leave me right here, Lark, honey. This is why I came to England."

I laughed. I had thought Ann would fall in love with York. "We can spend all day tomorrow exploring the city."

Jay sighed. "I wish I could join you."

Someone beside me cleared his throat.

"Sorry," I said automatically. We were blocking the sidewalk.

"Are you Mr. and Mrs. Dodge?" A stocky fortyish man with a fresh complexion and bright blue eyes gave us a tentative smile. "I'm Harry Belknap."

A flurry of handshaking ensued. The chief inspector seemed pleasant and eager to put Ann and me at our ease, which was kind of him, considering we'd come uninvited. We explained about the car rental, and he offered to take us to the car-hire office after lunch. When we had deposited our luggage in the boot of his little Fiat, he led us down to the River Ouse to his favorite pub. It was, he said apologetically, a tied house, but the bitter was tolerable and there were tables outside on the bank of the river. Perfection. I don't remember the food or the beer. The setting was just right.

While Jay and Harry—by that time we were on first-name terms—drank another beer and talked about the upcoming conference, Ann and I went for a short walk on the wall. York Minster dominates that quarter of the city. Ann was agog to see it, and I was curious to see whether the fire damage to the south transept had been repaired. I also looked forward to showing Ann the Shambles—a warren of small shops in the shadow of the cathedral that was once the medieval butchers' precinct. To the southeast lay Clifford's Tower, the visible remains of York Castle, on its high mound. As a kid, I had scrambled all over the tower. I was feeling younger by the minute. I made a mental note to wear sneakers the next morning. London seemed farther than two hours away.

Harry drove us straight to the car-hire office. The rental was a sad blue Ford Escort, rather tinny. It had a stick shift. Like Jay, I found the idea of shifting left-handed alarming and I had specified an automatic. However, the Ford was the last car available, so we took it. Jay rode with Harry. They were deep in a discussion of search and seizure.

I unlocked both doors and offered Ann the keys.

"No way. I'll navigate."

I slid into the cramped driver's seat and hoped my knees wouldn't bang the dash when I braked. "How's your sense of direction?"

"Rotten. I've never in my life driven anything but an automatic, though. You're elected, honey."

" 'It is an honour that I dream not of.' "

She chortled and fastened her seat belt. "That's out of context."

"Pedant." I eased the car out of the lot. Harry's neat red Fiat was waiting. "I'm going to hang on his tail like a remora on a shark, Ann. You keep your eyes peeled. I want to find my way back here tomorrow."

"Right."

We chugged in convoy through York's modern suburbs and headed north. Driving on the left induced a high state of paranoia. At least it kept me alert. I had mastered the gearshift within three stoplights. I think we crossed the river. We reached Thirsk, a pleasant brick town with a busy market square, in less than half an hour, but it took us another half hour to find the bed and breakfast place.

We twisted east and north among rolling hills that looked like sheep country. The Hollies—the name *and* address of our b and b—lay in a tiny dorp of no more than ten cottages. There was a Saxon church. A large tithe barn across the green had been converted into a promising-looking pub called the Weaver's Arms.

Harry pulled in by the enameled blue door of the largest of the ten cottages and I parked behind him. By the time we had extricated ourselves and our luggage from the two cars, the blue door had opened and a rosy-cheeked woman of sixty or so stood watching us. She looked alarmed.

"You'll be my Americans. Oh dear, I wasn't expecting two couples."

Harry's forthright northern vowels reassured her. He performed introductions and took his leave, shaking hands all around and promising to return for Jay in two hours. The conference was set to begin with a dinner session that evening. Jay was going to read his paper on Saturday and sit on three panels Saturday and Sunday. No rest for the wicked. Harry had apologized several times to Ann and me for excluding us. We reassured him again that we'd survive without male escort and saw him off. He was far too courteous to say so, but I think our presence dismayed him.

Mrs. Chisholm, our landlady, led us up a steep stairway, almost a ladder, and showed us our spotless rooms. Ann's had barely enough space for a twin bed and a wardrobe and basin. Jay's and mine was much larger, huge by hotel standards. Besides a canopied double bed and the usual furnishings, it featured a table and two chairs next to a hearth with a neat artificial log. A dormer window commanded a clear view of the church and the hilly country beyond.

We were near the North York Moors National Park. The view was straight out of James Herriot—unsurprising, given that his veterinary office was in Thirsk. The decor struck me as a bit Laura Ashley, but I wasn't about to complain. Neither was Ann. When

Mrs. Chisholm showed us an ultramodern bathroom with an honest-to-God shower, our joy knew no bounds. I, for one, gushed. Ann pulled out all the graciousness stops.

Jay excused himself to shower and get respectable, but Ann and I took Mrs. Chisholm up on her offer of tea. She led us downstairs and out the back into a garden ablaze with scarlet and yellow tulips.

"Do sit there and be comfortable." She indicated a grouping of wrought-iron lawn chairs. "I'll just put the kettle on, shall I? Oh dear, perhaps you'd rather have a glass of sherry."

We assured her, I with fervor, that we preferred tea, and she went off.

I looked at Ann. "What do you think?"

Her eyes narrowed against the mild sunlight. "That we're paying less per night for this place than for that cellar in London with hot- and cold-running murder."

I laughed. "*And* we get breakfast. Glad you came north?"

"I may settle here, sugar."

"Me, too. A shower!"

"Fresh air! Tulips! York!"

"The acid test will be dinner at that pub."

"I shall eat it with relish," Ann said serenely, "even if it's fried oatmeal and blood pudding."

We fell silent. The day had not been strenuous, but I was tired. I leaned back in the lawn chair. A light breeze stirred the tulips. At the edge of my hearing, I sensed Jay's shower running and, very dimly, the shriek of the teakettle. A dog yipped once, far off. Otherwise, there was no noise—no jackhammers, horns, sirens, squealing brakes, beeping trucks, rumbling trains. Paradise.

"Quiet enough to think," Ann murmured.

"Mmm." I *was* thinking. I turned the events of the past ten days over in my mind and they whirled in the same sick loop, but I no longer felt caught in the action. We would have to return to London, but we had two days of freedom ahead of us. I meant to enjoy every minute.

"I hope you like watercress sandwiches." Mrs. Chisholm set the tea tray on the small table and beamed at us. "Isn't the weather lovely?"

Everything was lovely, including Mrs. Chisholm. We nibbled and drank tea and explained ourselves in prudently censored detail. We did not mention murder. When Mrs. Chisholm heard we were booksellers, she gave us the names of two proprietors in York and a secondhand shop in Thirsk.

138

She was not herself a great reader, she admitted, but her late husband, the vicar of St. Ethelburga, had collected works of natural history in a modest way. I gathered that he had been many years her senior. When he died, she bought the cottage and fixed it up as a refuge for city folk who came to the area to hike or fly sailplanes—a nearby scarp provided sufficient updrafts for sailplanes. She had been letting out her Laura Ashley rooms for two years and did rather well during the holidays, though she had been relieved when we reserved the rooms—a family from Manchester had had to cancel. The woman in the next cottage helped with cleaning and cooking. She would pack us box lunches if we wanted to picnic. Most of the guests did.

All of this information flowed out under Ann's expert questioning. I listened and kept an ear cocked for Jay, but he didn't come down. When we had drunk our tea and eaten the tangy sandwiches, I left the two ladies among the tulips and returned to my room. Jay was sitting at the table, absorbed in the printout of his paper.

"Stage fright?"

He looked up and smiled. "Terminal. They're not going to catch my jokes."

"You could do a Monty Python routine. Nudge, nudge."

"Good thinking." He yawned and stretched. "Harry will drive me back here tonight, Lark. I may be late. I gather there's a lot of socializing."

"Must be a bar on the premises."

"Something like that." He sighed. "Maybe I'll cut out tomorrow and go with you and Ann to York."

"Do your paper, darling. The city has been there since roughly the year one. It will keep. We can poke around Monday. The train doesn't leave until five."

"Okay." His eyes strayed to his masterwork. I effaced myself and started unpacking the two garment bags. It didn't take long. We had traveled light.

Harry showed up at two minutes past five and Jay, who had put on a necktie at the last moment, went off with Mrs. Chisholm's last house key. I wondered at the necktie. It looked faintly regimental. I had once bought Jay a necktie that looked regimental, a stiff ocher design on a stuffy blue field. Close inspection revealed that the design was composed of bare footprints. Jay had been a surfer. I mused over the possibility of a necktie with a sober blue field and a design of bare fingerprints—or, for the conference, little DNA helices. It was a good thought.

Ann and I took a spin through the countryside amid much shifting of gears. We wound up at the closed gates of Castle Howard. Eight o'clock on a spring evening, time to head back to the pub for dinner.

We had a good, plain meal in the pub's private room (lamb chops for me, mixed grill for Ann) and returned to the Hollies as Mrs. Chisholm's other guests, a young couple from Hull, came back from their hike on the moors. They were not at all standoffish. I asked whether they jogged. They said yes, but when I suggested a run the next morning, they laughed. The husband pointed out the perils of running in open country where every household kept at least one unleashed dog. I was disappointed, but I did see the logic. I wondered whether running were an urban prediliction in Britain.

We trotted off at that point to our separate rooms and I went to bed with a guidebook.

Jay tiptoed in around midnight. I had dozed off over the *Guide to Rural Yorkshire* and was deep in one of those dreams where you run and run and never get anywhere. Ann was running with me in her nice shirtwaist dress. We were chasing Milos. Unleashed dogs, some of them miniature poodles, yipped at our heels.

"Hush." Jay touched my face. "It's just me. Nightmare?"

I sat up sleepily. "Frustration dream. How was boys' night out?"

He grinned and tossed the necktie at the table. "Not bad. Half a dozen policewomen and a female forensics expert showed up, but it was mostly men."

"Good beer?"

"Very good. I had three."

I blinked. "Must have been good." He seldom drank more than two. "Come to bed?"

"Soon as I can. How was the pub food?"

We chatted in the comfortable way married people do while he undressed. Then we snuggled, also connubially, and both fell asleep almost as soon as the light was out. As usual, I woke early. Mrs. Chisholm's breakfasts were served from eight-thirty to nine. I thought about running and about the dogs. Jay was still sound asleep, so I took out the guidebook and read some more.

I was looking for nearby wonders and marvels for Sunday. Ann had taken it into her head that we (meaning me) should drive to Haworth on a Brontë pilgrimage. Haworth wasn't far by American standards, but it was farther than I wanted to drive the Escort. Scarborough had Sitwell associations. No, too far and too crowded on a bank holiday. Whitby, ditto. There was always Castle Howard, but it was bound to be thronged, too. I wondered whether Ann would settle for Rievaulx Abbey. I read on. It was a good guidebook, detailed without pedantry and full of historical snippets. The directions seemed clear.

A stirring in the hall assured me that getting up was allowed. I slid from bed and into my robe. The female hiker from Hull, hair turbanned in a towel, smiled at me as I ventured out. I mumbled good morning. As I approached the bathroom, I heard her observing to her husband that it was a pity there was no proper bathtub.

The shower felt glorious. Only strong civic-mindedness prevented me from standing in it until the water ran cold. Jay and I were downstairs in Mrs. Chisholm's sitting room reading old copies of *Country Life* at 8:30. We had risen to go in to breakfast when Ann also appeared, wearing a dress and sandals. I was in jeans. I decided not to change.

Mrs. Chisholm's neighbor cooked an all-out Yorkshire breakfast. Bangers and lean bacon, grilled tomatoes, fried eggs, racks of toast—pure cholesterol. We wolfed it all down. The coffee was almost potable.

Jay was supposed to be at his conference by 9:30, so we hopped in the Escort. I drove and he navigated, and Ann sat in the backseat and exclaimed over the scenery. The conference site was a vast manor house that had been converted to a teacher training school sometime in the forties. Jay said it was painted institutional green inside, but the grounds were impressive. He gave me a nice kiss and opened the car door.

"Break a leg," I called after him.

He gave a half salute, grinning, and marched up to the main entrance. He was wearing the tie again. Men are slaves to fashion.

York was grand, especially the minster. We shopped in the Shambles and walked on the wall. We did everything but the Jorvik Viking Center, an archaeological exhibit. The lines to it coiled around the modern plaza as if the exhibit were a ride at Disneyland, so we took our box lunch down to the castle grounds and sat on the grass and watched the holiday crowds. I made Ann climb the walls of the tower. They lean out slightly, so scaling the spiral staircases was an odd, unsettling business, but the view from the battlements was almost as splendid as I remembered. We strolled back by the river and took in the county museum on the site of the ruins of St. Mary's Abbey. It was six before we retrieved the car from the city car park—a thoroughly satisfying day. Ann's feet hurt.

Dinner (she had lamb chops; I had the mixed grill) was fine and the public was working up a good head of noise by the time we wandered back to the Hollies. I had lobbied steadily for Rievaulx Abbey and environs for Sunday.

Ann finally gave in. "I'll come back next weekend, anyway, God willing. I can see Haworth and the Dales then." She yawned.

"That's the spirit."

We made an early night of it and I took the guidebook to bed again. This time, I was looking for stately homes and quaint villages. The site of a deserted village near the abbey sounded interesting—Wiganthorpe.

I drowsed off again, this time without a nightmare, and Jay was stroking my back and murmuring nonsense in my ear before I realized he'd returned.

"Mmm. That's nice. How was the paper received?"

"They liked it, I think. I had a long talk with an assize judge who made a speech about the problem of conveying technical information to juries. He wanted a copy."

"Bravo!" I gave him a squeeze. "How were the panels?"

He groaned a satisfied groan. "Terrifying. Thank God my mother taught me to keep my mouth shut when I don't know anything. There's a lot I don't know, lady."

I gave him another, more obvious squeeze. "And there's a lot you do know. Show me your expertise."

"Who's an expert tease?"

We had a nice, quiet romp and fell asleep still tangled together. Jay was up, showered, and dressed before I stirred Sunday morning.

He was sitting at the little table scribbling notes. "Good morning, merry sunshine."

"Umm. What time is it?"

"Half past seven."

"Wow, I'd better get cracking." I gathered my wits and sponge bag and went off to the shower.

As I was dressing, Jay said, "How are you fixed for cash?"

"Hurting."

"I'll give you what I have. I won't need much today, though I'll have to cash a traveler's check sometime soon. Where are you headed?"

"Rievaulx Abbey." I explained the itinerary and took the money. The trouble with bank holidays is that they *are* bank holidays. I was out of traveler's checks, anyway, unlike Jay.

We deposited him at his conference and took off. We found

Rievaulx melancholy and fascinating, though it was aswarm with families out enjoying the weather. Nearby Helmsley Castle had an impressive earthwork. By then, it was noon and picnic time, so we found a grassy spot down the road to Wiganthorpe and pulled over. We munched our sandwiches and eyed the sheep in the next field. It was the third straight day of sunshine. Amazing.

I knew Ann was disappointed not to be exploring the Brontë country to the west, so I whipped out the guidebook and began reading her the chatty little piece on the deserted village. The site lay on the grounds of a manor belonging to Lord Tennant, although His Lordship's principal seat lay in County Durham.

"That's nice," Ann murmured. "Who's Lord Tennant?"

"Hmm. It says that he still styles himself Lord Tennant of Wiganthorpe, even though the village has been deserted since the late middle ages and the house is a museum. 'Lord Tennant, like Lord Henning of Hambly—' " I broke off.

Ann sat bolt upright, scattering crumbs. "It's a house! Hambly is a house, not a village."

"No wonder we couldn't find it in the atlas. Lord Henning . . ."

We stared at each other.

"Milos is at Hambly." Ann struggled to her feet. "Come on. We have to find him."

"And phone Thorne."

"Yes." She was gathering up the lunch debris. "And those hypocrites at the Henning Institute—that smarmy woman in the office knew where Milos was all along. She was laughing up her sleeve at me, the unprincipled bitch."

I stood and shook out the rug Mrs. Chisholm had loaned us. "But we still don't know where Hambly is."

"*The Blue Guide,*" Ann said tersely. "Failing that, the book on stately homes sitting in plain sight in Mrs. Chisholm's parlor." She stomped over to the car. I followed.

Hambly, it turned out, was in Shropshire, near Ludlow and the Welsh border. Rather near Hay-on-Wye. We found the information in Mrs. Chisholm's stately homes book.

Our landlady was spending the day with her daughter in Leeds. Jay was due to sit on a panel at the conference at three. It was Sunday. I sat in the shadowy parlor and brooded while Ann went to the pay phone outside the pub and telephoned.

If Milos were indeed at Hambly, then the Henning people must have believed he was in danger. They had to be protecting him from

143

the British government as well as from his shadowy assailants. Ann's decision to report Milos's case had probably created considerable embarrassment. I felt rather sorry for the woman Ann was going to chew out.

Ann's calls didn't take long. She came in, her face a pale blur in the dark room. "I called Thorne, but he's still off duty. Sergeant Baylor answered."

"And?"

She plumped down on an armchair. "I opened my mouth to tell her where Milos is and I just couldn't. What if the Henning people think he's in danger from the British?"

"That did occur to me. Did you call the institute?"

"Nobody answered."

"It's Sunday."

"And a bank holiday tomorrow," she said impatiently. "I know. We'll have to handle this ourselves, Lark."

"We?"

"You and I."

"What about Jay?" When she didn't answer, I added, "He is my husband." And an ex-cop on first-name terms with a chief inspector of British police.

She took a deep breath. "All right. You stay here and I'll take the car. What time is Jay coming back?"

"Ten or so. It's the last full session." And if the bar was open afterward, he might be even later. The conference members seemed to be a sociable lot and Jay was enjoying them.

Ann met my eyes. "Will you give me until he gets here? I can drive to Shropshire in a couple of hours and check the place out."

"Ann, darling, you can't drive at all—remember?"

"I'll manage. I once drove Uncle Billy's tractor."

That was so absurd, I hooted.

She blushed, but I could see from the set of her jaw that she wasn't going to give in.

"All right," I said, "let's think this through. If the Henning people have Milos, then he's probably getting proper care. They did remove him in an ambulance. He's in no immediate danger."

Ann began pleating the skirt of her dress.

I went on, "We don't need to rescue him, Ann. *They* aren't sticking slivers under his fingernails and igniting them."

Her mouth trembled. "We don't know their agenda for sure, or his. We don't know what was in those papers. Until we do . . ."

I stood up. "It's two. My father should be up. My turn to telephone."

I jogged across the green and charged yet another international call. I got my parents' answering tape. Nobody was home. When I returned, Ann was upstairs packing.

She took the absence of news from Dad with calm. "If you'll drive me to York, I'll go to Ludlow by train and worry about a car when I get there."

I sighed. "I'll drive you to Shropshire. I have to let Jay know what's happening, though. I can't just take off."

She opened her mouth as if to protest, hands full of underwear. Then she focused on me and apparently read my determination. "All right. I'm sorry to be such a hard-nose, honey. I'm sure Jay won't do anything to put Milos in jeopardy, and I am grateful. It's just that I'm so worried about Milos. And so confused."

I could relate to that. I went into the Laura Ashley bedroom, stuffed my clothes in the garment bag, and sat down to compose an explanation for Jay. I meant to take it to the conference site in case he wasn't immediately available. Just to be safe, I repeated the gist of the information and placed the first note in the middle of our bed.

When we reached the former teachers' college, I left Ann in the car and went in search of my husband. I was stopped in the hall-way—which was indeed painted an institutional green—by a sixty-ish man in a dark suit and tie who demanded to know who I was.

I explained that an emergency had come up and that I wanted to speak to my husband.

Cerberus pursed his tight little mouth and asked me the nature of the emergency.

I never lie well under pressure. I said I had to make an unex-pected trip to Shropshire and that I wanted to tell Jay the circum-stances before I left.

"I'm afraid that won't be possible, madam. I cannot interrupt a session of the conference for a merely personal matter."

I started to blurt out that it was a *police* matter, then bit my tongue. I had to tell Jay about Hambly, but there was no reason I had to tell the entire constabulary. "I want to speak to whoever's in charge."

His eyebrows rose. "I am, madam." He was getting smugger by the second and I was getting angrier.

I decided to cut my losses before I said something unforgivable. I took out the note I had written and scrawled Jay's name on the outside, adding in parentheses "c/o Chief Detective Inspector H. Belknap." I held it out. "Very well. Will you see to it that James Dodge receives this message?"

He took the note with a bland smile. "Certainly, madam."

I startled Ann when I opened the car door.

"Back so soon? What did Jay say?"

"I left a note for him."

She refastened her seat belt as I slid into the driver's seat. "I hope he won't worry about you."

"So do I."

"We're off?"

I nodded and turned the ignition. "We're off."

14

◆ ◆ ◆ ◆ ◆ ◆

I trust you brought the AA atlas." I shifted to accommodate a steep hill. The Escort groaned.

By way of response, Ann lifted the huge book of maps from beneath a pile of guides and magazines in the backseat.

"Get me onto the A One. We need to find a gas station."

"All right," she said in a small voice. She refastened her seat belt.

I shifted into fourth and let the car roll downhill, accelerating slightly as we approached a curve. "I'm not mad at you, Ann. Just worried."

"We may be on a wild-goose chase."

"I don't think so." I forced a lighter tone. "And anyway, you wanted to tour the Welsh marches."

"That's right, honey." She added, incorrigibly the English teacher, "It's A. E. Housman country."

"So it is."

She gave me a swift glance and returned her attention to the atlas. " 'Oh, I have been to Ludlow fair / And left my necktie God knows where / And carried halfway home or near / Pints and quarts of Ludlow beer.' "

The sound of Housman's neat quatrain in Ann's plummy Georgia accent cracked me up. Then I thought of Jay's necktie, God knows why, and cracked up again. I was still chuckling when I saw the sign for the first roundabout. There was an exit posted for the A1. I extricated the car from the vicious circle, headed off in the right direction, and, as we topped a gentle rise, saw the BP logo floating in the near distance. The station was open. I filled the tank and we were on our way. The signs were auspicious. I felt a surge of optimistic energy. At least we were finally doing something.

We reached the vicinity of Ludlow by six. Traffic had been heavy but not impossible, and I had used the motorways, a hairy experience. Thanks to well-posted exits and Ann's heroic navigation, I bypassed Leeds and Birmingham and turned off on a highway that promised to lead to Ludlow, or, possibly, Kidderminster. By that time, my eyes hurt from squinting, My teeth hurt from clenching, and I was sure my spine had adopted the curve of the driver's seat.

Ann cleared her throat. "I need to find a loo."

"Okay. Look for a likely pub."

We chugged in silence along the secondary highway I had entered. After another half mile, Ann gave a subdued shriek and pointed. Spraying gravel, I pulled the Escort into the car park of a half-timbered building, rather large, that announced itself as the Royal Oak. That sounded nautical to me, odd so far inland. However, there were lights and the car park was almost full of station wagons and Land Rovers.

Our luck held. The Royal Oak was a country inn rather than a pub. We used the loo and looked the place over. In addition to a large and very noisy bar, all dark paneling and beveled glass, there was a dining room posted to open at seven. When Ann's attention strayed to a display of tourist brochures on a long refectory table, I cat-footed it to the registration desk.

The blond man behind the counter gave me a harried smile. "May I help you?"

"Two for dinner."

"Ah. Yes, of course. You'll have a half-hour wait."

"We could sit in the bar. . . ."

"If you will, madam, I'll call you."

I shot a glance over my shoulder. Ann was absorbed in a pamphlet. "Uh . . ."

"Yes?"

"Is there by any chance a room available for the night?"

He said doubtfully, "There's one left, but the tariff is rather steep. It's meant for a family group."

"How much?"

He told me. It was less than Jay and I had been paying Mrs. Chisholm.

I palmed my Visa card. "We'll take it."

"Very good, madam. For how long?"

"Just tonight."

"Shall I show you the room?"

I said expansively, "That won't be necessary. I'm sure it's very nice."

He whipped out his register and I signed. Fortunately, I had scribbled the car's license number on a bit of paper, so I had the necessary information at my fingertips. He took an impression of my Visa, which he insisted on calling a Barclaycard, and handed me a large key. The deed was done.

I tucked the key into my purse and moseyed over to Ann, who was reading brochures with maniacal concentration. "How about a beer?"

"Okay. This is interesting country. All kinds of stately homes." She snaffled another brochure and tucked it into her bag. "Lead me to it."

Most of the patrons were standing in the center of the room, drinking beer and shrieking like peacocks. All of them appeared to know one another. They had been to a race meeting near Ludlow. While Ann staked out a place on the periphery, I fetched two half-pints.

I set the beaded glasses on a table the size of the AA atlas. "Is bitter okay?"

"Yes." She leaned against the settle, wriggling her shoulders. "My word, I'm tired. I marvel at your driving, Lark, honey. Why you took those nasty old roundabouts smoother than a London cabdriver."

I smiled and sipped my beer and let her lay on the compliments. When she wound down, I said, "I saw a signpost for Ludlow at the last roundabout. Thirty miles."

"Yes. We're almost there, thank God."

"What do you propose to do?"

She blinked at me over her beer glass.

"When we reach Hambly."

"Find Milos?" Her voice wavered in that nice southern uncertainty that is half statement, half question.

"So we just march right up to the front door and ask the lord of the manor if he has a stray Czech stashed in his back bedroom?"

She reddened. "Well . . ."

"We ought to think it through."

"I've been trying to think it through since we left Yorkshire," she confessed. "I guess we need to see Hambly first."

"Case the joint?"

She winced. "Really, Lark."

The desk clerk appeared in the door arch. I caught his eye and nodded. "What we need is food and logic. Let's try out the dining room."

"But there are hours of daylight left."

There were perhaps two hours of daylight left. I adopted a tone of sweet reason. "We did skip lunch. We have to eat sometime, Ann, and you know how things are on Sunday." I got to my feet. "We may not find another restaurant open and I'm not in the mood for pickled onions. I need sustenance."

She rose, too, and shouldered her tote. "I guess you're right."

Dinner was very English—soup, good roast lamb with real mint sauce, three kinds of potatoes, and boiled green cabbage leaking liquid. I ate with deliberation. The dining room filled with families. Ann and I talked sporadically but didn't advance beyond our need to find Hambly, the house. There was bound to be security, I pointed out, if only a handful of family retainers. Probably, if the Henning Institute folks were in the habit of secreting political refugees on the premises, there would be battalions of guards. Ann's gloom deepened as we ate.

She ordered the trifle. That was too much Anglophilia for me. I asked for coffee and the cheese board, a wise choice. The cheese was ripe and Stilton, and the coffee, had it not been for whole cream and Demerara sugar, would have peeled my tonsils.

Ann ate a last delicate bit of what looked to me like vanilla pudding. Then she glanced at her watch. "My goodness, it's almost nine!"

"Heavens to Betsy." I sipped coffee.

"It must be dark out."

"Must be."

She stared at me. "You knew the meal would take forever."

I fished in my purse. "Well, yes. What's worse, I rented a room for the night." I held up the key. "Bed and breakfast. I suggest we retire to our room and map out our strategy."

Her mouth compressed. Our eyes locked. Finally, she leaned back in her chair. "I declare, you're as strong-willed . . ."

"As a mule in a hurricane?"

"You took the words right out of my mouth."

In deference to fishermen and the commercial travelers who were its mainstay, the Royal Oak served breakfast early, from seven-thirty to nine. Ann and I had reloaded the car and were waiting outside the breakfast room's door at 7:30.

Our bedroom had been a marvelous jumble of antiques (a wardrobe and dresser), cheap modern stuff (three beds and a cot), and that bizarre domestic technology the English specialize in (an electric pants press). Floor levels on the way to the bathroom varied wildly, which indicated that the place probably did date back to the reign of Charles II, he of the oak tree hideout.

We had stayed up until midnight planning alternative courses of action, and I had gone down to the foyer twice to call Jay at Mrs. Chisholm's. I'd dialed six times and each time the line was busy. That had worried me. I had left two separate notes describing where we were going and why. Jay might find it annoying to be stranded in the country without a car, but he could ask Harry Belknap for a lift or call a taxi from Thirsk. I had told myself that over and over until I finally fell asleep.

The weather had changed slightly the next morning. It was misting out, what the Irish call "soft weather." A chatty salesman who breakfasted at the next table said he thought the sky would clear by ten. That promised well. Breakfast was gammon and eggs. I kept hoping one day I'd run into a place that served smoked haddock for breakfast, or kedgeree. However, the gammon was good gammon. We were on the road before nine.

With a night's rest and a solid breakfast under her belt, Ann's mood had swung. She hummed to herself as she scanned for our turnoff. A roundabout shot us off on a B road—paved and well-maintained but rather narrow. Because we were in territory warmed by the Gulf Stream, everything had leafed out, and flowering shrubs blossomed in the misty fields and gardens. Spring was further along than it had been in Yorkshire. By ten, the sky had cleared.

The road twisted and rose. There was quite a lot of traffic—and sweat-making blind corners—so I concentrated hard on the mechanics of driving safely. At a quarter to eleven, we nosed into the village Ann claimed was closest to Lord Henning's estate. It was tiny, perhaps twenty houses, a church, one shop with the red POST OFFICE sign affixed, a pub, and an upscale antique shop. The street had been laid out well before the invention of the automobile. I spotted a small car park beside the pub, so I turned around at the church and went back, parked the car, and got out.

151

Ann extricated herself from the passenger side. "Hambly can't be more than ten miles from here." Her cheeks were pink with excitement.

"Good. I need to find a phone." I had tried Mrs. Chisholm's number before we left the Royal Oak and got another busy signal. I was beginning to think there was something wrong with the line.

"The pub won't open until eleven."

"Maybe there's a pay phone in the post office."

We walked to the shop, but it was closed up tighter than a drum. When I peered through the window, I saw no evidence of a public telephone. The antiques place was also closed but promised to open at 11:30. That left the pub.

We stood by the car, not saying much, until the door to the pub opened. We asked for a pot of tea and a phone, and the barmaid, her eyes bright with curiosity, pointed down the dank hallway that led to the rest rooms. I tried Mrs. Chisholm's number three more times. The line was busy. I held my breath against the odor of disinfectant emanating from the loos and dialed again. This time, a woman answered.

I said carefully, "This is Lark Dodge. May I speak to my husband?"

The woman—it was apparently the cook—asked me to repeat myself, so I did, explaining that I had stayed there Friday and Saturday nights and that I was anxious to talk with my husband.

"Oh dear, lass, he's gone, hasn't he? That copper with the red auto drove him to York this morning early."

"I see," I said, feeling rather blank. "May I speak to Mrs. Chisholm?"

I was given to understand that she was off visiting friends in Thirsk. I thanked the woman and hung up. I supposed Jay must have decided to leave on an earlier train. We had been scheduled to return at five. I wondered how early was early. On the off chance the he might already have reached London, I dialed the flat, but no one answered. I walked back into the saloon bar of the pub with my feet dragging.

Ann poured me a cup of tea. "That nice woman says Hambly is about five miles down the road that runs past the church. It's open today, Lark. Isn't that a stroke of luck? She says they don't open it to the public very often, but there's some kind of stately home tour going on over the holiday and Hambly will be open until four or five."

I sat and sugared my tea. I needed energy. "I've been on stately home tours. Everything will be cordoned off and there will be a volunteer or a staff member in every major room watching to make sure nobody snatches the porcelain knickknacks."

"Don't be negative, Lark."

I sighed. "I'm sorry. Jay checked out early and I don't know how to reach him. He isn't at the flat."

"Try again in a couple of hours, honey. He's bound to show up."

"You're probably right, but it is worrying. Ah well, let's go to Hambly and see what we can see."

We drank our tea and left, pulling out behind a dark sedan that picked up speed as the village ended. I kept to a more cautious pace and the sedan disappeared from view. The road narrowed beyond the church. A stone wall, at head height and in good repair, followed it on the left—not conducive to trespass. I had set the odometer at zero. When it registered 5.2 and we still hadn't found Hambly, I began to wonder whether the barmaid had been fictionalizing. Perhaps the odometer was calibrated in kilometers.

"There's a sign!" Ann leaned forward. "The car park's off there to the right."

I drove into the grassy plot and bumped over uneven turf, past dozens of other vehicles, to a spot beneath a large tree. A meadow had been roped off and a piece of generic farm equipment, quite new, sat idle at one end. Two other cars—they must have come from the opposite direction—had turned in after us. A boy in a school blazer and shorts directed them to form a new row. Clearly, the opening of Hambly to public viewing was something of a local event. An enterprising soul had brought in a mobile canteen. Candy wrappers and soft-drink cups littered the grass, and two port-a-potties already had customers.

Ann had undone her seat belt and was rummaging in the backseat for her purse. "What a relief there are so many visitors. We can blend in with the others. And with any luck at all, there will be gardens." She opened her door.

"Gardens?" I grabbed my own purse and got out the other side.

"If the gardens are on show, we have an excuse to ramble around the grounds." She fumbled her bag open and took out a coin purse. A crudely lettered sign had indicated a 50p charge for parking.

We strolled over the grass to the kid who was directing traffic and paid him. He gave us a polite smile and waved another car into the new row. It was the dark, rather dusty sedan we had followed from the village. When we had crossed the road and queued up behind a family group to pay the admission charge, I glanced back. Two men in dark suits, one wearing sunglasses, had gotten out of the sedan. They did not look like garden-club enthusiasts.

We took our tickets and went on up a graveled drive. Two of the children in the family ahead of us had already darted off into the shrubbery. The mother was pushing a baby stroller. Her husband, casual in jeans and a light jacket, was chatting with an older woman who had obviously gussied up for the occasion. She was mincing along the gravel in high heels. An older man called to the children "not to muck about in them flowers."

I glanced behind us. A foursome of middle-aged women in neat spring outfits was following us. The men from the sedan were paying for their tickets, saying something to the woman in charge.

We passed a clump of evergreens and yellow-flowered shrubs and came in view of the house, perhaps a quarter of a mile off. The drive led down past stone outbuildings and a greenhouse, dipped toward a small stream, then rose again to a lesser height as it neared Hambly. It was a rambling, pleasant house, constructed of what I took to be local stone. The brochure we were given as we entered indicated that the family had added a neoclassic wing in the early nineteenth century to a seventeenth-century structure. Hambly was large by American standards but not a swollen palace like Castle Howard. It looked as if a family—and perhaps twenty servants and as many guests—could have lived in it.

The greenhouse was open for viewing and an array of potted primroses had been set out for sale. We ducked inside. Ann began interrogating the plump, besmocked woman in charge in a manner that suggested she knew plants. I feel a vague benevolence toward plants, but I do not have a green thumb, so I stood near the open door and watched the passersby. The four matrons were drooping over the potted flowers and the men from the sedan had gone on toward the house itself. A large group—probably a coachload—of well-dressed adults swarmed up the drive toward us. They seemed to be making for the greenhouse, too. I thought we could blend in with them if the need arose.

Having established her bona fides as a plant fancier, Ann joined me in the doorway.

"Where now?"

"The house?"

"Right." We moved out ahead of the large group and approached what turned out to be the neoclassic wing of Hambly. The main entrance lay around the side. It faced down another slope, toward a spot where the stream widened into an ornamental water. A humped bridge of improbable quaintness led to a tiny island with a gazebo. I was fairly sure the Henning people were not holding Milos in the gazebo.

Ann took a deep breath and heaved her huge purse to her right shoulder. "Ready?"

I began to climb the wide, graceful steps that led up to the main entrance. "What are we looking for, apart from Milos?"

"A way into the private part of the house."

A way in. My cheeks felt hot and I was sure I had turned red in the face in anticipatory embarrassment. We were going to make nuisances of ourselves. My qualms were trivial compared to Milos's safety, but I felt them nonetheless. Ann sailed serenely on.

The main hallway was marble, stark and bedecked with armor, probably of the Renaissance, since it looked more ornamental than useful. Earlier armor—the kind fashioned before the widespread use of guns—tended to be plain and businesslike. A smiling man with a flower in his lapel gestured us on to the grand staircase that swept up to the next story. Ann was having none of that. She paused and in her best imitation of a dizzy tourist began interrogating him about Hambly.

To my surprise, she pressed the right buttons. He expanded visibly and began describing the general plan of the house. We were to see the public rooms only, as I had expected, and they occupied the first floor—the second floor, to Americans—of the central portion of the H-shaped building. The neoclassical wing to the right, he said with ponderous good humor, had modern plumbing and wiring and composed the family's living quarters. The older, Queen Anne wing to the left had been given over to the Henning Institute some years before.

Ann gushed about the work of the institute.

I cleared my throat. "Then that wing contains offices and records and so on?"

"Certainly, my dear. And living quarters for some of the institute staff, too, though they complain about the heating system. I'm afraid it's not terribly efficient."

Ann thanked him lavishly for the information and sauntered up the steps. As I followed, I heard him greeting the advance guard of the coach party.

At the landing, the stairs branched left and right. A pedestal in the exact center held the bust of an eighteenth-century statesman.

Ann stopped to contemplate the bust. "Milos is in the old wing, I'll bet my bottom dollar."

"That does narrow things down." I led the way on up to the left.

"I'm immune to sarcasm," she said cheerfully. "Oh, look, isn't it gorgeous?"

The first of the public rooms was hung in green silk—not wallpaper—and contained a variety of musical instruments, notably a harpsichord and a lute that was lying open in its case, as if the musician might return to play it at any moment. A tall window provided the only illumination, but the sun was doing its best and we could see pretty well. A charming volunteer told us more than we wanted to know, under the circumstances, of the Henning family's musical proclivities.

We thanked him and moved along the rope to the next room. There were no halls—and no closets to hide in—so one room debouched on another through white framed doorways, each gracefully ornamented. The walls were hung in silk and decked with vast gilt-framed oils, all of them dark with age. In none of the rooms did we see a means of access to the old wing of the house. Apparently, it had been entirely sealed off.

That was disappointing. We trudged gamely on, following a clump of mixed visitors. A large, well-lighted picture gallery formed a bridge across the area above the head of the stairs. To the right, the rooms seemed friendlier.

A formal dining room was set with Spode and heavy silver as if for a banquet. It did have doors—closed and connecting with the newer wing—but everything was cordoned off behind a protective rope, and a stern-faced docent watched everyone narrowly as he reeled off the room's provenance. A formal waiting room or reception room and a faded pink sitting room for the ladies completed the roster of the rooms that were open for viewing.

We drifted slowly down the stairs, trailing a group that included the two men in dark suits. The thinner of the two had taken off his sunglasses. As he turned to say something to his companion, he was momentarily profiled against a tall window.

Ann stopped dead.

I bumped into her. "What is it?"

She grasped my arm and pulled me aside. "Wait."

The men had gone on out the main entry. When a laughing group from the coach passed us and went out, too, Ann's grip eased.

"What's wrong?" I asked, low-voiced.

"One of those men in suits, the thin one, was the man who stabbed Milos."

My heart thudded. "Are you sure?"

"Hope to die."

"My God."

"Move along, please," the guide Ann had questioned said in a firm, polite voice.

We went out into the sunlight and stood blinking on the stone porch. I could see the two men. They were strolling along the path to the older wing of the house.

"Whatever shall we do, Lark?"

"Find a phone," I said grimly. "And keep them in sight." Mutually impossible aims. I trotted down the wide stairs and moved to follow the men.

"Wait." Ann reached the drive beside me. "Won't they recognize us?"

I was wondering whether they would do worse than that. I was wondering whether we had led Milos's enemies to Milos's sanctuary.

15

♦   ♦   ♦   ♦   ♦   ♦

The coachload of gardening enthusiasts surged from the house like a spring tide. They were chattering about herbaceous borders and seemed to have a definite destination in mind. We moved along in their wake.

The two men glanced back as we cleared the corner of the house, caught sight of the advancing horde, and stepped down into a sunken garden area. I tried to keep some of the taller men from the coach between me and our quarry, because it seemed likely I was the one the assailant would recognize. After all, he had snatched Mrs. Watt's Harrods bag in the mistaken belief that she was Ann, but he must have had a good look at *me*. I had been standing right beside Milos, talking to him, and at six feet, I am not inconspicuous.

The gardening enthusiasts eddied and swirled down into the sunken garden, which held dormant rosebushes boxed by low, severely clipped hedges, and provided no cover. Ann and I remained on the upper level, I effacing myself behind a fancifully pruned yew and Ann peering past it at the garden.

"What are they doing?"

"Talking. The heavier one seems to be laying down the law

about something. The man who attacked Milos is just listening. They're looking up at the house. Oops, here they come."

I edged farther around the yew.

"And I just love all those masses of tulips," Ann was saying brightly. "Don't you, Myrtle? I reckon I'll do the whole front yard over next winter if I can find out where they sell the bulbs, those fringy scarlet ones." She lowered her voice. "I think it's okay. They gave me a glance and kept right on walking."

"Myrtle?"

"Sorry."

I peered past her. The men had reached another set of stairs halfway along the house and were walking down them toward an expanse of rolled lawn. "Something doesn't compute."

"What?"

"I'm not sure." I walked cautiously along the path until I could see the men again. They were heading over the lawn on a narrow walkway, away from us, away from the house. I lurked beside another topiary fantasy and watched them. "Do you think they've been following us all along?"

Ann meditated. "From Yorkshire?"

"From London to York, and so on."

"Surely we would have noticed."

"Not if they're pros." The idea of that thug watching us as we picnicked made my skin crawl. I couldn't feature very close surveillance, however. Certainly not at Rievaulx Abbey.

Ann said, "Maybe they haven't been following us at all. Maybe they already knew Milos was here and just waited until the house was open to the public to make their move."

I kept my eyes on the goons. They had gotten far enough from the house for a good view of the whole structure. The heavier man was pointing at something. I looked toward the area he was indicating, but our angle was wrong for me to see much above the first floor—we were too close. I had the impression of windows blanked with blinds or drapes. The facade did not look as if it could be scaled without special climbing gear. Thugs, of course, would have access to special equipment. Hambly would probably be duck soup to a cat burglar.

I turned back to Ann. "It may be that they've been waiting to make their move until they could get into the grounds. It's even possible they had as much difficulty as we did figuring out where Hambly was. But Inspector Thorne must have known."

Ann made a distressed noise. "Are you sure?"

"As I recall, we asked him if he knew of a town or village called Hambly. He said no, which was the literal truth. I wonder if it's general knowledge that Hambly is Lord Henning's seat."

"Would the Englishman in the street know of it?" Ann was craning around the bush, keeping her eye on the thugs. "The barmaid did, but she's local. And the house is not ordinarily open to the public—it's not a National Trust property."

"I may be maligning Thorne," I muttered. "He did seem genuinely puzzled over Milos's disappearance, though he knew a lot more about Milos's papers than he admitted. I wish Dad would get those papers translated. Maybe then, everybody's motives would be clear."

"They're coming back," Ann hissed. She started to move toward the front of the house, but I pulled her in the opposite direction. It was fortunate that the topiary shrubs had been planted in a row the length of the house. We ducked behind a yew shaped like a tall urn as the men came back up the stairs. I was gambling that they'd go on to explore the rest of the other wing, and I intended to eavesdrop. To my surprise, they wheeled to the right and headed toward the front of the house at a brisk pace.

Ann and I looked at each other. Her eyes glinted with excitement. "Shall we follow them?"

"We might as well. There's no public phone here, anyway."

We kept back and kept quiet until the men had reached the newer wing of the house and turned the corner. We almost sprinted until we had them in sight again. There were a lot of people on the walkway that led up from the neoclassic wing to the greenhouse, and it was not difficult to keep a screen of visitors between us and the goons. Their dark suits made them stand out among the holiday crowd, though not as dramatically as they might have in the United States. They marched along and did not dally to admire the landscaping. They had seen what they came to see.

Ann and I tagged behind a family group carrying a picnic basket. Just before we reached the gate, the family cut off across the rolled lawn, and we had an unimpeded view of the two men. Had they turned around, the reverse would also have been true. Fortunately, they didn't, and a trio of sightseers heading toward the house screened us as the men crossed the road.

We paused for a coach to pull out, crossed the road openly, and sauntered along our row of vehicles. Milos's assailant was unlocking the doors of the dark sedan, facing our direction but bent over. The other man had his back to us. The assailant walked around behind the sedan as we reached the Escort. I groped in my purse, found my keys, and unlocked Ann's door. By the time the sedan began to make its way toward the exit, I had the engine running. The sedan turned right, away from the village we had come through.

I had never followed another car surreptitiously, certainly never on the left-hand side of the road. I hung back and tried to remember to watch out for other vehicles, dogs, cats, and pedestrians, as well as the sedan, but there were a few moments of pure fright. The road was narrow and well traveled, and I almost slammed into the side of a Land Rover that was pulling out of a driveway. Fortunately, the driver spotted me and stopped. As I squeaked past, I saw his face contort in a voiceless snarl.

After about eight miles, the road entered another, larger village of the sort that is labeled "quaint" by tour directors. It became even more difficult to watch the sedan and drive safely.

I geared down and stopped at a zebra. A woman with two children in tow pushed a pram across the street. "Keep your eyes on him and tell me where he turns."

"Left at the next block."

"Okay." I crept around the corner as the sedan drove into a public car park that had been tucked discreetly out of sight of the main shopping area. I slid the Escort into a spot two rows over, beside the kind of station wagon the English call a "shooting brake." There was a maroon and silver coach on the other side of us. It hid us neatly. Ann was out of the car before I cut the engine. I scrambled out and locked the doors.

The men were just emerging from their car. The heavy man stretched and yawned, looking idly around while the driver locked the sedan. Ann and I waited. I held my breath. Then the knife artist said something, and the heavy man laughed and gestured at a well-marked path. They moved toward it—away from us.

"Whew!" Ann shrugged the strap of her purse higher on her shoulder. "What would you have done if they'd spotted us?"

"Ducked down and looked at the tires. People are always looking at their tires."

She chuckled. "Clever. Come on, we don't want to lose them now." I think she was enjoying herself.

I followed in her wake. "I'm going to have to find a telephone very soon, Ann—if only to call Jay. We ought to call Thorne as well."

"But Milos . . ."

I kept my voice low. The asphalt path led between two rows of houses; the men had reached the far end of it. "I was willing to keep Thorne in the dark when it was just a question of Milos's whereabouts, but we know this man is a violent criminal, probably a murderer. If I thought Thorne would buy the story, I'd say we spotted the goon while we were sight-seeing, but Thorne won't swallow that. And we didn't let him know we were leaving Yorkshire."

We reached the end of the path. It opened on the village green, a parklike area of generous dimensions. We looked around.

"There they are," Ann said, pointing to the right. The men were entering what looked like a large eighteenth-century coaching inn.

I had spotted a public telephone booth a few yards to the left. "Okay, I'm calling Jay. We can talk about whether to call Thorne later. While I'm telephoning, you follow those men."

"Into the hotel?"

"You've already gambled that the knife artist didn't recognize you. We can't lose them now."

"Right." She trotted off without further protest, like a detachment of the Georgia militia.

A plump woman in scarlet spandex pants and an embroidered tunic was using the telephone. After what seemed like an hour but was probably five minutes, she hung up, gave me an appraising glance, and walked off. I had a fistful of change ready in case the phone wouldn't take my card. Fortunately, it did. I punched in the London code and our number.

Jay picked the receiver up after the second ring. "Hello?"

"It's me, darling."

"Lark?" He cleared his throat. "Where the fuck are you? And what kind of stunt are you trying to pull?"

"You can yell at me later. I'm calling from a pay phone in Much Aston."

"You'll be in much trouble if you don't tell me what the hell is going on. . . ."

"I am trying to," I said, separating each word with care. "The name of the village is Much Aston." I spelled it. "It's in Shropshire, south of Much Wenlock, east of Ludlow, about eight miles from Lord Henning's estate. My note explained about Hambly."

"Right. A house, not a village, where you think Vlacek is being held." So he had received at least one of my messages. He sounded calmer.

"I'm *sure* Milos is at Hambly. When we got here, we took a tour of the house and Ann spotted the man who stabbed him. The man was touring the house, too."

There was a moment of dead silence, then Jay let out a whistle.

Now that he had stopped emoting and was listening to me, I described how we had trailed the men from Hambly to Much Aston.

"Okay. I'm writing this down. Can you go back to the parking lot and get their license number?"

"I memorized it," I said grimly. I had been staring at the license plate for the past twenty minutes.

He took down the number. "Great! I'll call Thorne and he can contact the locals."

"Tell him the men are in the Greyhound Hotel. Ann followed them in there and I haven't seen them leave."

"Jesus, is that wise? Those boys play rough."

I said coldly, "Ann is an intelligent, adult *woman* and equal to half a dozen boys, rough or smooth."

"A slip of the tongue. I have no doubt Ann could lick her weight in boys, but that bozo who stabbed Vlacek is a hard case. He probably killed your landlady."

Jay was stating the obvious. He was also scaring me. I held on to my temper with an effort. "I'd be happy to ooze silently away and I'm sure Ann would prefer to be rifling through the used books in Hay-on-Wye, but we do feel a certain responsibility. It's possible we led those goons to Milos. We can't let them get at him."

He sighed. "Okay, darling, I see your point. In fact, I saw it yesterday. If I hadn't called the car-rental outfit this morning, you'd be on the wanted list yourself."

I had forgotten all about the car-hire contract. We had intended to return the car—in York, at noon. I thanked Jay.

He said handsomely, "You can't think of everything. Now, Lark, I want you to go over to the Greyhound Hotel and book a room. You'll need a place to stay. Then sit in the lobby, you and Ann, right out in the open, and wait for the cops."

"But what if the men leave?"

"Let them. It's out of your hands now." He paused, as if shifting mental gears. "Your mother called about half an hour ago. She said your dad is arriving at Heathrow early this evening."

I digested that. "Did he get the papers or is he just being paternal?"

"I'm not sure. That is, he has the papers, but Mary doesn't know what's in them." Mary is my mother, the poet.

I groaned. "Wonderful."

"He booked the flight last night. Mary sounded a bit confused." He paused again. I could hear him thinking. "Listen, I'm going to call Thorne right now. What is it, five-thirty? I'll pick George up and rent a car at the airport. We'll drive out to Shropshire from Heathrow and see you tonight. Book two rooms."

"Three. You forgot Ann." I was mightily relieved. "All right, darling. I'm sorry if we worried you, leaving like that, but there wasn't much else we could do."

"I'll probably forgive you. Take care, Lark."

"You, too." When I had disconnected, I headed for the Greyhound through a coachload of sunburned, cross-looking tourists who were being herded in the direction of the car park.

I entered the hotel, blinking as my eyes adjusted to the dimmer light. Ann was standing at the registration desk talking to the clerk in a low voice. When I touched her arm, she jumped.

"Heavens, you startled me." She turned back to the clerk, a boy of about seventeen, and thanked him warmly.

We walked over to an ancient leather sofa that was placed to give patrons a view of the green and sank down on it.

"Did you reach Jay?"

"Yes. Where are the men?"

"They have a room here. They got their key and went upstairs. That nice boy at the desk said the heavy man has a Libyan passport."

"Libyan?" Czech I had expected. Something in the man's air and the cut of his suit had suggested that he was not English, but it hadn't occurred to me that he wasn't European.

"Libyan," Ann repeated. "Isn't it odd? The man who attacked Milos is English, though. He gave a London address."

"You're a wonder, Ann. If I'd taken five more minutes, I'll bet the kid would have let you look at the register."

"Oh, I did, honey," she said calmly. "The clerk went into the back room for a minute or two, and I just took a little peek. Their names are Mohammed Fasel or Faisel, something like that, and John Smith. Probably fake names. It's a pity English hotels don't take their guests' passports."

I grinned. If the clerk had had the passports in his possession, I felt sure he would have shown them to Ann.

"How is Jay?"

"Jay is a prince." I told her that my father had received the papers and was flying in that evening. She was excited. I had begun to be, too, and we spent perhaps ten minutes speculating over the possible meaning of the papers. Then I remembered the rest of Jay's instructions.

"Good God, I'm supposed to book rooms." I jumped up. "I'd better do it now before the men come down for dinner or whatever and spot me at the desk."

Ann rose, too. "The bar's open. They could come down any time. I'll watch the stairs."

The clerk assured me that he had three very nice rooms available overlooking the green, which was illuminated at night. If I'd come a day earlier, he would have had to turn me away, but most of the holiday guests had checked out that morning. There was a car park behind the hotel, though it was rather full just then because of a birthday party going on in the saloon bar.

Ann had really warmed the clerk up. He chatted amiably as I filled in the guest information, and told me the gentlemen who were coming in later that evening could ring for the night porter even if he had gone off duty himself.

All that palaver took a long time and I kept expecting Faisel and Smith to barge down the stairs. Finally, however, my Barclaycard worked its magic. I took two of the keys and went over to Ann.

"I'm going back to the car park for our bags."

"Can you manage?"

"Yes, and I'd rather be elsewhere when our friends decide to come down and patronize the bar."

"I'll wait for you on that sofa and keep an eye out for the men."

"They could sneak out the back."

"Probably, but why should they? I don't think they saw me. They were on their way upstairs when I came in here."

I hadn't told Ann that Jay intended to call Thorne, an honest oversight. We had been distracted by our speculations about my father's arrival. I hesitated a moment, then said, "Jay called Inspector Thorne, Ann. We're supposed to wait here in the lobby until the county police arrive and make the arrest."

She sighed but didn't protest. "I wish I could warn Milos."

"You could try calling Hambly."

She brightened. "I could, couldn't I? There's a phone back in that little hall that leads to the bar."

I glanced up the stairway. "I'd better scoot. See you in a few minutes."

"Okay." She was fumbling in her purse.

When I returned with the two bags, she was sitting on the leathery sofa, looking glum.

"Did you get through?"

"The clerk told me the number is what they call 'ex-directory' —unlisted. I did ring the Henning Institute in London, but nobody answered. They should get an answering tape."

I set the bags down. "Frustrating. Want to go to your room and freshen up?"

"Lord, yes, and use the loo. I've been crossing my legs for at least half an hour." She lifted her bag. "There's one of those creaky little elevators by the phone. I'll take it up."

"Okay." I wondered whether the goons had used the elevator. Maybe they were already in the public bar making whoopee. Maybe they had slipped out the back and gone off to Hambly to murder Milos.

I waited for Ann, who returned, fresh as a daisy, in another flowered dress. Then I took a chance on the elevator and found my own room without incident. It did indeed have a view of the green. From that height, I could see the stream that meandered through it. Two boys were fishing from the bank.

I changed from jeans to tailored pants and a blazer. After all, my father, my spouse, and the law were coming. I needed to look adult and responsible.

As I opened the door to go out, I heard men's voices coming closer. I closed the door, then opened it again a crack just as Smith and Faisel passed by. They passed so close, I could see that Smith was wearing the brown pinstripe he had worn when he stabbed Milos. I held my breath, but they kept going. They were saying something about eating in the pub. Their voices faded.

I inched the door wider and peered down the hall toward the stairs. They had disappeared. I went to the squidgy little elevator. It was an antique, with a cage for hapless passengers and cables that moaned as I pressed the button. As the lift creaked upward, it occurred to me that the elevator door opened into the passage that led to the bar. I left the lift waiting and walked down the hall to the stairs, hoping the would-be assassin hadn't forgotten his wallet. When I reached the ground floor, however, the men were nowhere in sight.

Ann was sitting on the sofa looking alert and bright-eyed. "They came and went into the bar."

"I know," I said hollowly. "I almost bumped into them upstairs. Their rooms must be just down the hall."

"Room," Ann corrected. "They're sharing."

"How thrifty of them. No sign of the police?"

"Nope. I reckon we'll just have to wait. I wish we could go to supper. I'm starving."

"Jay said to wait in the lobby. It's only six-thirty."

She settled back on the sofa and I sat beside her, sluing sideways so I could check to see who was coming and going in the back. A party of tourists rambled in and headed toward the bar.

"This could get boring."

Ann rummaged in her bag. "Have a pamphlet."

I read all her pamphlets and an old copy of the *Manchester Guardian* someone had abandoned. She pulled out a guide to the Midlands. From time to time, she read me a choice bit. The Cotswold villages, it seemed, were even more picturesque than Much Aston. We were not far from the Cotswolds. She had always wanted to visit Chipping Camden and Chipping Norton, she said, because of the names.

At half past eight, the men came out of the bar and went up the stairs. We waited. No police, no Jay.

All that time, people had been coming and going. The party in the saloon bar was really warming up, and the dining room had opened.

My stomach grumbled. "I'm hungry."

"Me, too. Shall we send out for pizza?"

"Sadist."

At 9:15, the men came downstairs, tossed their key on the main desk, and strode out the main entrance without so much as a glance in our direction. I was at the window in a flash. They were heading toward the car park.

"What now?" Ann asked.

"Jay said to wait."

"Yes, but it's pretty clear the police aren't coming."

"He said to wait," I repeated, "even if the men left."

"Jay is bound to concern himself with your safety, Lark, but surely there's something we can do."

"What, for example?"

"Lord, I don't know. Are they out of sight?"

"Yes."

"I suppose it's too late to follow them."

"And too dangerous. We've already pushed our luck."

She said fretfully, "I wish I could call Hambly."

"We could tell the village constable."

We stared at each other. I tried to imagine explaining the situation to a rural policeman and failed. We were foreigners and women. He would probably dismiss us as crackpots.

168

I brooded. My stomach rumbled. It had been a long time since the Royal Oak's gammon and eggs.

Ann took up her guidebook again, but I could see that her heart wasn't in it. I walked around the lobby and killed five minutes watching passersby. A nearby pub had spilled its patrons out onto the sidewalk. They looked happy.

The clerk, who was having a brief respite from hotel patrons, came over to us. "Are you all right, ladies? Shall I have the porter bring you something from the bar?"

"Oh, mercy, yes," Ann said. "We're hungry as wolves."

He looked bewildered.

I interpreted. "I think he means a drink."

"You could go in to dinner," he offered. "The dining room closes in half an hour, but I'm sure they can seat you."

Ann sighed. "We would just love two half-pints of bitter, honey. And we wouldn't say no to a packet of crisps."

He smiled. That, he could cope with.

When the porter came, the dear man brought two handsome plates of assorted cheeses, hard rolls, and butter, nicely garnished with lettuce, pickled onions, and chutney. The beer was wonderful. So was the ploughman's lunch.

We dispatched the food and drinks in short order and Ann carried the tray back to the bar. While she was gone, my brain kicked in. It was all very well for Jay to tell us to sit on our thumbs, but Faisel and Smith might be getting away with murder. We couldn't telephone Hambly, but I could drive out there and try to warn the Henning staff. I could drive right up to the main gate. If there was a guard, I could warn him.

When Ann returned, I was on my feet, car keys in my hand. I told her what I had decided.

"I'm coming, too."

"No, absolutely not. Somebody has to wait here in case Jay and Dad arrive while I'm gone. I won't be long."

"But . . ."

"You can't drive the car, and I can," I said brutally. "I go. You stay. I'll be back in forty-five minutes."

I covered the distance to the car park at a half trot. All the coaches had gone and only half a dozen cars remained. A sign said there was no overnight parking. When I came back, I would have to move the car to the hotel lot, but first things first. The villains had a half-hour start on me.

There was very little traffic, fortunately. I zipped along the road with my high beams on most of the way. I narrowly avoided running over a cat as I approached the estate. I drove along the wall and, after several miles, pulled over at the edge of the meadow that had served as a parking lot. The gate—which was tall and beautifully ornamented with gilt oak leaves and acorns around a monogram *H*—was locked tight. I found a button and pushed it. Though I waited almost ten minutes, no one responded. It was after ten by then and the moon was out. I peered through the gate and tried yelling, but I was wasting my time. I heard a dog barking far off but no encouraging sounds. No one was coming.

I gave up, got into the car, and turned back toward Much Aston. I poked along, trying to think of an alternate course of action, but nothing came to mind. Then I spotted the sedan.

They had parked it on the right-hand shoulder, almost in the hedge that bordered that side of the road. It looked abandoned. I drove about fifty yards farther along until I came to a gate that led into a field on the right. On the left, the wall of the Henning estate stretched unbroken as far as I could see. I parked the Escort beside the gate and sat for a moment, working up my courage. Then I locked the car, having stowed my purse behind the front seat, and walked back toward the sedan—slowly, making as little noise as possible.

The sedan was empty but unlocked. I could see nothing on the seats or dash but an ordinary road map, and I hesitated to get in. The boot was ajar. I opened it, wincing as the hinges creaked, but I saw nothing out of the ordinary. I closed it again very slowly until it latched.

I looked across at the wall. Had Smith and Faisel gone over it? It was about six feet high and, though it was surmounted by a course of jagged stones, I thought it was scalable. A car zipped by, going the way I had come. I watched its taillights recede and wished I had had the wit to flag it down.

A wisp of cloud passed over the moon, altering the light, and something glinted on the wall. I crossed the road for a closer look. At first, I saw nothing at all, but I ran my hands over the area from which the gleam had come and felt metal: two large hooks. I lifted them, careful to make no noise. They were attached to a rope ladder, or chain ladder, to be specific, of the kind sometimes used in home fire escapes. The cables had been wrapped in tape so they wouldn't clank.

I deduced that the men had used the ladder to climb the wall, then repositioned it as an escape route. They had been at their business, whatever it was, almost an hour. They could return at any moment.

I pulled the ladder back over the wall as quietly as I could. At least I could slow their exit a bit. Then I looked at the ladder and temptation overwhelmed me. I climbed to the top of the wall before I could have second thoughts, teetered a moment on the jagged surface, then jumped down inside.

The goons had chosen their spot with care—the edge of an evergreen copse. The ground was covered with needles. I made very little noise landing, though my flats slipped and I fell on my tush. I got to my feet, wishing I had taken the time to put on sneakers—and a darker shirt. My blouse was a ladylike print, pink and purple, and I was afraid it would show up white against my dark blazer. I buttoned the jacket.

I stood for a long moment, listening to the silence, then began moving along the edge of the woods. I could see very little and I was worried about bumping into one of the men in the dark. One of them would surely be acting as a lookout.

Within ten groping yards, I emerged at a "ride," a wide swath through the woodland, cut to permit ancient Hennings to exercise their horses. At the far end, a good half mile away, a light in the house shone small as a star.

I saw no one on the ride. I supposed the goons had not expected trouble from my direction. The lookout would be posted nearer the house. I began to run toward it. I am a good runner. In spite of my flats and the uneven sod beneath them, I covered most of the distance quickly, stumbling but not falling. The third time I slipped, I stopped and took off my shoes.

I was breathing hard, more from fear than from the run. I quieted my breath and went on at a quick walk. The turf felt cool and soft through my nylon footies. When I reached the end of the ride, I was still at some distance from Hambly and directly behind it. Ann and I had not circled the place completely. I wished we had. I wished I knew exactly what Faisel and Smith were up to. It gave me satisfaction to name them in my mind, even if the names were faked.

Lights showed in the new wing, in one corner of the second floor: family apartments. The ground floor showed only dim illumination and most of the drapes had been pulled. There were no lights in the central portion at all, but the institute's wing was patchily lit on the second and third floors. Milos was probably housed there.

I had taken a few steps in the direction of the older wing of the house when the heavier man, the Libyan, emerged from that direction and began to walk up the long rolled lawn toward me.

16

◆ ◆ ◆ ◆ ◆ ◆

Faisel was walking straight toward me across the quarter-mile expanse of lawn that separated the house from the ride. I leapt into the shadow of the trees and froze in place. He was carrying something in his right hand—a gun or a knife—that glinted in the moonlight.

I felt like a deer caught in the scope of a rifle. He kept coming. When he was about a hundred yards away, he glanced over his left shoulder toward Hambly. I was on his right. I took two cat steps back and tried to look like one of the flowering shrubs at the edge of the ride. His head whipped forward and he kept coming, trotting now, gun hand at his side, eyes scanning ahead of him. If I had twitched an eyebrow, he would have seen me.

He looked over his shoulder again, a long look, as if he was expecting to see or hear something from the direction of the house. I took three desperate sideways steps and gained the protection of a rhododendron. It had large pale blossoms with velvety dark hearts. I held very still. Then he was past me and I could breathe.

I counted to twenty very slowly, one one thousand, two one thousand, three one thousand. . . . Then I turned my head with exquisite care in his direction. He was trotting along at a good clip, almost running. I waited until he was a blob in the shadowy distance. Then I did what I probably should have done as soon as I sighted the house. I ran to the new wing, found the entrance, raced up to the door, and began pounding on it.

I was yelling nonsense—help, fire, murder. Open up, come on, you limey bastards. I pounded on the stout door with both fists, bashed the iron knocker, leaned on the bell when I spotted it, all the while shouting at the top of my lungs.

I kept glancing back toward the ride. Surely, Faisel could hear me, even at that distance. I didn't see him returning, though. I pounded and yelled.

Light illuminated the narrow windows on both sides of the door and the fan-shaped arch above. I kept pounding.

When the door opened, I almost fell into the arms of a stout man with glasses.

"Here, what is it? What's the matter?"

"You have intruders," I retreated two cat steps onto the porch and stood there, panting.

He raised both eyebrows. "I certainly see one intruder."

I gulped for air. "You have a man here, a Czech named Milos Vlacek. Two men are on the grounds. They're going to try to kill him."

He stared at me for a blank minute in which I came close to despair. Maybe the people in the family wing didn't know about Milos. Maybe the man would think I was crazy.

Then he wheeled without a word, trotted to an small alcove down the hallway, picked up a telephone, and punched a number. "Yes. Williams here. Someone has broken into the grounds and is after your friend. Move him to the family wing now. Hurry."

He slammed down the phone and turned back to me. "Stay where you are." He punched out another number. After a pause that may have lasted three rings, he said, "Williams here. There are apparently intruders near the house. Where's McHale? He what? Well, find him."

I listened to him and stayed on the stone porch, but I was dancing with impatience. I stared off into the dark, trying to see whether Faisel was returning, whether Smith had heard me yell.

The man who had identified himself as Williams turned back and advanced toward me. His teeth bared in a smile and his eyeglasses glinted. "Now, madam, whoever you are, I should like an explanation. . . ."

I squinted into the darkness. "Look out, there he goes." It was Smith and he was running hell-for-leather toward the ride. I had tensed to move when a tremendous explosion knocked me off my feet. Glass shattered outward on both sides of me.

I scrambled up. I must have been yelling as I ran, something about not letting the bastards get away with it, but I didn't hear myself because the noise of the blast had deafened me. I ran desperately, flat out, in my ladylike nylon footies.

I ran up the long slope of lawn and onto the ride. Smith had probably been knocked down, too, and he ran like an amateur, arms flailing, feet flopping. I caught up with him about a third of the way along the ride. In the last couple of yards, he may have sensed me coming, though I think we were both still deaf, for he started to turn and stumbled to one knee. His face was a white blur. He regained his feet and had turned to face me, knife in hand, when I slammed into him. I knocked him flat.

A fire burned in my head, fueled by adrenaline and rage, so I suppose we were equally matched. I was taller by a couple of inches and he outweighed me. He was a street fighter; I was an athlete. I had knocked the wind out of him, but he had the knife. We grappled.

At the edge of my consciousness, I was aware of the turmoil behind me. I paid no heed. I was wrestling with Smith, still atop him. I clamped the wrist of his right hand in my left, digging my fingernails in, but, though I had a fistful of his hair and was smashing his head on the ground, he kept his grip on the knife. He gasped for air. His body heaved and jerked. He pounded and tore at me with his left hand, trying to overturn me.

I knew at some dim level that if he reversed our positions and pinned me, I was dead meat, so I kept low to the ground and dug my knees into the springy sod on either side of his waist. My hearing returned, and there were noises—shouts, dogs barking, a woman screaming, rumbles and crashes from the damaged house. Somewhere an engine started and, very far away, the Klaxons of emergency vehicles from the direction of Ludlow and Much Aston ripped at the night.

Lord Henning's beagles found us as Smith's heels finally dug in. He arched his back, twisted viciously, and rolled me over. He was screaming obscenities. The circling dogs ki-yied. He wrenched his knife hand from my grip as I clawed at his eyes. The knife plunged downward and I felt burning pain, but I found his throat with both hands, and I kneed upward. He let out a squawk and raised the knife again. As I blacked out, I heard heavy masculine voices above the shrill yelping of the dogs.

I have been told that I came to in the ambulance and asked after Milos. What had fueled my berserk rage was the instant conviction that he had been killed in the blast.

Nobody answered me. The paramedics, and the constable who rode along in the ambulance, had not the faintest idea who I was, of course. They asked. Apparently I told them I was Lark Dailey and that I had a room at the Greyhound in Much Aston. Then I passed out again. They radioed that information to the county police, and a car was sent to the Greyhound, where Ann was raising holy hell with the village constable. She set them straight about my name and what I was doing at Hambly. It was then about eleven, and Jay and my father had still not arrived.

At the Ludlow hospital, my injuries were assessed, I was given a transfusion, and the knife wounds to my shoulder and arm were stitched. I was wheeled into a recovery ward as ambulances began screaming in with other casualties from Hambly, including Mr. Smith. When Lord Henning's gamekeeper and groundsman took him into custody, Smith was howling with pain because my knee had found its target. He was also considerably bruised about the head and body, his right wrist was torn and swollen, and he had lost a handful of hair. They patched him up and hauled him off to the pokey under heavy police guard.

I knew none of this at the time. I had been sedated to prevent me from thrashing about and pulling out stitches, so I slept until six o'clock the next morning, awakening to find Ann at my bedside.

"Where's Jay?" I demanded—or, rather, that was my intention. What came out was a blurred moan.

Ann rang for the ward sister and took my right hand.

"Where's Jay?" This time the words came out, but I was feeling a lot of pain, so I gave another loud groan.

The nurse bustled in. "Are we awake, then?"

Ann ignored her. "Jay's just down the hall, drinking a cup of coffee, honey, and your daddy's here, too. I'll go get them." She gave my hand a squeeze and vanished.

Sister Owens introduced herself briskly and set about checking my vital signs. I am afraid I moaned and groaned a lot. She gave me two capsules, levering me up and holding a glass of water for me. I groaned again as she eased me back against the pillows, and at that heartrending moment, Jay and my father appeared in my field of vision.

"Wow, you made it," I moaned. "Where were you?"

Jay was at my side. He bent and kissed me on the mouth. Since my mouth was about the only portion of my anatomy that didn't hurt, I returned the kiss with interest and groaned some more. I am not stoical by nature.

Jay kept his hold on my hand but edged aside to let my father approach. Dad looked exhausted.

I met his eyes. "Am I good?" This inane question was childhood code. When I was about three, I had asked it after being scolded roundly for some misbehavior. My father's proper answer should have been "Thee is good," a gentle allusion to his own background and an infinitely reassuring bit of ritual.

This time Dad sighed. "Thee is alive, daughter."

I shut my eyes as tears welled. I could tell that George Fox Dailey and I were due for a long philosophical discussion.

My father is not a Friend, though he was raised in a traditional Quaker household, but he does not believe in using force, except when one is in dire and immediate danger of losing one's own life or the life of a child. He must have known by then that my attack on Smith was entirely voluntary.

Jay said, "It's all right, George. Leave me with her until the pain pills start working," and when I opened my eyes Dad had left the room. So had the nurse and Ann. Jay held my hand.

He told me he loved me, and I said, "Me, too." The pain pills were beginning to take effect. I lay with my hands in his warm grasp and felt my aches ease. My mind was a sluggish pond. Things moved below the surface. One of the nicest things about Jay is that he knows when to keep still.

After a considerable silence, I said sleepily, "I was so worried about you, driving on the wrong side of the road all that way. What took you so long?"

He cleared his throat. "It's a complicated story, darling, and I'm not going to tell it now."

I roused momentarily. "The papers . . ."

"George brought them. We'll talk about that later, too."

"Milos is dead." I began to cry.

"Hey, no. Who told you that? He's right here in this hospital."

"Really?"

"Yes. I guarantee it."

"Mmm. Tell Ann." If Jay said a thing was so, it was so. I was smiling when I fell asleep again. At least something good had come out of my foolish derring-do.

I woke again at noon and the pain was awful but no longer mind-numbing. When the pain pill—not a sedative, this time—started working, I became conscious of extreme hunger. Jay said later that I gave an excellent imitation of the voracious plant in *Little Shop of Horrors:* "Feed me!"

At one, the proper feeding time, I was brought a bowl of cream of celery soup and a fish-paste sandwich. I ate both without blenching.

A polite detective from the Shropshire force questioned me after lunch. He told me Ann had explained a great deal already and that he wouldn't tire me by going into my reasons for coming to Shropshire. I gave him as straightforward an account of the events at Hambly as I could. His sergeant took my statement down and read it back to me. Then the detective thanked me and left. Sister Owens was scowling the whole time from the doorway. She was very protective of me. Ann, Jay, and Dad had not yet returned from lunch.

My head was quite clear. I wanted out of the hospital and I wanted the answers to some questions—lots of questions. My aversion to the hospital had something to do with the food and a lot to do with my desire for privacy. I needed to talk with Jay, Dad, and Ann. I needed to know a lot of things, and I didn't want to worry that some stranger was listening. My medical care, then and later, when I was an outpatient, was a tribute to the National Health, but I did want out of that hospital.

I raised such a ruckus, they let me go.

Jay drove me back to the Greyhound in the Fiat he had rented at Heathrow, while Dad and Ann took the Escort. The police had retrieved it, along with my untouched purse, and towed the sedan. Jay told me Lord Henning's dogs had treed Faisel in the evergreen copse. The Libyan was too heavy and too out of shape to scale the wall without the rope ladder, and I had left the ladder on the wrong side of the wall. He shot two of the dogs before one of them crunched his gun hand. I wondered how the tabloid press was going to deal with a genuine dog killer.

As we drove along the familiar road to Much Aston, Jay also told me about the effects of the explosion. The chief constable of Shropshire had phoned the hospital. He told Jay they thought the explosive was a substance manufactured in Czechoslovakia. The police, including Inspector Thorne, who was in contact with the Shropshire force, believed that the plot against Milos had originated in Prague, despite Faisel's Libyan passport.

Smith had placed the plastic explosive on a second-floor ledge, carrying it up in a common nylon knapsack. It was on that floor—the third story, in American terms—that Milos had been hidden, guarded by an attendant nurse.

Smith had probably used an egg timer wired to a detonator to give himself time to escape. Perhaps climbing back down and rounding the house had taken longer than he'd anticipated, or perhaps the detonator had malfunctioned and gone off early. I remembered Faisel looking back at Hambly as he trotted along the ride. He was probably expecting Smith to join him before the blast went off. Further testing would go on for some weeks, but those were the preliminary findings.

"Smith must be a man of all work." I leaned my head back on the headrest and closed my eyes. "Have they charged him?"

Jay's hands tightened on the steering wheel. "With two counts of murder and one of attempted murder—so far."

"Two counts of murder?"

"Miss Beale's and Lord Henning's watchman, a man named Angus McHale. They found his body and his dog's in the brush near that whatchacallum, the ride. Apparently, the dog sensed the two men approaching and McHale went to investigate. The dog was shot, but McHale was knifed."

I fought a gagging sensation. "That's horrible." I swallowed hard. "But surely a gunshot . . ."

"Faisel—that's not his real name, by the way—used a silencer." Jay slowed behind a lorry that was laboring up a small hill. After a moment, he added, "There will be other attempted-murder charges. When the blast came, Milos and his attendant had already reached a corridor that leads across the central section of Hambly to the family's quarters. The attendant was pushing Milos's chair. Both of them were thrown to the far end of the corridor and trapped in the debris. A section of the roof fell in on them. It took the fire department two hours to pry them loose."

"But Milos, is he all right?"

"He's bruised and there was some internal bleeding from the earlier wound, but he's doing very well, Lark. Ann saw him yesterday and said he was in good spirits. The attendant, a young woman named Flynn, was struck by a beam. She has a skull fracture and several broken bones in her shoulder, but they think she'll recover."

"What about the family?"

His voice lightened. "They're in the Canary Islands."

"What?"

"It seems they take off for a little vacation in the sun every year at this time."

"While the house is being shown?"

"Yes. I imagine it would be uncomfortable having strangers poking around your living room."

I thought of the ornate public rooms of Hambly and smiled at his word choice, but the vision of what had been destroyed appalled me. All that silk and silver, the ancient musical instruments, the Hepplewhite furniture, family portraits by artists such as Reynolds and Sargent and Augustus John. "Was there a fire?"

"A couple of small ones started in the remains of the institute's wing, but they were put out quickly. There was heavy damage to the public rooms, but it's a well-built house. The family wing lost its windows. Williams told me they think the central portion can be salvaged and that the damage to the family wing isn't structural. The institute's wing will probably be pulled down."

"Williams. He was the one who opened the door. Who is he, the butler?"

Jay smiled. "He's Lord Henning's political secretary. He was in the library working on a speech for Henning to deliver in the House of Lords."

"Heavens. And he was all right?"

"A few cuts and bruises. He said to tell you his glasses flew off and were smashed in the explosion, or he would have run to your aid. He did tell the people who found you which way you'd gone, though."

"It's a good thing they showed up when they did."

"Yes."

I shot him a glance. His mouth was set in a grim line. "Hey, I survived."

"Yeah, and I am very carefully not yelling at you for taking off after an armed man. . . ."

"In my stocking feet." I felt a bubble of laughter welling up. I wondered what had become of my flats. My left shoulder was strapped up tightly and my arm was pinned in a state-of-the-art sling. Jay was going to be tying my sneakers for me for a while. I told him that and his mouth eased in a reluctant grin.

I sobered as we drew alongside the section of wall I had scaled. "You said there were other casualties."

"None of them serious, fortunately. The cook and butler— they're a married couple—were in their quarters in the family wing watching television. They were cut and bruised, and so was a Henning cousin who was down for the holiday from Oxford."

180

"There had to be more people on the estate than that."

"Most of the employees live in villages in the area and had gone home. The gamekeeper and groundsman have small apartments in another building. They'd just stepped out the door to look for McHale when the explosion went off. Neither of them was hurt. They let the dogs out of the kennel and ran to the house to see what they could do. I guess the stables were pandemonium. They keep five horses. The groom had his hands full."

"What about the greenhouse?"

"There's a greenhouse?"

I described our tour of the grounds in terse detail. We were approaching Much Aston and there was a big question that had to be asked. I had asked it several times already. I kept getting evasions.

"What took you and Dad so long to get to Shropshire?"

He didn't answer at once.

"Jay . . ."

"Daphne Worth was struck by a hit-and-run driver Sunday evening."

I went cold. "But she was going to go hiking in Dorset over the holiday."

He slowed as we entered the village. "She was struck as she walked back to her b and b from a pub in Dorchester. She wasn't identified until Monday, and when she was, Thorne tried to get in touch with us at the flat. I had already left for Heathrow. Thorne put out an APB. The police caught up with me as I was hiring the car. They took me in for questioning."

I was shivering. "Surely they didn't believe you did it!"

"No, and I don't really think they believed you and Ann did it, either, but they had to check with us for alibis. It's a damned good thing you called me when you did or I wouldn't have known what to say when Thorne asked me your whereabouts. I'd still be in custody. George drove the car in and waited at the flat for me. When we got away, it was after nine. I broke a lot of speed limits coming west."

He found the entrance to the hotel car park, a cramped yard behind the building, and negotiated the narrow arch with extreme care.

I was so cold, I wanted to rub my arms, but I couldn't. "Is Daphne dead?"

"She's unconscious and they did surgery to stop the internal bleeding. They may have to remove her spleen. They think she'll live, but Thorne won't be able to interview her for some time."

I was near tears. "Oh, poor Daphne. Poor Trevor. Did you see him?"

"Only at the police station," Jay said dryly. "They were questioning him, too."

He parked the car and made me wait while he went around to open the door for me. That gave me a few moments to compose myself. Getting me out of the Fiat was a sweaty ordeal for both of us. By the time I felt clearheaded enough to walk to the hotel's rear entrance, Dad and Ann had parked the Escort and were standing by. My legs were okay, though the soles of my feet were cut and bruised. Ann had brought me a dress to wear and a pair of low-heeled pumps. The pumps were pure torture.

We walked slowly and waited by the elevator while Jay went to get the room keys. When he returned, he looked harried.

"What's wrong?" Dad asked.

"The lobby is jam-packed with reporters."

Ann and I groaned.

17

♦ ♦ ♦ ♦ ♦ ♦

We were under siege. Dad's room and Jay's and mine adjoined, with a connecting door, but Ann had to go out into the corridor when she wanted to visit us. The rooms had no telephones, fortunately, and the hotel was fielding our calls with a cheerfulness born of the postholiday boom my notoriety had inspired.

Reporters of all media had taken the remaining rooms vacated by holidaymakers, and the representative of a major London tabloid was heard to complain that he was staying in a b and b so small he had to share the bathroom with the family. The hotel bars—both the public and the private—were doing a land-office business, and the harassed chef had had to send out for more brussels sprouts.

The evening of my release from the hospital I spent sleeping, waking to groan, eat, and take more painkillers, then sleeping some more. The worst injury was a fairly deep knife wound high on my left shoulder, and I had received another nasty slash in the bicep of my left arm. The rest were scratches, bruises, and cuts from the window glass I had stepped on as I dashed off after Smith. I felt rotten and very sorry for myself in my brief intervals of consciousness.

Pain makes people selfish. I spared a thought now and then for Daphne, but Jay, who had spoken to Thorne on the manager's telephone, reported no change in her condition.

I heal fast. By lunchtime Wednesday, I was almost ready to deal with the real world—and my father was ready to talk about Milos's papers.

I had not forgotten them, of course, and I could tell from Dad's gray exhaustion that he was suffering from something worse than jet lag. He had had at least one chat about the papers' import with Jay and Ann the evening before, when they'd brought me back from the hospital, but they had talked in Dad's room while I slept off the ride from Ludlow. By the time I woke up Wednesday morning, Dad had run the gauntlet of reporters and driven off in the Fiat. He returned at 11:30 looking more cheerful.

Ann ventured out at noon and bought picnic supplies in the village, a "photo opportunity" of which the resident journalists did not hesitate to take advantage.

"And there I stood," she said, exasperation turning her face pink, "my arms full of *squidgy* parcels, while they shouted their damn fool questions at me. That nice boy behind the desk—you remember him, Lark, honey—just *swept* to my rescue. I came real close to kissing him in a public place."

"I wish I'd seen that." Jay began unloading her as one might unload a pack camel. He set out beer, mineral water, a lump of pâté, two cheese wedges, a long cucumber, two tomatoes, a jar of mustard, a stick of butter, and four blood oranges from Spain on the small table in our room.

I watched, propped against the headboard, as Ann drew her Swiss army knife from the depths of her purse and set about turning the groceries into a meal. I could have sat at the table, but there were only three chairs, including the one Dad had brought in from his room, so I kept to the bed.

My father was watching Ann, too, and listening to Ann and Jay banter as they prepared a selection of goodies for me. I was still definitely one-handed. We all ate our fill from the paper plates Ann had brought.

"It's been years since I tasted one of these." Dad popped the last segment of blood orange in his mouth. "A treat, Ann. Thank you."

She smiled at him and went to rinse off her sticky fingers at the hand basin with which all English hotel rooms are furnished. "Mama had a cousin down in Florida who raised the sweetest blood oranges? He lost the tree in a hurricane. Took the heart right out of him."

Dad sighed. "That's my problem. This monograph of Milos Vlacek's has taken the heart out of me."

Ann went back to her chair. "What do you intend to do about the papers, Professor Dailey?"

"What *are* they?" I interrupted. "Come on, guys, I've got a vested interest. . . ."

Jay shot me a warning glance. I bit my lip.

Dad was rubbing the bridge of his nose. He does that when he's putting his thoughts in order. My father is not a blurter. We waited. Finally, he sighed again. "They are documentation of evil, Lark. And your friend is a witness of unimpeachable integrity. His word will have weight."

"Milos is a distinguished poet, Lark." Ann's eyes shone.

"And one of the Czech intellectuals who signed Charter 77," my father added. "Have you heard of that, Lark?"

I shook my head. I was busy digesting the fact that I had embroiled myself in the life of yet another poet. I am haunted by poets.

"Charter 77 is a human-rights declaration, and its signers pledged themselves, among other things, to monitor violations of human rights in Czechoslovakia. You may think of them as a network of witnesses. A good many of them, including your friend Vlacek, have been imprisoned by the Czech government."

Jay retreated to the connecting door and closed it. He didn't say anything, but he was watching Dad with frowning concentration.

I forced myself to keep still.

"When the parcel arrived Friday," Dad went on, "I took it to Erzibet Rosen. You remember her, Lark."

"Yes, of course." Professor Rosen taught Slavic languages and literature for SUNY and had been a friend of my parents since she escaped from Czechoslovakia during the Soviet invasion of 1968. "She must have translated the document right away."

"She brought me an English language printout at noon Saturday and we had . . ." He hesitated. "We had an impassioned discussion of what should be done about it. She wanted to take it directly to the press and the FBI." He glanced at Jay. "I was not confident that was the wisest course. In the end, we compromised and I decided to fly to England as soon as possible."

There was another pause. He was rubbing his nose again.

"When he was released from prison last year, Mr. Vlacek found work as a janitor in a factory town. In December, Flight 103 crashed at Lockerbie. Almost at once, Vlacek began to hear rumors among clerical workers in the factory that the Czech government had supplied certain terrorist organizations with the explosive, semtex."

A plastique manufactured in Czechoslovakia. My mind was working slowly, but I drew the new connection.

"Oh, no." Nausea rose in my throat. One of Dad's most promising students had been killed on Flight 103 and my father was devastated by the tragedy. "Oh, Dad, I'm sorry."

He got up and walked to the window, staring out at the village green below. "Vlacek began to gather testimony—and, through the underground network of dissidents, to arrange interviews with key observers. He has documented the government's complicity in the bombing. The names in the papers are coded. When I called on Vlacek at the hospital this morning, he assured me that he could supply the key. Indeed, he dictated it to me. He had memorized it."

I recalled Milos's facility with quotations from Shakespeare. He knew *Macbeth* by heart—in English. He had an excellent memory.

Dad said, with deliberation, "I came to England, Lark, to assure myself of your safety, and, if I could, to ask Milos Vlacek what he wanted me to do with the information."

"But the British government has a copy."

"Yes. Even without the names of witnesses, the document is . . . powerful. I trust the London police have given the information it contains to the commission investigating the crash."

I shifted on the bed, easing my physical discomfort. My mind felt leaden. There had already been shocking suggestions that the CIA was warned of the impending crash, that the airline itself was warned, but that the warnings had not been passed on to the passengers. I did not have to be told that information could be suppressed.

Dad sat down again, heavily, like an old man. "Vlacek left Czechoslovakia in February and friends in London found work for him. A young dissident, a musician, was able to smuggle the document out of Czechoslovakia the week you and Ann attended the booksellers' convention."

"It was the kid in the bomber jacket," Jay said. "The one who delivered the manuscript at the Barbican."

"Milos says he's a rock musician," Ann added, eyes gleaming. "The Czech government *persecutes* rock musicians, Lark. Can you imagine?"

Thinking of the forces of repression running rampant in the United States, notably in Ann's neck of the woods, I could easily imagine the persecution of rock musicians. I nodded. "Go on, Dad."

"Vlacek's friends arranged with the Henning Institute to spirit him away from the hospital as soon as he could be transported. They do not trust the present British government to make the information public. They were also concerned lest Czech agents make another attempt on Vlacek's life. Until the information was general knowledge—or at least too widely disseminated to be suppressed—his life was in danger."

I levered myself up. "Take the document downstairs and hand it out to the press."

Dad frowned. "That was Erzibet's first impulse. And I do understand her . . . urgency. And the need to protect Vlacek. However, there is a criminal investigation going on. I think the proper course is for me to give the document to the Scottish authorities at once."

"People should know," I burst out.

"People will know," Dad countered. "Apart from the photocopy you sent me and the transcription on Erzibet's hard disk, I sent fifty copies of the translation to leading historians in the United States and Europe. This morning, I mailed them copies of the key with a covering letter. I asked them to hold the information until the Scottish inquiry is officially ended. If the Czech government's involvement is not made public by that time, I will instruct my colleagues to release the information to the media."

I reflected. "But an official investigation could take years. What about Milos's safety?"

Jay said, "I suggested George tell the press the truth, that Vlacek is being hounded by agents of the Czech secret police. He is a poet, after all."

"Without mentioning Lockerbie?"

Dad gave a small, almost mischievous smile. "Freedom of expression is a hot issue. There is this business of Salman Rushdie. I'll suggest that a similar attempt is being made to silence another creative voice."

"Both of you have Byzantine minds." I eased back on the pillows. "Ma knows every publisher of poetry in the Western World. Couldn't she arrange for one of them to bring out an edition of Milos's work in translation?" When they looked at me, Ann with sparkling eyes, I added, acidly, "A touch of verisimilitude for an otherwise bald and unconvincing narrative."

Dad's smile broadened. "An excellent idea. I'll call Mary from the manager's office. She's waiting for an update on your condition, anyway, Lark, and contacting publishers will give her a salutary distraction from worrying about her daughter."

I felt the deft sting of parental guilt and winced. "I suppose you're going north to Scotland."

"Ann has agreed to accompany me as far as York," Dad said placidly. "We'll return the Escort to the car-hire office and I'll take the train to Edinburgh from there. I have an appointment in Glasgow Friday afternoon with an officer of the Galloway and Dumfries constabulary." He sounded almost cheerful, and it occurred to me that being able to do something, even after the fact, might help ease his grief. I hoped so.

Ann began to tidy away the remains of our picnic. "I'll hire a car with an automatic transmission in York so I can visit Haworth. Then I'll come back to London."

"Do we have to go back to London at all?" My question was disingenuous, mere griping. With Daphne in the hospital, I knew Thorne would want us under his eye. And we would owe Trevor and Daphne another week's iniquitous rent.

Lord Henning was sprung on me that afternoon without warning. By then, I was feeling much better, but I took a nap after lunch on general principles. I was wakened by the rumble of voices in Dad's room.

I levered myself to sitting position with my good arm and sat on the edge of the bed, contemplating the shadowy hotel room. The drapes were drawn and all three chairs had vanished.

When the worst twinges subsided, I rose and picked my way over to the basin. The mirror above it assured me that bruises turn green. A nasty one had slid down my left cheek. My hair stood up in cranky curls. I took my hairbrush to it, dabbed on a bit of lipstick, and smoothed my blouse. The sling still pinioned my left arm. I was wearing jeans, and I didn't bother to put on slippers. My feet were bandaged, anyway. I padded across the flat gray carpet.

Dad's door stood ajar. I pushed it open and stood on the threshold, blinking.

Two men—strangers—leapt to their feet. Dad rose more slowly. Jay, who had been leaning against the far wall, straightened, and so did Ann, who was perched on the edge of the bed. All five of them stared at me, as if I had caught them talking about me. I probably had.

I blinked again. "Don't let me interrupt." I recognized one of the strangers. "Hello, Mr. Williams. I thought you were the Hambly butler."

"I performed that office, certainly." Williams's eyes smiled behind horn-rimmed glasses. He must have had a spare pair. "Your summons was, er, peremptory."

The other man took a step toward me and held out his hand. "How d'ye do. I'm Henning." He was older than Jay, dark, with a slight overbite.

I bit back the impulse to say, "I'm Dodge," and murmured something vague as we touched hands. Lord Henning's was rather cold. Ann was watching me with shining eyes. I wondered whether she expected me to curtsy.

The three men fussed, settling me into one of the chairs. Jay and Ann held off. When I was seated, Dad said, "Mr. Williams believes you should hold a press conference, Lark."

"Me?" I gaped at him.

Jay ruffled his mustache, hiding a grin. "He thinks the press would back off if you made a statement."

I turned to Williams, who was sitting on my left. "That's a wonderful idea. I can see the tabloids now. YANK BIRD BASHES DOG KILLER, LEAVES STATELY HOME IN RUINS."

Lord Henning gave a small cough.

I rounded on him. "I wish *I* was in the Canary Islands. You were crazy to fly back."

"Er . . ."

Williams said gravely, "I'll write the statement for you, Mrs. Dodge. Something brief and unsensational."

"Dad!"

My father looked guilty. "I think it's a good idea, my dear."

"You didn't see the noxious tripe they printed when Miss Beale was murdered. Tell them, Ann."

Ann said, "I'll be with you, honey."

"Traitor." I shut my eyes and tried to think. They were bullying me. On the other hand, the press were keeping us penned in. "All right. I'll do it." I opened my eyes. "On my terms."

Jay didn't bother to hide his smile. The others looked relieved. Williams said, "I've prepared a rough draft, Mrs. Dodge."

"I'm sure it's eloquent. You haven't heard my terms, yet, though."

"What do you suggest?"

"A joint conference tomorrow morning when Dad has had a chance to talk to Milos and my mother. Dad and Ann and I can make brief statements, and Lord Henning, too, if he's willing. *You* can field their questions, Mr. Williams."

Ann was making distressed noises. Served her right.

I said, "I won't be exhibited all by myself like some kind of freak giraffe."

Lord Henning cleared his throat. "Not a bad notion. Unusual, of course."

Williams was frowning. "I'll consult the chief constable. If he has no objections, I daresay I can arrange for a briefing session in one of the hotel's anterooms."

Henning interrupted. "At Hambly, Rhys. More dramatic."

"But Mrs. Dodge's health . . ."

"I feel fine." I beamed at Lord Henning, who blushed. "I think that's a great idea. The photographers can take pictures of the rhododendrons or something."

Lord Henning ducked his head to hide a small smile. "The glaziers will have finished with the ground floor by tomorrow. Blue salon, Rhys. It's large enough to accommodate the gentry."

There was more discussion and Williams trotted out his draft of my statement. I felt mild resentment that he was so ready to put words into my mouth, but I suppressed it. He meant well and God knew his experience of the British press was greater than ours. Also the question of what we should say about Milos required delicate handling.

Williams went downstairs to telephone. There were several awkward pauses in the ensuing conversation. After the third ghastly silence, I realized that Lord Henning was shy, an insight that surprised me so much, I was struck dumb. Ann stepped into the breach. She told Henning how much she had admired his house and how sorry she was about the destruction. I rallied and said I had been saddened to hear of Mr. McHale's death and the watchdog's. His Lordship responded with half a dozen sentences so stiff I could tell he was distressed. I began to feel agitated myself, remembering.

Dad intervened with a tribute to the Henning Institute, and Ann drew from his lordship the information that his mother was an Irishwoman and the institute was her particular interest, though his grandfather had established the London office and the fund-raising apparatus shortly after World War II. My father had spent some time in London working for the Friends Field Service Committee in the early fifties, so there was historical overlap, and Dad made the most of it. Lord Henning seemed to find the reminiscences soothing. Jay kept quiet, though I could tell he found the interplay of personalities interesting.

Presently, Williams returned. He was smiling. "All set. I spoke to the chief constable and made a brief announcement to the journalists in the lobby. Tomorrow at eleven. They'll pass the word."

They left soon after that, the shy baron and his gregarious secretary.

Perhaps Williams's announcement did some good. We went down to dinner at eight. Although a flashbulb popped in the lobby and dining among the news hawks felt like the old nightmare of nudity in public, we weren't harassed directly. Ann and Jay and I even went for a cautious stroll on the green in the long English twilight. My father called home.

Afterward, we had a brief council of war in Dad's room. Williams had vowed to join us for breakfast with fresh drafts for Ann and me, and Dad was preparing his own statement, so we didn't talk long. When Jay and I went to our own room, a roll-away bed lay by the open window.

"What's that?"

Jay said, "I slept on it last night, Lark."

"Well, once is enough. I feel a lot better."

He put his arms around me in a gingerly embrace. "Guess what?"

"You can tell?"

He kissed me, a nice, long, leisurely kiss. Then he helped me into my nightgown and we made cautious trips down the hall to the loo and retired to the double bed. I felt better, but I did not feel up to strenuous lovemaking. We lay side by side, talking a little, while I waited for the single pain pill I had taken to do its work. Eventually, I drifted off.

When I woke, it was dawn and Jay was not beside me. I groped among the bedcovers with my good hand, making sure, then sat up and looked around. He lay sprawled on the roll-away bed. I opened my mouth to say something rude, but he looked so deeply asleep, I hadn't the heart to wake him.

It wasn't until I had tiptoed down the hall to the loo and returned to the room that the significance of the separate beds came to me. I ought to have thought how all that stress, on top of detailed discussion of the Lockerbie crash, would affect Jay. He was having nightmares again, and when Jay had nightmares, he thrashed around. Ordinarily, I could put up with a little thrashing, but he was afraid of hurting me in my damaged condition. He might have.

I sank onto the bed. I wondered how long it would take before Jay would talk openly with me. We had been married nearly five years and there were still gulfs of reticence between us. I was a straightforward person. God knew, I loved Jay. Short of ax murder, he could admit to almost any fault and I would not just forgive it, I would find excuses for it or turn it into a virtue. Weak-minded of me.

My momentary anger gave way to despair. We would have to fly home in less than two weeks. Jay would deal with the flight as he dealt with the nightmares, and never mind that he shouldn't have to deal with either. I lay back on the bed and had a quiet cry. It didn't do me much good.

My GP, a brisk woman with ingenuous blue eyes, made a house call after breakfast. She changed the dressings on my arm and shoulder, said the cuts were healing nicely, and told me I could take a bath. That was a relief. I do not like what my mother calls "Pullman baths."

I wallowed in the huge Victorian tub. Jay pulled me out and Ann hustled me into a dress and pumps, then I was whisked off to Hambly in the Escort. True to his word, Williams had showed up at breakfast with statements so innocuous, I wondered why any journalist would want to hear them. Ann liked hers. My father was prepared to make any number of generalizations about terrorism and the forces of repression in the modern world.

As we drove to Hambly, I asked Jay about the nightmares. He admitted that they had recurred. That was that. He was not going to elaborate.

For me, the worst part of returning to Hambly was that it looked untouched—an illusion, of course. Still, the broken glass in the family wing had been replaced and we drove directly to that entrance. Williams met us at the door. A kindly groom took Jay's keys and Dad's, promising to park the cars out of sight. I didn't think the rentals were that awful.

We were ushered in to the main reception room, like honored guests, and Lord Henning materialized to offer us a cup of tea before the onslaught. A woman from the Henning Institute was showing the journalists the damage to the old wing of the house.

Henning—or, more likely, Williams—had brought in folding chairs for the press from the nearest Women's Institute. We were to face the reporters from stations in front of a handsome Adam fireplace. Comfortable chairs had been arranged for us as if for a conversation. The only flaws in the picture were the booms and lights and microphones the media seemed to require. I thought Williams should have brought in a spaniel to sit at my feet, just to improve my dog image, but I refrained from making the suggestion.

When the journalists entered, they seemed unnaturally subdued. At first, I believed they had been sobered by their glimpse of
destruction, but I soon realized that their restraint indicated mere
feudal deference. They were minding their manners. Once we had
issued our innocuous little statements, their questions were as
goofy as ever, though more politely phrased than in South Kensington.

We were trying to manage the news. Roughly summarized, we
told the press that the institute had given Milos asylum after his
stabbing, to which Ann and I had been witnesses. The Czech secret
police were trying to silence Milos, blah blah blah. Dad announced
that a leading university press (my mother had been busy) would
issue a collection of Milos's poems in translation, and that freedom
of expression was a right, not a luxury. He lectured a bit. I was
proud of him.

Then Ann explained that she had spotted Milos's attacker
while on a tour of Hambly, and that she and I had followed Smith
and the Libyan with the intent of revealing their whereabouts to the
police. She lied with delicacy and an air of total conviction. I was
proud of her. Then came the hard part.

I explained how I had driven out to alert the Hambly staff
and that I had spotted the abandoned sedan. Overwhelmed by the
conviction that the men had entered the grounds to make another
attempt on Milos's life, I had "effected" my own entry, run to
the family wing, and sounded the alarm just as the bomb went
off. In Williams's neat prose, I came across like one of those her-
oines of Victorian music halls—Grace Darling in her lifeboat, or
the young woman who hung on the bell rope to prevent curfew
from sounding.

Hang on the bell, Nellie, hang on the bell.
Your poor Daddy's locked in a cold prison cell.
As you swing to the left, Nellie, swing to the right,
Remember that curfew must never ring tonight.

After the explosion, I said, I had "detained the alleged assassin
until Lord Henning's employees could come to my assistance." My
injuries were slight and I was recovering nicely, thank you. I completed this sanitized narrative, reading too fast, and Lord Henning
made a colorless little statement deploring Mr. McHale's death and
the injuries the Hambly staff had suffered. He summarized the
damage to the house in some detail and gave an insurance com-

pany's cost estimate of half a million pounds. I thought that was grossly understated. He had, he said, flown home at once when he heard of the tragedy.

Then came the questions. Williams fielded them, answering the ones he could succinctly and rephrasing the others and distributing them among his "panel." Reporters from the more conservative papers directed some sarcastic questions at Lord Henning about the institute's supposed role in cosseting the Irish Republican Army. However, the questions were surprisingly mild.

We later discovered that Henning had been a Tory back-bencher, an early supporter of Margaret Thatcher, until his elevation to the peerage. His grandfather and his mother had been strong Labourites. Insofar as the institute had a radical agenda, its causes were not Lord Henning's causes. He seemed to view it as a well-meaning group devoted to the defense of traditional British liberties. The Tory journalists bought that, or appeared to. Everyone deplored the use of violence in rural Shropshire for whatever reason. Had the explosion occurred in Birmingham or Liverpool or London, the reporters would have found it much less interesting.

All that was strange and enlightening, but the bulk of the questions were directed at me and were of the "what were your sensations when" variety. There was sexual innuendo.

Ann answered as many of these probings as she reasonably could, pouring on the Georgia color. The reporters liked her, but they weren't entirely stupid. My sling and battered face made it obvious that my role had been active. This seemed to fascinate the television people. I kept my answers brief and colorless until a foxy-looking woman in the third row asked twice about my training in the martial arts and whether I thought women ought to be allowed to participate in combat. It was clear that she regarded me as an amazon and a freak.

Williams looked at me with a helpless expression and shrugged, as if to say, What can I do?

I drew a long, wincing breath. "I have no martial arts training whatsoever, ma'am."

She simpered. In British English, *ma'am* is reserved for royalty and the American usage is thought amusing. I thought of the columnist in the *Independent* and found myself telescoping the foxy reporter's smirk with that writer's self-righteous spite. If someone had showed me a poodle at that moment, I would have strangled it.

I adjusted the sling on my arm. "I'm a reasonably fast runner. When I saw Smith, he was running away from the house and I was afraid he might escape. The explosion deafened both of us, so he didn't hear me coming after him. I outran him and I knocked him down. Then I sat on him. I don't think that constitutes hand-to-hand combat, which I don't favor for anybody, male or female. I'm a pacifist."

"But what about—"

I rode ruthlessly over her. "I think women and men have a responsibility to society. I believed Smith had killed Milos Vlacek and I didn't think Smith should be allowed to escape. I tried to stop him. Any grown woman and most girls would feel the same way. I was angry and confused, but I was certainly not trying to kill the man, though he tried to kill me."

"Lark . . ." I heard Ann's voice—soft.

I didn't look at her. I kept my eyes locked on the reporter's. She was still smirking. "Now, the thing that's interesting to me in this rather nasty experience is that Smith kept calling me names. My hearing had come back by then. I heard him distinctly. He called me a *whore* and a *cunt* and a number of other terms I won't trouble to repeat, every single one of them sexually degrading. He had no other way of thinking about the situation. You seem to be suffering from the same inflexibility, *ma'am*. I'm sorry for you."

Much murmuring and shifting on folding chairs ensued. The foxy woman looked around as if seeking help. My father, Lord Henning, and Mr. Williams had all blushed red. Ann, who was sitting beside me, gave my right hand a squeeze. I couldn't see Jay.

Williams did his best. When the noise level reached the point at which he could be heard, he said sternly, "Mrs. Dodge acted very properly. When she knocked at the door through which you entered today, I myself responded. I can assure you her concern was for Milos Vlacek's safety."

"Did someone mention my name?"

Oh God, Galahad. St. George. Robin Hood. Never was medieval hero more welcome than Milos Vlacek to my sight. He was standing in the doorway, assisted by my husband and a person who turned out to be a nurse. Milos leaned artistically on a walking stick. Though he looked pale and thin, he had lost none of his pizzazz. He beamed at the assembled reporters.

"The free press, aha! I am glad to see you all. I am Vlacek and I tell you these American women are marvelous. Ann, I kiss your hand. Lark, my dear, you have saved my life. What can I say?"

He was awful, he was camp, he was terrific copy. Notebooks whipped out as Milos stumped up to to the Adam fireplace. I had

195

stood and so had Ann, who was making clucking noises. We seated Milos in Ann's chair. She stood behind him like Elsa the lioness.

Williams and Lord Henning had lost control. Williams rallied first. "Ladies and gentlemen, this is Milos Vlacek, the Czech poet whose safety provoked the attack on Hambly."

Five reporters shouted questions. Williams said, "Please, gentlemen"—never mind that three of the five reporters were women.

When the noise subsided, Milos drew his cane up under his chin and smiled. "You want to know what happened? Very well, I tell you everything. In December, there is the airplane crash at Lockerbie."

At the name, there was a general gasp, as if the house had caught its breath. My father's brows drew together.

Milos was now in dead earnest. His hand tightened on the cane. "The explosive that was used was manufactured in my country, and there are immediately rumors that the government supplied the terrorists. I am appalled. To kill innocent people, students, no, there is no justification. So I gather evidence of my government's role in the bombing. Then I escape to England, where I am given every consideration. It is a great country, England."

The reporters were coming out of their shock. They had begun to scribble frantically. The TV cameras ground on.

"I am working in the Hanover Hotel while I wait for my papers to be smuggled out of Prague. I meet Mrs. Veryan and Mrs. Dodge. We go to see *Macbeth* and my friend brings the manuscript of my report to the Barbican. It is storming, so I allow Mrs. Veryan to carry it in her bag. I am stabbed on the tube, but Ann has the papers, and this the secret police do not know. When I come to my senses, I expect only trouble, but these lovely American women, they send the information to America and they search me out. They find my place of hiding because they are concerned for my safety. They raise the alarm. I am saved, the document is saved, and all because of these wonderful ladies. Ann, Lark, I salute you."

Well, hey, I was ready to salute, too. Milos had just blown our elaborate cover-up out of the water, and never mind that Ma had arranged for his poems to be published.

As if by unspoken agreement, the tabloid reporters faded into the background and the representatives of the responsible press began digging at his story. They had a full account within fifteen minutes and seemed to believe it within half an hour. Print reporters broke for the few telephones available, or for their cars. The television cameras ground away.

I looked over at Jay, who was still standing in the doorway. He met my eyes and made a slashing motion across his throat. He was grinning.

18

♦   ♦   ♦   ♦   ♦   ♦

We took Milos to dinner. Lord Henning apologized for his understandable lack of hospitality and suggested a good restaurant about five miles outside Ludlow. He even had Williams make reservations for us. Williams must have leaned on the proprietor, because we were taken directly to a secluded alcove and no reporter invaded our privacy.

Well before that, we had left Hambly. The journalists evaporated to file their stories, so there didn't seem to be much point in hanging around. The workers resumed hauling debris as soon as Henning gave them the all clear, and the air filled with constructive noise. Lord Henning was flying back to his family that evening.

Milos's miraculous appearance was easily explained. My father had told Milos of the press conference, and Milos had charmed an off-duty nurse into driving him to Hambly from the hospital. Since he had once again discharged himself, she drove him home to her mother afterward for a long rest. The mother lived in a modern house in an unquaint village nearby. Dad and Ann picked Milos up at eight and brought him to Appleby's. That was the restaurant's name.

I, too, had needed a rest. Milos's sensational revelations had diminished Ann's and my newsworthiness somewhat. Even so, photographers and TV cameramen dogged us at the Greyhound. I was depressed by that—and depressed in general. Jay, on the other hand, was so cheerful, he whistled in the elevator.

When Ann and my father showed up in our room with the makings of another picnic, I said I wasn't hungry and just wanted to sleep. They carted their feast into Dad's room, meek as sheep. They took the chairs again, too.

Jay waited until they had busied themselves setting out the food, then sat beside me on the bed. "What's wrong?"

"I hurt." I was lying on my right side, waiting for the pain pill to work.

He began to massage my neck. "I know you hurt. Besides that."

"Nothing."

He rotated a thumb at the base of my skull.

"Ow."

"Tell me."

My eyes teared. "I made a fool of myself. I lost my temper with that . . . that . . ."

"Bitch?"

"Now *you're* doing it!" I wailed.

"A mistimed joke."

"Go away and eat something."

"Not until I know what's bothering you."

"I told you." I flopped onto my back and stared at the ceiling. The molding was ornamented with plaster curlicues.

Jay turned my face toward him.

I blinked my tears back. "Go away."

"I guess I don't understand. She—that reporter—was goading you. I thought you kept your dignity. You meant what you said, didn't you?"

"Yes, but . . ."

He brushed the bruise on my cheek with a feather-light touch. "But?"

"I *hate* getting angry."

"It's never a pleasant feeling, but you were justified."

"It's a woman thing," I mumbled.

Jay understood anger well enough. What he didn't understand was the shame a display of anger produced. I was conditioned not to lose my temper in public, not to use four-letter words, even somebody else's, not to avenge an insult. And maybe my conditioning was right. Civilized.

I said, "I made an enemy of her. That was stupid."

"Does it matter? You don't have to read what she writes, and a lot of the other reporters were nodding and taking notes."

Wonderful. "I embarrassed Dad and Lord Henning."

"They'll live."

"I embarrassed *you.*"

"Nope." He kissed me. "I was ready to applaud."

"You're just saying that."

"You don't embarrass me, Lark." His eyes had gone dark the way they do when he's thinking long thoughts. "You can make me angry. You puzzle me sometimes. Every once in a while, you scare the shit out of me. But you don't embarrass me. I was standing there in the doorway at Hambly, watching you and thinking how lucky I am."

I kept my eyes on his. "No lie?"

"Cross my heart."

"I'm the lucky one." I was about to cry again, so I kissed him instead.

I slept three hours and woke feeling good—good and hungry. Ann fixed me pâté and crackers.

Appleby's was the kind of restaurant the English mention when foreigners criticize English cookery. The menu was straightforward without being folksy, the ingredients were absolutely fresh and prepared with loving attention, and the service, though obsequious by American standards, was excellent. The odd thing about such establishments is that they aren't where an American would expect them to be. They are hidden on unnumbered, sometimes unpaved roads in remote corners of the kingdom, and they do not advertise.

My father claimed the best British restaurant he had eaten at was on the Isle of Mull off the coast of Scotland, inaccessible three-quarters of the year and twenty miles along a single-lane road from the nearest population center. I had thought that was Dad indulging in unaccustomed fantasy, but Appleby's, not quite so remote, convinced me otherwise.

At first, we didn't talk about the events at Hambly. We were too busy soaking up the ambience and the mushroom tartlets. Dad and Milos discussed the role of the intellectual in political change and we all ate. A couple of times, I caught Milos watching the waiter with a critical eye, notably as he removed our polished-off bowls of green pea soup. To die for. The fish was sole, delicate, melting,

201

wonderful. The discreet waiter brought us rack of lamb, mine tactfully dissected.

Jay turned to Milos. "So why did you decide to blurt out the whole story, Mr. Vlacek?"

Milos sawed at the lamb. "I put them in danger—Lark and Ann, as well as the two who were killed and my poor friend from the institute. I am opposed to terrorism, but if I agree to conceal the information from the press, and if something then happens to innocent bystanders . . ." He gestured with his knife. "If I allow that, then I am in danger of becoming a terrorist myself."

Jay chewed. "Okay, I can see that. But why didn't you warn George you had changed your mind?"

Dad glanced at Jay and back at his wineglass.

"This is tender lamb." Milos kept his fork in his fist, European style. He seemed unembarrassed. "I call the hotel. Already Professor Dailey has left for Hambly. A headache is nibbling at me. I brood about the harm my singular crusade is doing and I wonder how to pull the plug." He loaded the fork with meat and veg.

"Maximum publicity," my father murmured. He sipped his wine.

Milos beamed. "Openness. Is it Bacon who says that the simplest solution is best?"

"Occam's razor." Ann had been uncharacteristically silent. "What are you going to do now, Milos?"

He chewed and considered. "Find another job. I cannot return to the Hanover. A good waiter is supposed to melt into the background. I have trouble with this. It is not my nature."

I had to laugh. After a moment, everyone did, though Ann cast me a reproachful glance.

As we drove home, Jay said, "He's impressive—Vlacek."

Though I had drunk only about a tablespoon of the wine, I was sleepy. I yawned. "Impressive?"

Jay made a cautious right turn onto the road to Much Aston. "I don't know what I expected. He's straightforward and down-to-earth."

"He likes openness. That's what all the furor was about, in a way—secrets within secrets, secret plots, secret alliances, secret police. God knows, the free press is a pain sometimes, but I prefer it to cover-ups. We were wrong to try to hide what we knew. I'm glad Milos set us straight."

My kindly thoughts about the press wavered as we approached the Greyhound. Jay parked the car in the hotel lot and we used the rear entrance. My shoulder ached. As we stood in the dark corridor, waiting for the elevator, I leaned on Jay's arm. "At least it's over."

"Mrs. Dodge?"

I straightened, prepared to say "No comment" until the elevator arrived. Jay and I turned.

"If I may have a word with you, Mrs. Dodge." It was Inspector Thorne. He gave me a tentative smile. "And with Mrs. Veryan."

My heart sank. "Ann rode with my father. She'll be back soon."

"Good. That's very good. May I?" He gestured at the brightly lit elevator as it creaked to a halt. The iron lattice groaned and the door opened.

Jay was frowning. "Are you all right?"

"Yes."

He turned to Thorne. "Very well, but my wife is supposed to rest. You can have half an hour."

Thorne sighed. "That should do the trick."

We entered the lift and it creaked upward.

I said, "How's Daphne Worth? I was shocked to hear of her accident."

" 'Twas no accident. I've come for the villains' automobile. The lad's seeing to the paperwork."

"Sergeant Wilberforce?"

"Aye." The elevator stopped. Thorne held the ancient door open for me, and he and Jay followed me down the hall to our room. "They transported Miss Worth to London yesterday, to St. Botolph's. She's still unconscious. She's mumbled a word or two, calling for her mum and her brother, but nothing to the point. Happen forensics will be able to tie the auto to the crime. Parks fingered our friend Smith for the burglary, but he's said nowt so far of Miss Beale's death."

Jay unlocked our door and we entered the room.

I flipped the light on. "Why don't you retrieve the chairs, Jay?"

He had already opened the communicating door and entered my father's room. Thorne followed him while I sat on the foot of the bed and tried to wake up. Obviously, it wasn't over. Inspector Thorne represented the loose ends. I hoped he would tie them up quickly.

Thorne took me through the events of the bank holiday weekend, starting with Saturday. I gave him my version, slowly, naming places and routes, which he wrote down in a small black notebook. When I got to the part where we headed south, I balked.

"Look, Inspector, why don't you wait for Ann? She has the AA atlas in her room and she can show you where we went. I drove; she navigated. I don't remember the highway numbers. The inn we stayed at Sunday night . . ."

"That's crucial."

"Well, it was called the Royal Oak and it was north of Kidderminster, but Ann can *show* you where it is. She'll be here in a few minutes."

"All right." He set the notebook on the small table. "I heard of your adventures at Hambly, lass." He appeared to hesitate. "Will you tell me your impressions of the two men you followed into the grounds?"

I felt blank. "You know what they look like."

"Not that." He gave his head an impatient shake. "Personalities."

"Ah." I closed my eyes and focused my mind. "Faisel seemed to be directing operations, a sort of field supervisor. Out of shape, a bit pompous, not physically courageous. It seemed to me that he thought Smith was expendable."

"Very likely. And Smith?"

"Pure testosterone."

His brows shot up. "Eh?"

"No social inhibitions whatsoever. Not bright, but skilled and satisfied with himself. It was almost as if he were laughing up his sleeve—at Faisel and maybe at the world in general. Smith was cold." I hesitated. "You did ask for impressions."

He nodded, his hands folded, eyes intent.

"Faisel is a bully, a controller. Smith is something nastier, if that's possible. A tool who prides himself on being an efficient tool. A professional killer." I stumbled on the word. "Alleged killer."

Thorne gave a wry smile. "I'm not a solicitor, Mrs. Dodge. And I've laid down my notebook. Then you think Smith could have killed your landlady?"

"Yes. In cold blood. He hates women." I glanced at Jay. "*Despises* is probably more accurate. Ann and I followed those two men around Hambly as if we were invisible to them. They didn't notice us." I paused and considered. "Or maybe they did but they couldn't conceive of us as a threat to their plans."

Thorne cleared his throat. "If Smith's telling the truth, they had no idea who you were, Mrs. Dodge. They noticed Mrs. Veryan as they were leaving the hotel for Hambly, but they dismissed her presence as a coincidence."

Ann—we—had had a close call. I shivered. "At Hambly, it was Faisel, not Smith, who killed the watchman's dog. I don't know that that means anything. They're both killers."

Noises emanated from the hallway, then from my father's room, and the connecting door opened. Jay said, "I think they're back."

"Ah, there you are. . . ." Dad stopped in the doorway.

I rose from my perch on the foot of the bed. "It's Chief Inspector Thorne, Dad, from London. Is Ann . . . ah."

My father entered with Ann on his heels. Jay made the introductions, and Dad and Ann shook hands with the inspector.

Ann said, "I hope you're well, Inspector. You look bone-tired. Surely you're not still on duty? We brought a bottle of whiskey for a little nightcap."

Thorne was smiling at her. "I might be persuaded, lass."

She beamed at him like a moon goddess and went to round up glasses. I was glad I had not taken a pill. Whiskey sounded far more appealing.

It was an unpronounceable single malt Dad had spotted in the bar. His mind must have been in Scotland, explaining the day's debacle to the Galloway and Dumfries constabulary. He swore he had once drunk the stuff in Edinburgh during an April blizzard.

We all sipped and made approving sounds. I drink scotch about once a year, so my grounds for comparison were not wide, but it went down smoothly and the base of my spine tingled.

Thorne looked blissful. Presently, he asked Ann for the AA atlas, copied out our stopping places, and took us through an account of our movements. He expanded a bit on Daphne's condition, which was grave. Trevor had quit his job to take care of his sister. When and if she should be released, she would need careful nursing. Parks had confessed his own part in the burglary and named Smith as Milos's assailant. By tacit agreement, none of us mentioned Milos's papers.

Thorne said nothing of them, either. He had kept his silence almost from the beginning. Someone had told him the papers were classified, someone with sufficient authority to make Thorne keep to his silence, even when the rest of the world was talking about Milos's revelations.

I liked Thorne, but he had lied to us when he said the papers didn't bear on the case. We might have believed him.

By then, it was eleven and I was falling asleep sitting up. With some prodding from Jay, Thorne rose to go. He promised to see us soon in London.

He threw us a curve as he left. "We must inspect the auto you hired in Yorkshire." He had the grace to look embarrassed.

Dad ran his hand through his hair. "But you've charged Smith . . ."

"With Miss Beale's murder," Jay murmured.

Thorne nodded. "Aye, that's it. The odds are we'll charge the pair of them with attempting to kill Miss Worth, too, but we've no evidence they were in Dorset Sunday evening. That being so, we have to eliminate other possibilities."

I said with some heat, "We have no motive for harming Daphne Worth."

"I don't have to establish motive, lass, just means and opportunity. And I'd be no kind of investigator if I didn't have your auto checked."

"But we have to return the car tomorrow, Mr. Thorne." Ann had meant to ride with Dad to York in the morning.

"I'll tell the boys to step lively, then. Happen they'll be finished by afternoon. I'll not take the keys from you now, but don't use the Escort until I give you the word."

My father said, "We'll cooperate, of course."

Thorne shook hands with Dad, who saw him to the door, and made a sketchy bow toward the rest of us. Then he was gone.

Ann plopped onto the foot of the bed next to me. "I can't drive that car. Whatever shall we do? George has to catch the train to the north." She was now on first-name terms with Dad. Despite his somewhat pedantic style, my father is not at all formal. Ann's deference had given way to her natural friendliness.

The only solution to the car problem had been for Dad to return the Fiat to Heathrow and fly to Glasgow. The rest of us hung out at the Greyhound until the police finally released the Escort at 2:30. It was clean, they said. Actually, it was covered with road grime. Jay drove us lickety-split to York, using the motorways, because otherwise we would have had to pay a surcharge for returning the car to the wrong place.

Jay left Ann and me to forage for sandwiches while he turned the car in. We had half an hour to admire the walls of York before we caught the train south. We reached the flat in London late, around ten, all of us exhausted and me hurting. I took four aspirin and went straight to bed. I heard the phone ring a couple of times at the edge of awareness.

Next morning—I slept until eight—Jay told me both my parents had called the previous evening—Dad from Glasgow, my mother from New York. Dad's reception in Scotland had been chilly because of the publicity the press conference had received. He was coming back that evening and would take a cab from the airport. My mother, apparently unaware that it was midnight when she reached Jay, had wanted a thorough explanation of the press conference. When she'd asked to speak to me, Jay had said I was asleep, bless him. Sooner or later, I would have to talk to Ma about my escapade, but I could not have defended myself that night.

Jay served me tea and croissants for breakfast. He had gone out for the newspapers around 7:30, and by the time he came back, the press were in place, cameras at the ready.

"Did they corner you?" I took a bite of croissant.

He grinned. "They tried. I spoke Spanish to them, *muy agitado,* until they gave up."

"Why didn't I think of that?"

"Probably because you don't speak Spanish, darling. More tea?"

I held out my cup. "Did they recognize you?"

"I don't think so. It's a good thing I stayed off camera in Shropshire."

I showed him the *Daily Blatt.* "You didn't. There you are leaving the Greyhound with Ann."

He took the paper from me. "Nobody could identify me from that. I look like a bandito. Shall I shave off my mustache?"

"Sure." I knew he wouldn't. "And I'll shave my head, and nobody will recognize either of us. Give me back the *Blatt.*"

He complied. "You feel better, don't you?"

"A lot. Dr. Mayfield said I could take my arm out of the sling from time to time." That reminded me that I'd have to report to the outpatient clinic at St. Botolph's to have the dressing on my shoulder changed.

We were trying to decide whether to call a taxi when Ann drifted in, yawning. She had been rather mournful on the ride back from York because of missing Haworth again, but a night's sleep had restored her to her usual cheer.

Jay made coffee for her and I warned her about the press siege.

She groaned. "I have to go out. I promised Milos I'd talk to his landlady and rescue his belongings."

"That does it," Jay said. "We'll call a taxi. Ann can ride with us to the hospital. There's strength in numbers."

"If you go with us, you'll blow your cover." I explained to Ann about Jay's Spanish impersonation and she was enchanted. She decided to speak Latin.

Jay came with us, anyway. We reached St. Botolph's around ten, thanks to another blasé cabdriver who shot right through the cordon of reporters. Ann patted me on my good shoulder and reminded me to ask after Daphne. Then she went off on foot in search of Milos's apartment, which was near the Gloucester Road tube station.

My kindly Shropshire GP had smoothed the way for me by telephone and I was accepted on a local physician's list with a minimum of fuss. Finally, I was called. Jay said he'd wait.

He was browsing among the National Health pamphlets when I returned with my arm in less restrictive strapping. He saw me and rose, smiling. "How are the stitches?"

"The doctor doesn't think there'll be much of a scar on my shoulder, but I may have to have a plastic surgeon look at the arm."

"You could pretend you'd undergone some kind of initiation rite."

"Or become a Hell's Angel Woman. Right." I wriggled my arm. "I was lucky Smith didn't hit a tendon."

"Or your aorta." Jay gave my good arm a pat. We made our way to the lobby. "Where's the rest room?"

"WC, please, or loo. It's down there." I pointed down the short corridor to my right. "I'll ask about Daphne at the desk while I'm waiting for you."

"Good idea." He strolled off down the hall.

My friend, Mrs. Philbrick, was on the desk. She had seen me on the telly and made much of me for a good five minutes while the other patrons looked on. I finally edged in a question about Daphne. She wasn't allowed visitors outside the family, but, translating the hospital jargon, I concluded they thought she'd survive. Her condition was "guarded." I asked whether there was a flower stall nearby.

Mrs. Philbrick gave an approving nod. "But do find something cheery, love, something with a bit of color. Her brother, such a handsome gentleman, took up a bunch of dreary mums, all white like a funeral, not fifteen minutes ago."

"Oh dear." I wondered whether white chrysanthemums were universally associated with funerals.

"Men!" Mrs. Philbrick gave me a matey wink and turned to help an elderly woman with a question about her niece's kiddie in the pediatric ward.

I drifted to my left, toward the plastic couch I had sat on the week before. The lobby was fairly busy. Medical types scurried down corridors. Patients and visitors knotted and separated, rather like fish swimming among coral. I garnered some curious looks, but only the younger children stared openly.

As I glanced around, I caught sight of Trevor Worth. He was sidling down the left-hand corridor in the direction of the main entrance. Though he wore one of his natty suits, he looked rumpled, almost distraught. I hesitated, hoping he hadn't had bad news but decided I had better explain Dad's presence in the flat.

I cut him off by one of the administrative offices. "Hello, Trevor. How's Daphne? I hear she's better."

He stared at me. For a moment, I thought he didn't recognize me, and my cheeks went hot with embarrassment. Then his eyes shifted. "Oh, hullo. Yes, better. Sorry." He started to edge past me as the office door opened.

A woman in a business suit emerged, followed by two men in the uniform of a delivery firm who were carrying a filing cabinet between them. They blocked Trevor's way to the street. The administrator was giving the two men directions.

"If you have a moment . . ." I began. Something was wrong. Trevor looked wild-eyed.

I hesitated, spotted Jay, who was almost upon us, and turned to him with relief. "Oh, Jay, here's Trevor. He says Daphne's better."

"That's good news." Jay held out his hand.

Trevor said something desperate under his breath and shoved past us. He ran about five steps toward the entry and careened into the workmen, who dropped the file. A drawer popped open and papers spilled onto the tiled floor.

"Here, watch it, mate." One of the men grabbed for Trevor but slipped on the loose papers and toppled sideways, swearing.

Jay said, "Sorry," just like an Englishman, and moved off after Trevor. I watched Jay hurdle past the workmen. He avoided knocking into a woman in a flowered hat who was coming up the steps, then disappeared to the right.

I gaped after them. The workmen scrambled up and were trying to gather the papers. The lady with the flowered hat had backed against the edge of the door, hands out defensively.

"Where did he go? Did you see him?"

I whipped around.

Sergeant Baylor, her face pink, trotted up to me. She was carrying a small hand-held radio with an antenna.

I pointed and she dashed off, sliding by the bewildered workmen as if they weren't there. The woman with the hat began to scream, though she sounded more excited than frightened.

I decided I might as well join in the chase, too, whatever it might mean.

I scooted past the filing cabinet. "Sorry."

One of the men trotted after me. "What the bloody hell . . ."

I was wearing jeans and sneakers, so I moved fast. I stopped at the top of the wide stairs and glanced wildly around. Jay and Trevor had crossed the Fulham Road at the zebra and were half a block down a narrow street that led north. Jay was gaining on Trevor, running hard, and Sergeant Baylor chased after them, going flat out. I sprinted across the zebra and went after them.

Trevor was running toward the warren of streets that lies between the Fulham and Old Brompton roads. He flashed around a corner when Jay was within arm's length of him, and I lost sight of them. Then Sergeant Baylor rounded the corner, too.

My arm was beginning to hurt. I hoped I hadn't jarred it. I slowed to a trot, nursing the sling. Behind me, I heard a police siren and the squealing of brakes and beeping of horns as the traffic responded in the main road. The side street I was running along was almost deserted.

I turned the corner and slowed to a walk. Trevor was standing halfway down a quiet residential street, by the iron railing of a basement areaway. Jay had a grip on his arm. Trevor's shoulders slumped. I couldn't see his face.

Sergeant Baylor stood facing the two men. For an insane moment, it looked as if they were having a nice three-way conversation. I picked up my pace and neared them as Sergeant Baylor began to inform Trevor of his rights.

When Jay saw me coming, he grimaced and gave a short shake of his head. No. I stopped and leaned against the square pillar at the edge of the railing. Neat steps led up to a bright yellow door with a polished brass knocker. There was a small neo-Gothic church across the street.

Sergeant Baylor's radio squawked as the police car rounded the corner and pulled up sedately beside the little tableau. Two uniformed men got out. Trevor was handcuffed and put in the backseat with a minimum of discussion. Sergeant Baylor leaned down to the driver and said something, low-voiced, and the car drove off. It was almost as if Trevor had called for a taxi.

"Now, sir . . ." Sergeant Baylor turned to Jay. "Mr. Dodge!"

I said dryly, "My husband, Sergeant. We bumped into Trevor in the lobby of the hospital. What happened?"

She blinked. She was puffing a little. "Your husband just assisted me in apprehending a murderer."

Murderer? Surprise struck me dumb.

Sergeant Baylor drew a long breath and tucked a stray curl behind one ear. "Mr. Worth was spotted not ten minutes ago in hospital trying to smother his sister with a pillow. We have reason to believe it was he who ran her down on Sunday in Dorchester."

Jay said, "I was afraid of something like that when I saw him in the lobby. He looked as if the devil was after him, and I knew Inspector Thorne hadn't been able to place the other suspects in Dorset at the crucial time."

"Trevor tried to kill Daphne? But that's awful," I burst out. "Why? I don't understand."

We were walking slowly back toward the hospital. Sergeant Baylor said, very cautiously, "Chief Inspector Thorne has never been satisfied that the men who burgled your flat also killed Miss Beale."

"But I thought Parks . . ."

"Parks confessed to the burglary and to abetting the assault on Milos Vlacek, but he swears neither he nor Smith had anything to do with Miss Beale's murder."

"So he says." I was having trouble admitting to myself that I had been attracted, however briefly, to a murderer. I stumbled on an uneven paving stone.

Jay took my good arm. "Different MO."

Sergeant Baylor had been walking slightly ahead of us. She turned, her eyes earnest. "That's it. The burglary was a professional job, but the murder seemed to be improvised on the spot. Very amateurish."

"But effective," I croaked.

"And vicious." She shook her head. "That poor little dog."

We walked on, silent, giving Rollo his due.

At last, she sighed and went on, "The Chief Inspector had Smith charged after the explosion at Hambly because of Miss Beale's Czech connections. It seemed possible that the murder was part of the international conspiracy, after all. There was, er, a certain amount of pressure. . . ."

From the press or from the Home Office? I wondered.

"So Thorne reconsidered when the sedan came up clean?" Jay sounded as if he were trying to read Thorne's mind.

Sergeant Baylor stepped boldly onto a zebra, the traffic halted, and we followed her across. "I'm sure he'll explain his reasoning to you, sir. There is circumstantial evidence in the first murder, and, of course, the second attempt on Miss Worth's life settles it. The man's guilty." We were walking three abreast toward the hospital.

She picked up the pace. "I don't mind admitting I thought Mr. Thorne was daft to post me at the hospital when Miss Worth's assailant was under lock and key in Shropshire. But the inspector was right. He usually is."

Jay said, "Will you tell us what triggered the chase, Sergeant?"

"I was standing at the nurse's station when the sister on duty let out a shriek. She'd gone in to adjust the IV and she found him at it. She pulled him away. Mr. Worth crashed into me as I tried to enter the room. Knocked me down."

I wondered whether Trevor had said "Sorry." "What did you do?"

"I radioed for help, but he'd disappeared down the stairs by the time I ascertained that Miss Worth was still breathing."

I drew a sharp breath. "She's alive?"

"Oh yes." She walked on for several silent paces. "Do you know that ghastly hypocrite brought her flowers? We'd have caught up with him eventually, but I'm most grateful to you, Mr. Dodge. I'd not like it on my record that I lost him."

We were approaching the hospital. At the entryway, she stopped. "We'll want statements from both of you, of course, but you may return to your flat and wait there if you like. I know Mrs. Dodge is unwell."

Mrs. Dodge was dumbfounded but otherwise hale.

Sergeant Baylor offered to send us home in a police car. She checked in with Thorne via the radio. Jay thanked her but declined the ride. She shook hands with both of us and disappeared into the lobby.

Jay and I stood on the sidewalk, staring at each other. After a moment, Jay began to chuckle.

"What is it?" I was rather cross that he had figured Trevor out and I hadn't.

"All the time I was chasing after the guy, I was wondering whether a noncitizen can make a citizen's arrest. It's a good thing the sergeant showed up."

"You must've been damned sure Trevor was guilty."

"I did call out to him, asked him what was the matter. When he heard me, he really started running." He sobered. "You liked him, didn't you? I'm sorry, Lark."

212

I gave him as much of a hug as I could with one arm. "He talked about cars all evening. I thought he was boring." A taxi approached, cruising. "Hey, the little yellow light isn't on. Hail it. Quick."

We rode home in comfortable silence. I was trying to sort things out and was so absorbed, I forgot to worry about the reporters. They were still there.

As we emerged from the taxi, a young woman stuck a microphone under my nose. Flashbulbs went off. "Mrs. Dodge, tell us your sensations when . . ."

I said, "You really ought to pop over to the Chelsea police station. Miss Beale's murderer was just arrested." In the breathless pause before the new questions began, we dashed up the stairs and Jay unlocked the door.

"Who did it? Tell us who did it, Mrs. Dodge."

I turned on the step and gave them all a huge smile. "No comment."

19

◆　◆　◆　◆　◆　◆

I wondered what was keeping Ann.

Jay and I kicked our heels at the flat, waiting for the police to come for our statements. Remnants of the press battalion still lurked around the entryway, so there was no inducement to go out. We talked about Trevor's arrest and what it meant, but not exhaustively. Jay is trained not to theorize ahead of the facts, so I think he was a little embarrassed by his leap of intuition. I like to jump to conclusions as well as anyone, but I was feeling chagrin that I had so seriously misjudged Trevor. Of the two siblings, I would have cast Daphne as the murderer. Though I had come to like her, she had seemed the less stable personality.

We ate a snack. Ann still hadn't come. I hoped the errand she was running for Milos hadn't tangled her in some political web or bankrupted her. I hoped she wasn't going to pay Milos's rent. I stewed about that. Her funds had to be getting low.

Jay told me what I needed was a good run, and he was right. Unfortunately, my feet weren't up to it, as my brief sprint that morning had taught me. I had applied bandages to the half-healed cuts and was scuffing around in slippers when the door buzzer sounded.

Jay went to answer it and returned with Inspector Thorne. Thorne was accompanied by Sergeant Baylor and Constable Ryan, and all three looked pleased with themselves. Sergeant Wilberforce sent greetings from Shropshire.

I offered coffee or tea and they settled for tea—or Thorne did. Though he was in high good humor, he made poor Ryan go out to keep the press at bay. Sergeant Baylor came with me to the kitchen and showed me her tea-making technique. I put the remainder of the ginger digestive biscuits on a plate and we took the tray to the living room.

After tea, Thorne took our statements, with Sergeant Baylor doing steno duty. Thorne was thorough, as usual, but this time he didn't fish for our subjective interpretations. In my case, that was just as well.

He seemed interested in Jay's part in the chase. "Betty here tells me you hared off after Worth before she appeared on the scene. Did you suspect him all along?"

"He was behaving strangely this morning." Jay rubbed the back of his neck. He looked embarrassed. "I can't say I pegged him from the first, sir. I thought he was a pleasant guy but not very bright. The thing is, he has expensive tastes."

Ah, the Porsche. I should have brooded about the Porsche.

Jay went on, "And then he sells used cars. . . ."

"What?" I suppose my eyeballs bulged. *Used* cars?

Jay fiddled with his watch strap, avoiding my stare. "That agency deals in new and used vehicles, all upscale, but he said he handled only used cars. He tried to sell me one. The commission on used cars—even used Jags—can't be all that wonderful. And this is an expensive town to live in."

Thorne said he himself commuted from the southern suburbs because rents in Chelsea were so steep.

Jay waved an expressive hand at the zebra-striped decor. "Ann and Lark have been paying outrageous rent, and the incursion of a lot of well-heeled temporary residents into an area is bound to inflate all rents."

Thorne nodded. "Go on, lad."

I squirmed. Jay's observation was true, of course, and exactly what Daphne's group had been protesting, but hotel rates were even more outrageous than the rent we had paid Miss Beale.

Jay was saying, "I suspected both of Miss Beale's heirs even before I left home. When I met them, though, I didn't think Miss Worth was particularly interested in money or social prestige. I

216

also didn't think her brother would settle for the wrong kind of address."

"Daphne hated the commute from Chiswick," I objected.

"But she was involved in that activist group, trying to do something constructive about rents in general. People who think that way don't usually succumb to selfish motives."

Thorne smiled at Jay as if he was a pupil who had come up with the right answer on an exam. "Greed and debt. Worth's overdraft was stretched to the limit. He owed his tailor a whopping tab, too. Miss Beale had bailed him out once and told him she wouldn't do it again. By all accounts, she was fond of her nephew, but she had strict notions of fiscal rectitude. That and the prospect of inheriting were more than enough to provide temptation when the moment came."

Jay smoothed his mustache. "Miss Beale's murder looked like an opportunistic crime to me. When Lark told me about the burglary and its aftermath, she mentioned that both of the Worths had been in the basement flat when the crime was discovered. I suppose Worth saw his chance and took it. There was a strong possibility the burglars would be blamed."

Thorne chuckled. "Or your good wife."

Jay's mouth twitched at the corners. "Or Lark, or Ann, or both in collusion."

"He didn't like Rollo."

All three of them looked at me and Sergeant Baylor's eyes narrowed.

I held my ground. "The first time I saw Trevor Worth, he cuffed Rollo, who was yipping at us the way poodles do when strangers invade their territory. I didn't think much about it at the time. Rollo was just being a poodle, but the noise was irritating. I have since been, er, sensitized to British feelings about dogs. Trevor's behavior was not typical."

"Ah, the newspapers." Thorne must have read the *Independent* column, too. "D'ye know what set old Sparks talking?"

We shook our heads.

"He was willing to admit his role in the stabbing, and burglary's his trade, poor sod, but what he couldn't thole was being sent up for coshing a dog. Tears in his eyes. I had to believe him. Mind you"—Thorne thumped the arm of the chair for emphasis— "Parks is an old-fashioned crook. Smith is another sort of villain altogether."

I leaned forward. "Is that why you asked me about Smith's personality?"

"Aye. I was trying to see him bashing in the dog's head and tossing Miss Beale down four flights of stairs. I daresay Smith wouldn't have had qualms. He's a killer, true enough, but he likes to use a knife and he's quiet with it. You said he was cold, lass. That was my impression, too."

I shivered. "Efficient."

"Aye, and there was nowt in Miss Beale's death to suggest the killer was either quiet or efficient."

I sighed. "It's hard to imagine Trevor bludgeoning his aunt and Rollo with a blunt instrument. He may be greedy, but he's fastidious, too."

"Not when it comes to battening on his female relatives," Sergeant Baylor interposed. When we looked at her, she flushed but didn't retract. Something going on there.

"Ah, well, Worth's a wide boy," Thorne said. "He's not talking. Advice of counsel. The family solicitor's a nice, quiet chap. He's scurrying about looking for a QC to defend. Good luck to him. If Worth hadn't tried to smother his sister, he might've got away with it. Thanks to you, sir, we have him in custody."

Jay said, "Sergeant Baylor was right behind me. I had no excuse to hold him, you know. I was damned glad to see her. Have you found the car Worth used in Dorchester?"

"No, but he had access to any number of used vehicles. We're working on that angle now. It's a matter of time."

I stood up. "Shall I brew another pot of tea?"

Sergeant Baylor was ready to head for the kitchen again, but Thorne shook his head. "No, lass, thank you. We've a mort of paperwork to see to yet."

I cocked my head. "I know I'll be called as a witness—in both cases, probably."

"Aye."

"And I'll have to fly back to London."

"True." He cleared his throat. "The department has funds. . . ."

I said, "That is a consideration, but I was wondering whether Jay will have to return, as well."

"For the Worth trial?"

Jay didn't say anything and I avoided looking at him.

"It seems a bit much." I was keeping my tone casual. "I have a fairly open schedule, but Jay's tied to the school calendar. Can't you take a deposition from him before we leave?"

Thorne thought it over. Then he nodded. "I'll arrange for a deposition." He levered himself up. "I'm sorry I missed seeing Mrs. Veryan."

"She'll be called, too, won't she?"

"She will that." The thought did not seem to displease him. "She's a fine woman." He shook my hand and Jay's, and Sergeant Baylor did, too. Thorne said he thought we could leave London in a day or two.

When they had gone, Jay said, "I can fly back here if I have to."

I gave him a passing kiss. "I know, but I don't see why you should have to." I went into the kitchen and started to tidy it. "You'd better go out and buy something for dinner."

Jay braved the press circus again and bought baguettes, pasta, garlic, tomato sauce, and mince. My spaghetti is not bad, and it's an infinitely expandable dish. Dad might need a meal when he got in.

There was still no word from Ann, but the buzzer sounded while I was making the meat sauce. Jay went to investigate and presently I heard Ann's voice in the foyer. The door reopened. Ann and Jay entered, guiding Milos between them.

"Now you sit right down, Milos Vlacek," Ann scolded. "And don't lift a finger. Jay will help me with your things."

I suppose it was inevitable. I gave Milos, who looked ill and rueful, a welcoming smile. "Would you like a drink, Milos?"

He sank onto the zebra-striped couch, coughing. "Professor Dailey's whiskey?"

I went back to the kitchen, found the water of life, poured a healthy slug of it into a wineglass, and brought it to Milos.

He sipped, eyes closed. His dark hair stuck to his forehead in sweaty hanks.

I said, "I suppose you decided to return to your flat."

"Yes. This morning, I hitch a ride to London with my nurse friend's young man, but my landlady has already let my room." He sipped again. "I am standing on the doorstep, wondering what to do with my belongings, when Ann appears. A ministering angel."

That I could imagine. "Well, she should have brought you here right away. You don't look very strong."

He sighed and opened his eyes. "No, I am like a kitten—weak and not very intelligent. I insist that we find my young friend Kohut in Bloomsbury, so we spend several hours, and many pounds on taxis, searching for him. We find him at last, but he is living in student digs—is that the term?"

"Close enough. He didn't have room for you?"

"No." He swallowed the rest of the whiskey. "Ah. He is worried, of course, and tries to think of a solution. He telephones his friends. Then Ann says I must come here. I am sorry to intrude, Lark. Really."

"It's okay." I could hear Jay's low laugh and Ann's expressive drawl from the foyer. "We have room."

Jay entered, staggering under the weight of a large carton. Books, I supposed. Ann followed with two suitcases. She looked flustered but determined.

I took one of the suitcases, which weighed a ton, in my serviceable right hand. More books. "Where to?"

She blushed scarlet. "My bedroom."

"Right."

"I'll sleep in the armchair."

Dad had dibs on the couch, which was a Hide-a-Bed, but I thought we could come up with a better arrangement for Ann.

Jay and I followed Ann into her bedroom and deposited Milos's earthly goods.

"He has a fever." Ann's chin was up. She looked guilty and funny and I wanted to give her a hug.

I said, "We have orange juice and aspirin. Better put him to bed. I'm making spaghetti, so there's plenty to eat."

She expelled a long breath that puffed a strand of blond hair from her forehead. "Just so you don't misunderstand."

"We like Milos, Ann." I exchanged a quick look with Jay. "Uh, maybe you'd better sit down a minute. We have some rather startling news."

"They haven't escaped, have they?"

"Who? Oh, Smith and Faisel. No, but Trevor Worth has been arrested for murder. What's more, he's guilty. He tried to kill Daphne today in the hospital."

Ann plopped onto the foot of the bed. "As I live and breathe..."

"I was surprised," I admitted. I outlined what had happened and Ann exclaimed and tut-tutted. She sounded less surprised than I had been, but she may just have been distracted by Milos's plight. She congratulated Jay on his role in the arrest.

The story of Trevor's thwarted attempt on Daphne took Ann past her embarrassment. I wondered why in the world she should feel embarrassment, then reminded myself she was only recently divorced and probably uncomfortable about her single status. And she was about to install a man in her bed. YANK BIRD IN LOVE NEST WITH POET.

220

We went out into the living room to tell Milos what had happened, then I dashed back to the stove to rescue my sauce. Fortunately, it hadn't scorched, though orange blobs spattered the countertop. I turned the burner down low and came back as Ann, embroidering freely, was retelling the saga of Trevor's arrest. Milos looked bewildered. It occurred to me that he had been in the hospital and unconscious when Miss Beale had been killed. He probably had no idea who Trevor was.

I interrupted, "You can tell Milos the whole story later, Ann. Right now, I think he should go to bed. Do you have medication, Milos?"

"Um, pills? The antibiotics, yes. I am supposed to take them with water four times a day, but today I forget."

Jay went to the kitchen and came back with a tall glass of springwater. "Better get back on schedule, buddy. You'll wind up with pneumonia."

Milos took the glass. "That I don't need. I am grateful to all of you. . . ."

"Drink," Jay said. "And I'll help you to bed. You can toss bouquets at us later."

Milos gave a shaky laugh and obeyed.

I went back to the kitchen to put water on for the pasta and whip up a salad.

Ann followed me. "You're sure it's all right?"

"More than all right. It's a good idea. Milos needs looking after. Jay will poke the pills down him in fine style. He was a medic in the army."

"What a talented couple you two are."

"All that and spaghetti, too." I crisped lettuce and patted it dry. "The only person who could reasonably object to Milos's presence in this flat is in jail on a murder charge."

Ann shook her head. "I'm still trying to take it in. Poor Daphne! What a terrible thing to find out about your own brother. Did he hurt her?"

"Thorne says he didn't have time."

"He's a stupid man. Trevor, I mean."

"No genius, certainly."

"I don't quite know what to do next, Lark. I meant to go to York and tour the countryside, but I can't very well leave Milos in this state."

"Why don't you hire a car at Heathrow and take Milos north with you?"

Ann's eyes widened behind the pink lenses. "But . . ." I watched her consider the idea. "Maybe I will. He could rest for a few days here and build up his strength. Then we could explore England together."

"Go for it." I measured out the pasta. The water was stirring as if it meant to boil. "Will you set the table?"

"Sure." She took down four plates and wandered to the table, her eyes vague. "We could go to Haworth. And Hay-on-Wye."

"Or Scotland. Macbeth was king of Scotland."

"Macbeth? My land, I'd half forgotten the production at the Barbican. It seems years ago." She reached for salad bowls. "Milos will have to find a job eventually. . . ."

I hesitated. "Do you need money?"

Ann gave a small laugh. "Who doesn't, sugar? I'll just dip into my divorce settlement." Her smile widened to a grin. "Wait till Buford Veryan hears what I've gone and done with his money. He'll be beside himself."

I smiled, too. "With jealousy, probably. Besides, it's not his money. It's yours, and there's nothing wrong with your judgment, Ann."

Ann clasped a stack of salad bowls to her bosom. "Lordy, I wish I could see Buford's face."

The door buzzer sounded again.

"I'll get it," Jay called from the living room.

It was my father, back from Glasgow earlier than we had expected him. He had forgotten his house key. I measured out more spaghetti.

Milos slept through dinner. It was a verbal meal, what with Ann explaining Milos's presence and arguing with herself over the propriety of a middle-aged woman driving all over England with a poet, with Jay summarizing our eventful morning, and with Dad telling us about his trip. The Scots police had been polite, uncommunicative, and efficient.

My father saved Ann's honor, or perhaps just her sacroiliac, by booking a room at the Norfolk Hotel. Ann protested; Dad insisted. Jay said he would walk over to the Norfolk with Dad and help carry his luggage.

Ann and I did the dishes while the men went off to the hotel. When the kitchen was clean, Ann dragged out her maps and began planning a new itinerary. She decided to save Scotland for her next transatlantic adventure. When I first met her, she had talked about her visit to England as a once-in-a-lifetime thing. Her perceptions—and perhaps her plans—had changed.

She rummaged through her travel guides. "If I have to fly over here for the trials, I could go on up to Edinburgh afterward."

"It's cold and dark in winter."

"Winter?"

"Thorne said the trials will be scheduled in the autumn session. The docket is full for this term."

"Good. I can go back to work at the bookstore and pay off my Visa by then." She picked up the AA atlas again. "My word, Lark, the trouble I had getting a credit rating in my own name. I hope you've established a separate rating. Not that you and Jay are going to split up, but you never know."

I assured her that I had my own credit cards.

Her face went dreamy. "Scotland in winter. That sounds romantic."

"And Haworth and Hay-on-Wye now." I got up and peered over her shoulder at the atlas. "You might as well show Milos Chester and Shrewsbury, too, and come back through the Cotswolds."

"I could see about getting tickets for a play in Stratford."

"More Shakespeare?" I laughed and went back to the couch.

"Something cheerful like *Midsummer Night's Dream*."

"Milos would enjoy that."

She let the atlas fall to her lap. "I can't believe I'm doing this. I must be crazy."

"You deserve a good time after all the stress you've been under."

She brightened. "Maybe you're right, honey."

I heard Jay fumbling at the lock and went to open the door for him. "Did you settle Dad in?"

He gave me a hug. "Yes. Nice hotel. He wants us to join him for breakfast. I told him I thought you'd be up to the walk."

"Heavens, yes. What time?"

"Nine. I'd better wake Milos and stuff another pill down his throat." He went on into the bedroom.

I helped Ann pull out the Hide-a-Bed. Milos roused long enough to swallow an antibiotic and a couple of aspirin. Jay thought the fever was easing and that sleep was the best medicine—a good generalization. We all decided to call it a day, though Ann swore she was too excited to sleep.

Jay had plenty of time to check on Milos the next morning. His temperature was normal and he was hungry as a horse. Ann was feeding him eggs and bacon and her magical tour of England when Jay and I set off for the Norfolk Hotel.

There was a one-day tube strike scheduled, which explained the dearth of reporters on the doorstep. The traffic had clotted in irritable gridlock in the Old Brompton Road. The hotel was only a few blocks from the flat, however, and we had time to admire the ornate lobby before my father came down.

We sat at a small table in one corner of the large dining room and ordered the full breakfast. Dad had to assure the waiter that he was a guest of the hotel and would pay for all three meals before the man would take the order. Juice, coffee in a silver pot, and three racks of unbuttered, cooling toast appeared by the time we had exchanged pleasantries. Dad had called my mother from the hotel before he'd gone to bed.

"She wants you to call her today, Lark."

"All right." I poured him a cup of coffee. "Jay?"

"I'll pass." He took a sip of orange juice.

I poured my own coffee and looked at the toast. I hoped Ma was not in a reproachful frame of mind.

Dad was rubbing the bridge of his nose. "I understand you have a birthday this month, Jay."

Jay grimaced. "Too true."

Dad reached inside his suit jacket and drew out one of those slim folders travel agents give their clients for tickets and itineraries. "I hope you won't think me high-handed. I had some time to spare yesterday in Glasgow and I decided to book these." He handed Jay the folder.

A long silence followed while Jay looked at the contents. He handed the open folder to me. "Did you tell him, Lark?"

I looked. Dad had booked two one-way passages from Southampton to New York, one week from the next Wednesday, on the *Queen Elizabeth II*. For Mr. and Mrs. James Dodge.

I met Jay's eyes. "Not one word."

"Tell me what?" my father asked.

I opened my mouth to answer him and then I thought, No. Jay could explain or not, his choice. I had already intervened with Thorne.

Jay was tracing slow circles on the tablecloth with his juice glass. Finally, he raised his head. "I have a phobia, George. When Lark called to tell me about the stabbing, I knew I ought to come on the first available flight. It took me four days and a murder to work up the guts to get on an airplane."

He paused and I thought he would let it go at that. To my relief and surprise, he went on to explain how the phobia had come about

224

and something of the nightmares. It was a terse, halting account, and my father listened with frowning attention. Our coffee cooled.

Jay and my mother had hit it off from the first, but there had always been distance between Jay and Dad. They spoke well of each other and had never had a serious disagreement, but there was no friendship, either. That had bothered me. I am closer to my father than to my mother, with whom my relations are fond but edgy. For Jay to confide in Dad about the nightmares was a remarkable gesture of trust.

Jay fell silent. After a moment, he added, "I'm grateful for the tickets, George. I could probably get through the flight, but I wasn't sure I could deal with the nightmares much longer."

Dad heaved a sigh. "I am sorry you have a problem with flying, Jay, believe me, but I'm glad you told me. What you said makes sense of something I've wondered about."

Jay frowned. "I beg your pardon?"

"You've been married to Lark for five years now. We've visited the two of you in California every year—and enjoyed our time with you. Lark flies home regularly, but *you* haven't come to see us in Childers since your wedding. Mary and I wondered whether we'd done something to offend you." Dad took a sip of cold coffee and made a face. "Mary said I probably bored you with my fishing stories."

"I'm sorry." Jay sounded miserable. "It wasn't anything like that."

"Least said soonest mended." Dad smiled at him. "If you've no great objection, my boy, I'll come out this fall and you can take me up on the Rogue for steelhead."

Jay cleared his throat. "I'd like that."

"Excellent." Dad beckoned to the waiter. "Our coffee is completely cold. We'll need a fresh pot and cups."

"Yes, sir."

Dad looked at us with a lurking twinkle in his eye. "I'll have to make a clean breast of things, too, I can see. I thought up the birthday business last night after I talked to Mary. I am to convey her felicitations, by the way."

"Thanks." Jay's mouth had eased, but he was still a little flushed. He smoothed his mustache.

The waiter appeared with our coffee and replaced the cups.

I poured, and this time, Dad laced his with a healthy dollop of cream.

"I bought the tickets because *I* was having nightmares. All this talk of Lockerbie . . ." He shook his head. "I didn't want to worry about the two of you flying all that way." He took a judicious sip of coffee and set the cup down. "Ah, that's better. If I hadn't stumbled across the travel agency directly after my talk with the Scottish investigators, I probably wouldn't have caved in to my fears."

I had taken a warm, satisfying swallow of coffee, too. "That's all very well, Dad, and we appreciate your concern, but what about you? You're still flying back."

My father reached inside his jacket again and drew out another folder. It was identical to the one he had given Jay but slimmer. "No, I'm not."

EPILOGUE

JULY 1990

◆ ◆ ◆ ◆ ◆ ◆

I had a letter from Ann today.

Jay and my father and I sailed from Southampton after a pleasant
week and a half taking day trips out of London. We stayed on in the
flat so I could see my doctor. He said the wounds were healing fast.
I was sure of it.

Although Milos agreed to join Ann's impromptu tour, he insisted on looking for a job first. Fortunately, his notoriety in the
media made the task easier than it might have been. A Bloomsbury
bookstore hired him as a salesclerk. The proprietor gave him two
weeks to recuperate first and seemed genuinely interested in Milos's
welfare, though the salary was small.

Ann put the brief delay to good use. She hired a car with an
automatic transmission and bought tickets to the RSC production of
A Midsummer Night's Dream in Stratford-upon-Avon. She intended to take Milos to Hay-on-Wye so they could both stock up on
used books. Then she was driving north to Yorkshire. She had
reserved rooms at Mrs. Chisholm's bed-and-breakfast house for a
full week. I thought they would have a wonderful time.

Jay and I cashed in our plane tickets. The voyage across the Atlantic was delightful. Neither of us got very seasick. We had dinner at my father's table every night, and danced and swam and did connubial things in our tiny stateroom. Jay only had one nightmare. I told anyone rude enough to ask about my scars that I'd been in a car wreck.

My mother met the ship in New York and drove us home, and we spent a week in Childers. Jay and Dad fished and talked history. Mother took me to consult a plastic surgeon.

We flew home from Toronto on a direct Air Canada flight to San Francisco. Jay said he got a kick out of holding an airplane up over the Rockies. That may have been because I made him take two tranquilizers before we boarded the plane. It was good to be home. There had been a forest fire, but it had bypassed our house by several miles. My bookstore was still solvent.

I returned to London in December to testify in the trial of the man I knew as Smith. So did Ann. Milos was not there to meet us because he had flown home to Prague to take up an important position in the Ministry of Education. The Czech government had fallen in November.

Ann and I stayed with Daphne Worth. She was living in the zebra flat. She had stored the porcelain knickknacks and the antique furniture and had let out Miss Beale's flat to a family with two children. Her friend, Marge Perry of the tenants' rights association, had taken over the basement flat.

Daphne was recovering slowly. Trevor pleaded guilty, on the advice of his lawyers, and received a twenty-year sentence. Daphne had visited him once. He complained about the prison food. She didn't go back.

Ann and I were apprehensive about testifying, but we were well coached and survived the ordeal. British justice moves swiftly.

For me, the worst part of testifying was seeing Smith in the dock. He had the coldest stare of anyone I've ever encountered. Faisel had tried to plead diplomatic immunity. When the Libyan government didn't acknowledge him, he also pleaded guilty. He admitted he had hired Smith to kill Milos. Faisel refused to name his employers, though. There was much speculation as to who they were. Faisel got fifteen years, a stiffer sentence than his lawyers had expected, and a thorough drubbing in the tabloid press. After all, he had killed two dogs in the assault on Hambly.

Smith was sentenced to life in prison. It was unlikely he would ever be paroled. Chief Inspector Thorne, who took us out to dinner the day the trial ended, was jubilant. He flirted with Ann all the way through the meal. She smiled and flirted back, gently. She and Milos had been corresponding.

I flew home in time for Christmas. My parents flew to California, too. I think Jay was almost as glad to see them as he was to see me.

In January, we watched on television when Vaclav Havel was sworn in as president of Czechoslovakia. I thought I saw Milos in one of the shots, but I couldn't be sure because my vision was a little blurry. Yesterday, Havel announced that the Czech Communist government had indeed supplied the explosive that destroyed Flight 103 and so many young hopes.

Today, I received a letter from Ann. She never did open her bookstore, and she is teaching English again. The letter was postmarked Prague.

DATE			